The
Witching
St👁ne

I don't believe in witches!
I don't believe in witches!
I don't believe in witches!

DANNY WESTON

The Witching Stone

uclanpublishing

The Witching Stone is a uclanpublishing book

First published in Great Britain in 2020 by
uclanpublishing
University of Central Lancashire
Preston, PR1 2HE, UK

978-1-9129793-8-7

1 3 5 7 9 10 8 6 4 2

Set in 10/17pt Kingfisher by Toni Murtagh

A CIP catalogue record for this book is available from the British Library.

Printed and bound in Great Britain by Clays Ltd, Elcograf S.p.A.

This book is for Meg Shelton –
the moment I saw her grave,
I knew I had to write about her.

Danny Weston

CHAPTER ONE

THE VILLAGE

As days went, Alfie thought, this one wasn't looking promising.

It was a bright sunny afternoon in July, and he was stuck in a little village somewhere north of Preston. After a quick look around the place, the only thing he'd found that might be of any interest was the local graveyard.

Which, when you thought about it, was pretty depressing.

'Look,' Dad had told him, ten minutes earlier, as they stood in front of the offices of the local estate agent, Blackwood and Phibes, 'Here's the plan. I have to go in here for an initial meeting, just to say hello to the staff and so forth, find out what they want from me. I'll be there for maybe forty minutes . . .

an hour, tops. And then, we'll find somewhere to have dinner together.'

'Great,' said Alfie, trying, but failing, to sound enthusiastic.

'I mean, it beats me why we have to be in Woodplumpton in the first place,' Dad continued. 'I told them I could do everything remotely from my desk at home, but they insisted they wanted me here, to project manage the whole thing. And they were happy to pay for accommodation, so . . .'

'I know,' said Alfie. 'You don't have to explain.'

Dad clearly felt that he did. 'See, what I still don't understand, Alfie, is why you didn't just stay at home. You're old enough to look after yourself now. I could have driven back at weekends. You'd have been fine.'

'I just fancied a break,' said Alfie. 'I thought it would be fun.'

Dad threw a disbelieving look around the deserted streets, clearly not convinced. 'You'd have had so much more to *do* in Bristol,' he reasoned. 'And all your mates would have been there.'

Alfie shook his head. 'No, Dad. They're on their summer holidays. They're in Spain or Portugal or Ibiza, or whatever. It would have been dead.'

Dad looked wounded by the remark. 'Look, Alfie, I'm sorry we couldn't afford a holiday abroad this year, but you know that's just the way things are right now. Maybe once I've got the fee for this job tucked safely away in the old bank account, we can have a think about going somewhere a bit more exotic for Christmas.'

Alfie shrugged. 'Yeah, whatever,' he said. 'This place looks . . .
OK. Sort of . . . countrified. What's it called again. Wood . . .?'

'Woodplumpton.'

'Yeah. And, it's only for a few weeks, right?'

'Sure.' And then Dad had launched into his regular speech
about the gig economy and how he was a freelancer and how
freelancers always had to go wherever the work was. Which
is why the two of them were here in Woodplumpton, so Dad
could spend a month redesigning and project managing the
new computer network at Blackwood and Phibes. Happy days.

Dad looked thoughtful. 'The reason you came,' he said. 'It's
not because of what happened with Sophie, is it?'

Alfie tried not to scowl. He didn't even like hearing her name.

'Course not,' he said.

'Because, you know what people say. Plenty more fish in the
sea, right?'

'Yeah, sure. They do say that, don't they. No worries.'

And that was pretty much the end of the conversation. Dad
had gone into the estate agents' and Alfie had been left to
wander around the village looking for something – anything –
of interest. Which is why he was wandering aimlessly through
the stone gateway of the church, killing time and contemplating
the empty vacuum of the summer that lay ahead of him like a
great big yawning chasm.

OK, so Sophie was a sensitive subject. It had been three months now, but it still felt raw. She was the first girl he'd ever properly been out with. They'd been an item for a couple of months, and it had begun to feel really serious. And then, completely out of the blue, she'd dumped him and taken up with Brendan, one of his best friends. No big deal. Things like that happened every day, right? But, it still hurt to be reminded.

He trudged dejectedly along the flagged stone path that led to the church, cutting between rows of neatly tended graves, each one with its own bland inscription, most of them obscured by patches of moss and lichen. And he was just thinking about turning around and walking straight back out of there when he came to an oddity – a large round boulder just to the right of the path and beside it, a brass plaque that read *THE WITCHES GRAVE*.

He stopped in his tracks and looked down at it uncertainly, thinking that this was something he'd never seen in a graveyard before. Not that he'd spent much time in them, but still, it was unusual enough to make him pause. He moved a little closer so that he could read the rest of the words etched into the plaque.

BENEATH THIS STONE LIE THE REMAINS OF MEG SHELTON, ALLEGED WITCH OF WOODPLUMPTON, BURIED IN 1705.

'Yeah, right,' he said, scornfully. As he turned away somebody popped up from behind a headstone a short distance to his left, with a suddenness that almost made him jump out of his skin.

'Sorry,' said the girl. 'Didn't mean to startle you.'

'Oh, you didn't,' he assured her, a little too quickly to be convincing. She was dressed all in black and she had that kind of severe make-up that Goth girls seemed to favour – thick black mascara and crimson lipstick, with straight glossy black hair that hung to her shoulders. She had silver dangly earrings and was holding something in one hand, that looked like a square slab of crayon. Her fingernails were painted midnight blue with tiny white skulls on them. And that was the detail that got him interested in her.

'You said something,' muttered the girl, by way of explanation, 'I thought you were speaking to me.'

Alfie shook his head and pointed to the boulder. 'Nah, I was just . . .' But the girl had already bobbed down again, out of sight. After staring in her direction for a moment, Alfie felt compelled to walk around the boulder to see what she was up to. He'd imagined she must be putting flowers on the grave of a much-loved grandmother and prepared himself to be polite and sombre about it – but when he came around the far side of the gravestone, he saw that she had taped a large sheet of tracing paper over the front of the stone and was rubbing the brown crayon across it in order to get a copy of the words.

'School project?' he ventured.

She gave him a scornful look. 'Who does those any more?

No, I just thought this would make a cool T-shirt design.' Alfie stepped a little closer so he could read the inscription over her shoulder:

Remember as you walk on by
As you are now so once was I
As I am now so shall you be
Prepare yourself to follow me.

'Who'd wear that on a T-shirt?' he chuckled.

She didn't look up. 'Me, for one,' she said. 'And I reckon there might be a few others out there who'd buy it.'

'Isn't it a bit . . . gloomy?' he asked.

Now she did turn her head to throw Alfie a despairing look. 'Don't you ever watch the news?' she asked. 'There's some very gloomy stuff happening in the world right now. This might come as a shock to you, but art reflects life.'

Alfie watched for a moment as the girl's hand swept expertly across the gravestone, picking up all the little details of the old-fashioned font and the lichen-encrusted surface of the stone. 'So . . . er . . . how do you make that into something you can actually wear?'

'Purple Onion,' she said.

He stared at her, uncomprehending.

'It's a company I use online. I send the design to them and, if they get any orders for it, they make them and send me a cut.'

'Yeah? And you make money from that, do you?'

'Well, I'm not exactly ready to retire to a private island in the Bahamas,' the girl admitted. 'But it brings in a few quid. And anyway, it's just a sideline. I'm an artist really. Well, I'm trying to be.'

Alfie shrugged. 'Go you,' he said. 'I'm Alfie, by the way.'

She was interested enough to stop working for a moment, then stood and turned to look at him. 'I'm Mia,' she said. She started to reach out a hand, but then realised it was covered in brown crayon and abandoned the idea. She studied him for a moment. 'So, you're not from round here then?'

Alfie frowned. 'Is it that obvious?' he asked her.

'It's a small place. I know most of the faces here. Yours is new.'

'Er . . . yeah, well I live in Bristol most of the time. But my dad has got some work here and it was a bit too far to commute, so we'll be based here for the next month.'

'Couldn't you have stayed with your mum?' she asked him.

He shook his head. 'My parents split up when I was little,' he explained. 'My dad got to keep me. I still see Mum now and then. She's married to somebody else now.' Alfie saw the look of doubt on her face and added, 'Seriously, it's cool.'

'So, where exactly are you staying?'

'Oh, it's just this guest house in the village,' he said.

This seemed to pique her interest. 'A guest house?' she echoed.

'Which one?' But before he had a chance to reply, she added, 'Oh, please tell me you're staying in The Excelsior.'

He grinned. 'We are!' he cried. 'But . . . how did you know?'

Mia laughed. 'I didn't. But there's only a few to choose from and it would be just your luck to end up in that hell hole.' She grinned conspiratorially. 'I take it you've met Selena then?'

'The woman who runs the place?' Alfie frowned. 'I didn't catch her name, but she was there when we checked in. She seemed a bit . . .' he searched for an appropriate description and latched on to the only words that seemed appropriate '. . . up herself?' he ventured.

Mia laughed. 'Tell me about it! Selena Holbrook has a reputation around the village. Whatever you do, don't get on the wrong side of her.'

'I'll try not to,' Alfie replied. 'Er . . . how would I do that?'

'By being normal.' Mia seemed to remember something. 'You're not eating there, are you?'

'We haven't yet. We've only just arrived, but we're supposed to be having breakfast there every morning, so . . .'

'Avoid it if you can!' Mia urged him. 'Their food is legendary – as in, legendarily bad. I've lost count of the cases of food poisoning they've had. Her husband is the chef and he's *terrible*. I only tolerate them because of the Stan Lee connection.'

Alfie frowned. 'Stan Lee? What you mean, the guy who wrote *Spider-Man*?'

'Sure. Stan the Man. That was his catchphrase, right? Excelsior!'

'I'll take your word for it,' he told her.

Mia smiled. 'Not a comic book fan? We'll have to work on that.' She seemed to remember something else and turned her head to look towards the boulder. 'It seems you're a bit too ready to diss one of our local celebrities. "Yeah, right?" That *is* what you said, isn't it? In a sarcastic voice?'

Alfie turned his head to follow her gaze. He'd momentarily forgotten all about the stone and the inscription. 'Oh, that?' he said. 'Sure. Well, it's a load of nonsense, isn't it? I mean, witches don't exist, right?'

She put her hands in the back pockets of her black jeans and wandered over to the boulder. Alfie followed, happy to spend a little more time talking to her.

'I tried that inscription on a T-shirt once, but it didn't sell,' murmured Mia. 'Which is weird because this grave is famous.'

'Really?'

Oh yeah. People come from all over the world to have a look at it. As far as I know it's the *only* witch's grave that can be found in a churchyard. They didn't usually make it on to consecrated ground. They were usually buried at a crossroads with no marker. So, Meg being here is something of a mystery.'

Alfie chuckled. 'You talk about her as though she's real,' he said.

9

'Well, she *is*. Or at least, she *was*. Women were accused of witchcraft all the time back in the day.'

'Seriously?'

'Oh, I know what you're thinking. Pointy hats, crooked noses and broomsticks, right? But that stuff is just set dressing. Usually, they were lonely old women who had a way with herbs and probably knew a thing or two about midwifery.' She pointed to the inscription. 'Of course, poor Meg here, she's a late example. 1705. That's nearly a hundred years after the Pendle Witches.'

Alfie nodded, but his blank expression must have given him away.

'You've heard of the Pendle Witches?' she prompted him.

He shook his head. 'No. Should I have?'

'Well, they're famous.'

'Not in Bristol.'

'Hmm. Well, the clue's in the name. They came from Pendle, Lancashire, not so very far from here. They were accused of witchcraft and were taken to trial. I think ten of them were hanged in the end . . .'

'Hanged? You mean . . .' Alfie mimed the action of being strung up and stuck out his tongue.

'Oh, yeah. You can Google it if you don't believe me. It would have been around 1610, I think. People had grudges against them, you see. It was very easy to make up lies about them, say they'd been seen dancing with the devil or some such nonsense. Then the people that accused them could get their hands on whatever land the women owned. I imagine it was the same kind of thing with poor Meg, here.'

'Yeah, but you don't really believe there's a body under that stone?' insisted Alfie. 'For one thing, the grave wouldn't be long enough.'

Mia nodded. 'Not if she was buried in the usual way,' she admitted. She smiled oddly. 'But Meg was different. She was buried head down.'

Alfie couldn't tell now if she was messing with him. 'Get away,' he said. 'Why would they do a thing like that?'

'Because the first two times they put her in the ground, she dug her way out again. She was seen wandering around the graveyard at night.'

Alfie stared at her. 'No way' he said.

'Way. It was a bit of a problem, as you can imagine. The good people of Woodplumpton couldn't sleep safe and sound in their beds with one of the undead wandering about the place, could they? So they figured if she was head down, well, she'd just keep digging herself deeper and deeper into the earth, wouldn't she? And they put that big boulder on top just to make sure she'd never find her way out again.'

Alfie knew it was nonsense and yet he couldn't stop a cold chill running through him at the thought of a woman clawing her way through the dark, cold soil. He grimaced. 'That's just nonsense,' he muttered. 'That couldn't happen.'

Mia shrugged. 'I grew up here. Everybody knows the story and I'd say most people believe it. When we were kids, we used to dare each other to walk around the stone and . . .' She hesitated, as though reluctant to continue.

'Go on,' Alfie prompted her. 'And do what?'

'Well, it's just this local superstition. None of us were ever brave enough to try it.'

'Tell me about it!"

She sighed. 'You're supposed to walk around The Witching Stone three times and each time, you say . . .' Alfie noticed how she lowered her voice to a cautious whisper. 'I don't believe in witches.'

'That's it?'

Mia nodded.

'And what's supposed to happen if you *do* say that?'

'Well, they reckon . . .'

'Yes?'

'. . . that Meg will come after you.'

'And then what?'

She shrugged her shoulders. 'I don't know. But I don't expect it would be pleasant.'

Alfie laughed and rolled his eyes. 'I've never heard such tosh!' he said. 'Seriously.' He lifted his hands and arranged them into claws. 'Meg's coming after you. Wooooh!' He noticed how uncomfortable Mia looked, how she edged back a little from the stone as he spoke. 'You really went for that stuff, didn't you?'

She shrugged. 'I guess.'

'You'd do it now though, right?'

Mia shook her head. 'No way,' she said.

'Oh, come on! Why not?'

'You don't get it. You're not from round here. It's one of those things that you'd never risk. Just in case.'

Alfie felt a sudden powerful urge to impress her. 'Let's give it a try,' he suggested. 'Come on, what's the worst that could happen?' He started to walk around the stone.

'Don't,' she said quietly.

'I don't believe in witches!' Alfie replied.

'You've made your point,' Mia told him.

He ignored her and began a second circuit.

'I don't believe in witches!' he said, louder this time.

'Please!' said Mia. 'You don't have to prove anything to me.'

He began a third circuit.

'I DON'T BELIEVE IN WITCHES!' he yelled. And stopped in his tracks as he felt something cold and powerful fasten around his ankle, holding him in place. He stared down in shocked surprise and there must have been something in his expression that betrayed his dismay because Mia looked at him and gasped, 'Are you all right?'

And as suddenly as the feeling had come, it left him and he was able to move his foot. He laughed, a little uncertainly, and then looked at Mia. 'I was . . . just . . . kidding,' he said. 'You know, trying to spook you.'

'Are you sure? You've gone as white as a sheet.'

'Don't be daft. I'm fine.' He looked quickly around the graveyard, just to make sure that things were normal, and had the sudden weird impression that everything had been taken away and replaced with identical replicas of what had been there before. He glanced at his watch.

'I should go,' he said. 'I'm meeting my dad for dinner.'

'Not at The Excelsior!'

'No. We'll find somewhere in the village, I expect.' He looked at her. 'Well, thanks, er . . . Mia. It's been an education. Will I see you around?'

'Sure, why not?' She pulled a phone from her pocket. 'We can swap numbers if you like?'

'Cool.' He pulled out his own phone and they added each other to their contacts list. She was looking at him uncertainly the whole time.

'Are you sure you're all right?' she prompted him. 'You look kind of funny.'

'I always look like this,' Alfie quipped. 'Don't worry. If old Meg wants to come after me, she'll have a fight on her hands!'

He'd expected to get a laugh out of her but she just looked thoughtful.

'OK,' she said. 'Well, see you around.'

'Yeah, see you.'

Alfie retraced his steps along the path and was slightly puzzled. He had every reason to feel cheerful – he'd just met somebody he was really interested in and that didn't happen very often. Hardly ever. So why did he feel so . . . anxious?

He turned through the gates of the church and walked along the street beyond. As he went, he couldn't shake the powerful feeling that he was being watched. *Ridiculous*, he thought.

But when he turned and glanced back down the road, he saw that a cat was following him.

CHAPTER TWO

FELINE

The cat was strolling along the neatly flagged pavement, its gaze fixed intently on Alfie, as though deliberately coming after him. He had a moment of genuine surprise and then tried to dismiss the idea. *Don't be stupid,* he told himself. A cat of all things! It was like some ridiculous cliché from an old horror movie.

It wasn't a black cat, mind you, but a scrawny ginger creature with a head that looked somehow much too big for its body. It had pale yellow eyes, which seemed to be focused on Alfie's face as though trying to puzzle him out. There was something about the lithe, unhurried way the cat walked that unnerved him – as though it had all the time in the world, and nothing was going to deter it from its chosen path.

Alfie forced himself to laugh, a sound that sounded unconvincing even to his own ears. *This is ridiculous!* He turned away and quickened his pace, telling himself that the cat would soon get tired of the game – if a game it was – and would choose to follow somebody else, somebody who looked more likely to have food. That was why cat's followed people, right? Because they wanted to be fed? But whenever he looked back, there it was, still coming after him.

Impulsively, Alfie went to cross the road, not even pausing to check the way was clear. The sudden blare of a car horn made him jump. He ran to the opposite pavement as a car coasted past him, the driver flinging him an outraged look as he went by.

'Sorry,' muttered Alfie. He made it to the far side of the street and looking back, he saw to his dismay that the cat was also crossing the road. Unlike him though, it had paused to make sure that it was safe to do so. Alfie frowned. He stopped walking and stood there, hands on his hips, watching as the cat prowled nearer. When it was less than a metre away, it came to a halt, sat down and proceeded to lick a front paw with a bright pink tongue. 'I'm in no hurry,' those pale eyes seemed to say.

Alfie stared at the cat, annoyed with it now. 'Clear off!' he said and took a threatening step towards it, raising an arm in a show of defiance.

The cat got quickly back to its feet but instead of running, it backed away, still keeping its gaze fixed on Alfie. The sleek ginger face had no expression whatsoever. The cat seemed calm and controlled, and continued its retreat as Alfie advanced. When he stopped, however, the cat also hesitated and sat down again.

'What do you want?' Alfie asked, and for the first time, the cat's face registered an expression – a sort of puzzled interest. 'Clear off!' said Alfie, louder this time, but the cat just stared back at him.

'Oh, for God's sake, you're losing it,' Alfie told himself aloud – and noted the amused expressions of a couple of elderly ladies passing him in the other direction, pulling tartan shopping trolleys behind them. The two of them strolled towards the cat and were obliged to move a few feet apart in order to pass it on either side. The creature didn't even glance up at them but kept its gaze fixed on Alfie. He turned away, put his head down and, blushing furiously, began walking again, picking up his pace considerably and heading in the direction of the Estate Agent where he had left Dad. When he saw the familiar shop façade ahead of him, he stopped and turned back, aware of a powerful anger building within him. The cat studied him, as cool as ice.

'Get the hell out of here!' yelled Alfie.

'Well, that's nice,' said a voice behind him, making him start. He span round to see Dad , who had just stepped out of the shop doorway, his portfolio hanging over one shoulder, a confused look on his face. 'Who are you talking to?' he asked.

'Oh, just the c —' Alfie's words died in his throat. Looking back, he saw that his follower was nowhere to be seen. Not on the pavement. Not on the entire street. Alfie scanned the various side roads and shop doorways in the hope of seeing it crouched there, but no, it was gone. He pointed a finger to the place where he had last seen it. 'There was a . . . a cat,' he said. 'Right there.'

'Yeah?' Dad looked like he didn't really know what to do with that information, so Alfie made an effort to pull himself together. 'How did it go?' he asked brightly.

'The meeting? Oh, fine,' said Dad. 'The usual palaver.'

'Uh huh.'

'You know, if you want, I can give you a detailed breakdown of the kind of system I'm going to install for them . . .'

'Uh, no, that's OK.'

'I could make some spreadsheets and pie charts and show you them every night, before you go to bed.'

'Er . . . no, really, don't bother.'

'Funny, I thought you'd say that.' Dad grinned. He already knew that the intricacies of his work held no interest for his son. 'Come on,' he said, and started walking back along the street, heading in the direction that Alfie had just come from. 'Somebody told me the best place to eat here is a pub called

The Fatted Calf. I don't know about you, but I could murder a burger and fries.'

'Yeah, sounds good,' agreed Alfie, falling into step. 'Funny name for a pub, though.' As he walked, his gaze swept the street from side to side, but there was no sign of the cat anywhere – not so much as a glimpse of ginger fur. *How could it have disappeared so quickly? he wondered. Had it sprinted up a side street as soon as Dad had emerged from the estate agents? Had it ducked into a shop doorway? Cats didn't do that kind of thing . . . did they?*

'What have you been up to?' asked Dad.

'Hmm? Oh, I visited the local graveyard,' said Alfie.

'Yeah?' Dad gave him an amused look. 'You know how to party, don't you?'

'I'm known for it,' said Alfie, forcing a grin – but he still felt compelled to glance behind him every few minutes, just to make sure that nothing was following him.

***

The sign for The Fatted Calf turned out to be as odd as its name. Sure enough, there was a picture of a very plump looking bovine standing nervously in a stall. Around it, a bunch of quaintly dressed villagers looked on appreciatively, as though anticipating the feast to come. They weren't actually licking their lips, but their hungry expressions did not bode well for the calf's future. Inside, the dimly lit inn was all rough-hewn beams, antique lanterns and garishly coloured toby jugs; but the food on the menu seemed OK and the landlord, a big barrel-chested man in a clean white shirt and braces, seemed happy enough to have some custom. The place was pretty much deserted. There was a round mahogany table by a window which offered a view out on to the sunlit street, so Alfie and Dad settled themselves and ordered their food. Dad even allowed himself a pint with his meal, by way of celebration for having found some decently paid work. Alfie had noticed he drank a lot less frequently since Mum had left the family home. Before that, he had liked whisky and had been getting through half a bottle a night.

'Well, this is nice,' said Dad as they waited for the food to arrive, making it clear that it was just one of those things that people said in such circumstances. He rubbed his hands together. 'I'm looking forward to this,' he added.

'Yeah, me too,' said Alfie, determined to keep up his end of the conversation. 'So, what are they like? The people at . . . Blackwell and . . .'

'Blackwood and Phibes,' Dad corrected him. He smiled. 'Sounds like something out of a horror story, doesn't it?' He raised his hands and wiggled his fingers. 'They seemed like ordinary estate agents,' he said, in a movie trailer voice, 'Blackwood and Phibes. Coming to a cinema near you soon! Certificate 18!'

Alfie sniggered. 'Funny,' he said. 'But seriously?'

'Oh, they seem nice enough,' continued Dad. 'There's a bit of resentment, obviously . . .'

'About what?'

'Oh, you know, somebody coming from the big city to show them how to put their ship in order . . . you always get that.'

'They've got a ship?'

'No, it's a figure of speech, mate! People never like to be told what to do by somebody who's just blown in on a breeze, do they? They always think they know the best way to run things. But once they've spent a bit of time with you, they start to realise you're not totally up yourself and they relax a little. And they start to appreciate that you might actually know what you're talking about. I think it'll be fine. Hey, you never know, I could have this all sewn up earlier than I thought, so . . .'

Alfie shook his head. 'First rule of a freelancer,' he reminded Dad. 'Always make the job last for as long as they've paid for. That's what you've always told me, anyway.'

Dad smiled ruefully. 'I guess I do say that. I just don't want you to be bored.'

'Don't worry about me, I'll be fine.'

'Yes, you with your weird graveyards. That's an odd thing to take an interest in.'

'Oh, it's not really an interest. I just happened to wander in and . . . hey, did you know, they've got a witch buried in there?'

Dad grinned, as though expecting it to be a joke of some

kind. 'Oh yeah, what kind of a witch?' he asked. 'Don't tell me, I know. A sand witch!'

'I'm being serious. Meg Shelton, she was called. She was accused of witchcraft in . . . seventeen something or other . . . and they buried her there, head down. Then they stuck a flipping great boulder on top of her, so she couldn't escape.'

Dad gave him a look. 'Sorry?' he said.

'Well, it's just that the first two times they tried it, she dug her way out.'

Dad was studying him now with a frown on his face. 'I think somebody's been pulling your leg,' he said, and Alfie couldn't help but think of that curious tugging sensation he'd felt around his ankle just after he'd said the forbidden words for the third time . . .

He made an effort to concentrate 'No seriously. There's a plaque beside the grave and all that. I could show you if you like.'

Dad took a gulp from his pint. 'I'll take your word for it,' he said. 'Though I'm pretty sure it can't say all that on a plaque. Not unless it's the size of a hoarding.'

'Well, no, it just has the date and a line or two. Mia told me the rest.'

Now Alfie had Dad's undivided attention. 'And who's Mia?' he asked.

'Oh, she's just . . . this girl I met.'

Dad raised his eyebrows. 'In a graveyard?' he murmured.

'Yeah. She was like . . . sitting by one of the graves, doing this kind of . . . rubbing thing, you know where you get a copy of the words on a sheet of paper.'

'School project?' asked Dad, and Alfie gave him a look.

'Come on, who does those any more? No, she makes T-shirts and stuff. For money.' He tried to remember the company she'd mentioned. 'Red . . . onion?' he ventured, but it didn't sound quite right. 'Purple grapefruit? Something like that.'

The landlord bustled over with two plates of food and set them down with a flourish. He looked very proud of his chef's efforts and Alfie had to admit that the food looked decent enough. The man indicated a metal container full of condiments on the table. 'Anything else you need, just give me a yell,' he said. He looked at Dad with evident interest. 'You'll be the new chap they've got in at Blackwood and Phibes,' he observed. It wasn't so much a question as a statement. Dad looked suitably surprised.

'That's right,' he said. 'How did you know?'

The man grinned, displaying a pronounced gap between his top front teeth. 'It's a small place,' he said. 'Everyone knows everything about everybody here. You'll soon get used to our funny little ways.' He reached out a meaty hand to shake. 'I'm Fred Wilton,' he said.

'Mark Travers,' said Dad, amiably. 'This is my son, Alfie.'

'A pleasure to meet you both. If I can be of any assistance, you just let me know. The people at the estate agents are regular customers of mine.' He glanced, almost apologetically, around the deserted interior of the lounge bar. 'It's not normally this quiet,' he said. 'I blame the sunshine, myself. People aren't interested in pubs when it's hot. Not unless it has a beer garden.' He gave Dad a wink. 'You'll find it a bit quiet here compared to Bristol,' he added, and moved away in the direction of the bar. Dad gazed after him, thoughtfully.

'Nosy sod,' he muttered, and Alfie had to stifle a laugh. 'Seriously, how did he know where we came from?'

Alfie pulled a face. 'Everyone knows everything about everybody here,' he said, in the horror movie trailer voice and they both chuckled.

Dad lifted the burger from his plate and took a bite. He chewed noisily for a while and Alfie followed his example, aware that Dad was looking at him curiously as he ate.

'So, tell me more about this Mia,' said Dad, when his mouth was empty enough to speak clearly. 'I have to say, you're a quick worker.'

'Don't be daft,' Alfie told him. 'I don't know anything about her. She's just this girl.'

'They all say that. You don't want to be in a big hurry, you know, not after what happened with Sophie.'

'Nobody's in a hurry!' Alfie assured him. 'Stop jumping to conclusions! We just chatted.'

'Did you swap phone numbers?'

'Well, I . . .'

'Did you? I bet you did.'

Alfie turned his head to look out of the window and almost choked on his burger. There was a bus stop across the road and on the metal bench inside it, sat the ginger cat. It was staring straight in through the window of the pub. Alfie put his burger down and swallowed a chunk of meat and bread with difficulty. 'Dad, look at that,' he said. 'Can you see that cat?'

Dad glanced around the interior of the pub. 'What cat?' he asked.

'No, not in here. There! Look, *there*!' Alfie even got up out of his seat to point, but then lowered his hand as he realised he was indicating an empty bus stop. There was no cat on the seat and yet, an instant before, there *had* been, he was sure of that. He lowered himself back down and said something terse under his breath. 'I beg your pardon?' asked Dad, looking vaguely shocked.

'Er . . . sorry. I thought I saw a cat, that's all.'

'What's all this about cats?' Dad looked understandably mystified. 'You were jabbering something about them back at the estate agents'.'

'I just . . . thought I saw one, that's all. Sitting in that bus stop. No big deal.' Alfie stared down at his plate and realised with a twinge of surprise, that he really didn't feel hungry any more. He pushed his plate to one side.

'Is something wrong?' asked Dad, bewildered by his son's sudden change of mood.

'No, I'm just not in the mood to eat, that's all.' Alfie picked up a chip and moved it distractedly through a blob of ketchup.

What's going on? he asked himself. *There's something wrong here.*

And there *was* something wrong. He couldn't identify what it was – he couldn't exactly put a name to it – but whatever it was, it had unnerved him and set a series of jitters rattling at the back of his skull. He didn't know what to do for the best, but he was sure of one thing . . . it was going to get a lot worse, before it got better.

CHAPTER THREE

EXCELSIOR

The two of them strolled slowly back to the guest house along the deserted, sun-burnished streets and thankfully, there was no sign of Alfie's ginger friend. Dad seemed to sense his son's current discomfort and attempted to fill the silence with aimless prattle, commenting on the various shops and houses they passed along the way, wondering aloud how much the properties in a place like this cost, and asking various questions about Alfie's friends and what they were up to. But, Alfie felt too perplexed to join in. He kept trying to tell himself that he was letting his imagination run away with him, but as he walked, he began to notice a dull ache in his left ankle, something that definitely hadn't been there earlier.

But what did that mean? That Meg Shelton had reached up and grabbed his leg as he stood by her burial place? That was beyond stupid, the kind of thing little kids told themselves at Halloween to freak each other out – the kind of nonsense he'd never given any credence to. And yet, thinking back to the moment it had happened . . . it was weird, but just as he'd said those forbidden words for the third time, his leg had been held in place as though it was in a vice. It had only been for an instant, and yet . . .

They reached the big detached building that was The Excelsior guest house and went in through the white painted swing doors. The foyer had an odd smell about it, which Alfie decided was an unpleasant mingling of the aromas of meat and cauliflower. Selena Holbrook stood to attention behind the battered reception desk, as though she'd been standing there for hours waiting for them to return. She was a tall, thin, angular woman with a long face and a very prominent nose, which was made all the more noticeable by a large brown wart sticking out of one side of it. Her suspiciously black hair was worn in an old-fashioned beehive, which seemed to add another six inches to her already considerable height and she was wearing a long, purple dress that clung tightly to her skinny frame. As her two guests approached, she arranged her meticulously powdered face into what was probably intended to be a smile of greeting, but which actually looked more like a grimace of pain, as though somebody hiding under the desk was in the process of driving a long nail into her foot.

'Ah, good evening, gentlemen,' she trilled, in a broad Lancashire accent. 'And aren't you the lucky ones to have such delightful weather for your visit?'

Dad opened his mouth to reply, but before he could say anything, she continued in a rush.

'May I assume that you'll be taking your dinner with us this evening? Malcolm has managed to lay his hands on some spectacular brisket.'

Alfie wasn't really sure what brisket was, but decided he didn't much like the sound of it.

'I'm afraid we've already had our dinner,' Dad told her, sounding apologetic.

'Oh.' She raised a pair of painted eyebrows in an apparent show of disbelief. 'But it's barely five o'clock,' she exclaimed.

'Er . . . yes, well, we were hungry from the long drive,' explained Dad. 'We went to The Fatted Calf,' he added.

'I see . . .' Selena's face ran through a series of expressions: surprise, followed by disappointment and finally one of profound irritation. She reached down to the desk and made a big show of drawing a line across a sheet of paper in front of her. Then her face went back to that weird approximation of a smile. 'Perhaps we'll be able to tempt you another evening?' she said. 'Malcolm does some extraordinary things with a piece of halibut.'

'Does he?' said Dad, and made a point of not looking at Alfie, in case the two of them felt the urgent need to snigger. 'Well, I'm sure we won't want to eat at The Fatted Calf every evening, even though the food there is very decent.'

'Hmm. Though of course, here at The Excelsior, we're firm believers that it's quality not quantity that counts.' She paused as though expecting Dad to comment, but when he didn't she continued. 'Well, of course, we are always at your service, Mr Travers, night and day. I trust you've enjoyed your first look at our enchanting little hamlet?' She looked directly at Alfie. 'Not a great deal here for a young man like yourself,' she observed, and Alfie wasn't sure if that required some kind of answer, so he just shrugged his shoulders. 'Your mother decided to stay in Bristol, did she?' added Selena, somehow managing to make it sound like an accusation.

'Er . . . well, she . . .'

'You know, I think we'll head up to our rooms now,' said Dad, hastily. 'We haven't had a chance to unpack yet.'

'Very good, Mr Travers. Will you be requiring an alarm call in the morning?'

'No, thank you,' said Dad, not looking back. 'I can set one on my phone.'

'As you prefer. A newspaper?'

'No.'

'Don't forget, breakfast is served from 7 a.m.'

But they were already heading up the staircase to the first floor.

'Well, she's a treasure,' muttered Dad.

'Yeah, Mia warned me about her,' whispered Alfie. 'Said she was . . .'

'What?'

'A terrible cook – or at least, Malcolm is.'

'Oh great, that bodes well for the next month. You got your key there?'

'Yeah.'

'Well, we may as well relax for a bit. We can decide about going out somewhere later on, if we fancy it. Get your stuff unpacked. There's a TV in your room and you've got your phone. If you need me, I'm just next door.'

'Dad, I'll be fine. You get some rest. You're probably tired after that long drive.'

'Yeah, I am, to tell you the truth.' They came to Dad's room, number six, and he slotted his key into the lock. He pointed to the next door, a short distance along the landing. Number seven. Alfie found his own key and unlocked the door. He stood for a moment, looking in without much enthusiasm. It was a square, featureless room, the walls painted a pale shade of magnolia. There was a double bed under the window with a naff floral bedspread on it and the room was decorated with vases of imitation flowers. On the other side of the room, a small TV stood on a mahogany stand and there was an ancient looking wardrobe, which at some point in its life had been painted magnolia to match the walls – the paint was peeling off in places, revealing the original mahogany beneath. *This looks*, thought Alfie, *like the room I used to sleep in at Grandma's house.* He looked back along the corridor to nod to his dad and the two of them went into their rooms, closing their doors behind them.

Alfie walked over to the bed and sat down on it. He looked slowly around the room and let out a long sigh. Then, aware of another twinge in his ankle, he leant forward, undid his trainers and removed them. He kicked them off, rolled up the right leg of his jeans and eased down his sock. He looked at his ankle in dismay. A blue-black bruise encircled it, just above the joint. It was about ten centimetres wide – the width of a human hand, thought Alfie and then shook his head, not wanting to give that idea any credence. *No*, he told himself, *there has to be some kind of logical explanation.* Maybe he'd injured the leg earlier when he was wandering around the village, though he couldn't remember doing anything that would cause this kind of bruising. He turned the leg around just to assure himself that yes, the mark really did go all the way around.

Impulsively, he took his phone from his back pocket and hit the browser icon, intending to type in the words 'bruised ankle', but instead he found himself entering two different words – Meg Shelton. The top hit that came up was from Wikipedia.

Meg Shelton *(died 1705), known as the 'Fylde Hag', was an English woman accused of witchcraft. Her grave can be seen . . .*

It was all there, pretty much everything that Mia had told him – and there was also a photograph of the boulder that marked her grave. So, she hadn't been making it up and the story clearly was very well known. However, Wikipedia didn't tell him much he didn't already know, so he tried a more general Google search and was surprised to discover that there were plenty of sites devoted to Meg. After going through a bunch of them, he found that they all seemed to be repeating pretty much the same series of stories. The only new things he discovered were that she had been killed by a fallingbarrel crushing her against the wall of her house – though nobody seemed to have a credible explanation for how such a thing might happen – and there were a few really unlikely stories about her ability to transform herself into an animal of some kind.

The first one Alfie read concerned a local farmer who noticed that his cows weren't producing as much milk as usual. One day, he spotted a goose with milk dribbling from its beak. The farmer struck the goose with his stick and it immediately shattered into pieces. He realised that it had somehow turned itself into a milk jug, which he believed belonged to Meg.

A second story explained how, when pursued by another farmer, Meg had disguised herself as a sack of straw so she could hide amongst a pile of other sacks. The farmer, who knew of Meg's abilities, decided to thrust a pitchfork into each of them in turn. For a while, nothing happened – but then there was a horrible screech as one of the sacks transformed itself back into a furious Meg, now bleeding heavily from a wound in her arm.

As Alfie read on he came upon, undoubtedly, the most ridiculous tale of all. This was one in which Meg turned herself into a hare. A local nobleman wagered that if Meg could outrun his hound, he would let her have a fine house in which to live, rent-free. Meg transformed herself into a hare and raced off in the direction of her own home, hotly pursued by the hound. Just as she was drawing near to sanctuary, the hound managed to bite the hare's hind leg. Meg escaped with her life but from that day on, she walked with a pronounced limp.

Alfie gave a snort of indignation and switched off his phone. There was no way he was going to believe that kind of drivel, he told himself. It was pathetic, like something from a fairy story . . . and yet, looking down once again at his ankle, he couldn't deny that something had bruised it – and nor could he put aside the very real pain which throbbed beneath the discoloured skin. 'This is bonkers,' he muttered. He lay down on the bed and closed his eyes. The long journey from Bristol had tired him out and, early though it was, he felt a weariness pulsing through him. Perhaps, he thought, he'd just have a quick nap . . .

Within minutes, he was fast asleep.

***

He opened his eyes to find that the room was in darkness and he lay for a moment, staring up at the ceiling, trying to recapture his shattered thoughts. He'd been dreaming about something, hadn't he? It was something to do with walking through a forest, but try as he might, he couldn't glue any of the pieces of it together. He turned his head towards the window and realised it must be really late as it was already fully dark outside. He hadn't bothered to draw the curtains when he'd come into the room, so he could see the rectangular outline of the window, a deep midnight blue against a wall of inky black.

And then something turned cold inside him as he realised what had woken him.

A sound.

A soft scratching sound, coming from the direction of the window. But . . . that didn't make sense. He was up on the first floor, wasn't he? In the silence that ensued, he lay there, holding his breath and listening carefully. Just when he thought he must have imagined it, the sound came again: an urgent scratching, as though something sharp was being dragged across a rough surface.

Slowly, Alfie pulled himself into a sitting position. He stared intently towards the window, aware now that the silhouette of it was not completely rectangular. Halfway along the bottom edge, there was a humped shape, as though something on the other side of the glass was crouched on the window ledge. Alfie felt around on the bedspread and after a few moments, his fingers located his phone. He switched on the torch and turned the beam towards the window, illuminating it. The glare was reflected straight back by a pair of feral eyes, belonging to the creature that was sitting on the sill, staring in at him. The ginger cat.

Alfie very nearly yelled out loud but managed to stifle the cry. He stared irritably at the visitor and it looked fearlessly back at him, once again dragging the extended claws of a front paw across the rough paint of the sill, producing a loud scratching noise.

'Go away!' hissed Alfie, not wanting his voice to be loud enough to wake Dad, next door. The cat ignored him. It clearly wanted access to the room and was not going to be easily deterred. Alfie steeled himself and slowly got up from the bed. 'I don't know how you found me,' he whispered, 'but you're not welcome here.' He moved closer to the window, keeping the torch beam fully on the creature's angry looking face. 'If you don't clear off,' he whispered, 'I'll push you off that sill.'

If the cat heard, it offered no reaction; so Alfie reached out to the catch of the window, levered it down and pushed it slightly open. The warm evening air gusted into the room, bringing with it an unfamiliar fragrance, a strange sulphurous smell, as though somebody had just struck a match.

'I'm warning you,' whispered Alfie. 'You'd better move.'

The cat glared back at him, undeterred.

'Right,' said Alfie. 'You asked for it.'

He reached his hand through the gap, fingers extended to push the cat off the sill. But then, with heart-stopping suddenness, a hand closed tightly around his wrist.

***

He woke with a gasp of terror to find himself, once again, lying on his bed in the unfamiliar room. His first impulse was to cry out but, just as he had in the dream, he somehow managed to stop himself. He lay for a moment, puzzling things out. When he turned his head towards the window, he was relieved to see that the blue rectangle was no longer interrupted by the humped shape of a feline – and when his sleepy eyes came fully into focus, he was able to note that the window wasn't open. He had dreamt it. He lay still, allowing his breathing to fall back into a normal rhythm, telling himself that he only had himself to blame. He shouldn't have gone looking at all that nonsense on his phone, no wonder he'd had a nightmare.

But then it dawned on him, that the ache in his ankle had not gone away. If anything, it was worse than it had been before. And now, there was something else. Something new - a dull pulsing ache in his right wrist. In an instant, he was off the bed and making for the door. He felt his way along the walls – looking for a switch. His fingers found one and snapped it down. Bright, reassuring light filled the room.

Alfie stood there looking at his wrist in numbed surprise. He couldn't tell if it was bruised like his ankle, because it was encircled by something even more shocking – a dark, clinging bracelet of mud.

***

It took him some time to recover himself. For a moment, he thought about going next door and waking Dad, but then he pictured his father's startled face as Alfie explained the reason for waking him up in the dead of night.

'Dad, there was this cat that followed me home. It was at the bedroom window, scratching at the glass. When I reached out to push it off, it grabbed me by the wrist . . .'

Dad's expression turning to a look of astonishment. 'The cat grabbed your wrist?'

'Well, it didn't have paws, you see. It must have had hands . . .'

There was no way he was going to say any of *that*. Dad would think he'd lost his mind. Perhaps he had, but that wasn't really the point. Instead, he told himself, he was going to have to be rational about this. Methodical. There was an explanation for it all and he was going to find it. The first thing was to get himself cleaned up. He went to the bathroom, switched on the light and had a quick look around. The shower cubicle looked inviting and, he told himself, maybe a hot soak would help to relax him a little. Right now, he didn't feel like he'd ever relax again, but he had to do something.

He opened the shower door, reached in and switched on the water. A vigorous flow started to spray from the stainless steel head and after a few minutes, clouds of steam indicated that the water was good and hot. Quickly, Alfie stripped off his clothes, flung them into a corner of the room and stepped into the shower, closing the door behind him. He held his wrist under the flow and watched as the thick, dark mud flowed in rivulets down his arm. There were small bottles of shampoo and shower gel on the caddy, so he opened the latter and slathered a good measure of the contents on to his wrist. He scrubbed with his other hand, creating a lather and pretty soon the mud was gone and was making a dark pool around his feet. He inspected his wrist carefully, turning it around. It looked red but for the moment at least, there was no sign of bruising. Well, that was something, he decided.

Now he ducked his head under the flow of the water, helped himself to some shampoo and worked it through his hair. Once he'd got a good lather, he tilted his head back and allowed the water to soak his face. As he did so, he was vaguely aware of somebody coming into the bathroom. He cursed silently, realising that he'd probably been making more noise than he thought. He must have woken Dad up and he'd come to investigate.

'Won't be a minute!' shouted Alfie, but there was no reply

He dashed soap from his eyes and turned his head to peer through the steamed-up glass. Sure enough, he could just make out the dim outline of a figure standing a short distance from the cubicle, as if waiting for him to finish. 'Sorry, did I wake you?' he asked. 'I had a bad dream,' he added, by way of explanation. He turned away again. 'Might have shouted a bit. Nothing to worry about.' And then a troubling thought occurred to him. *The bedroom door had been locked. How did Dad manage to get in without a key?*

The silence felt suddenly wrong. He reached out and switched off the water. He turned slowly back towards the door. He couldn't see the figure through the glass any more. He edged the door open a little and peered out, only to find that the bathroom was completely empty. But . . . there *had* been somebody there, he was sure of that. Dad must have gone back into the bedroom to wait for him to finish showering. *But the key! He doesn't have a key to my room.* Alfie stepped out of the shower, reached for one of the white towels hanging on a rail nearby and tied it around his waist.

As he did so, he became aware of a sound from the adjoining room. Somebody was definitely in there, waiting for him . . . But then came the sound of someone tapping on the outside of his bedroom door. Dad's muffled voice called softly from the corridor.

'Alfie, are you awake?'

Puzzled, Alfie took a step forward, then stopped in his tracks, staring down in dismay at the bathroom floor. The immaculate white tiles were covered with a whole series of muddy footprints. Not shoe prints, but the unmistakable pattern of bare feet.

Alfie stood, looking down, his mouth hanging open.

Dad's voice came again from the far side of the locked bedroom door. 'Alfie? Are you all right?'

CHAPTER FOUR

BREAKFAST FOR TWO

Alfie and Dad sat at a round table in the otherwise-deserted dining room of The Excelsior, studying the breakfast menu in silence. The atmosphere was strained to say the least. Dad looked red-eyed and irritable, clearly not in the best condition for his first proper day at work.

He and Alfie had spent quite some time the previous night, mopping up the mess in the bathroom and bickering about it. Dad, quite understandably, thought that Alfie must have been the one who made the mess – either that or he'd had somebody else in his room. Alfie, of course, protested that he was as baffled as Dad. He had no idea who might have been wandering around making muddy footprints on the bathroom tiles. He'd come out of the shower and there they were. It was a total mystery. And anyway, he countered, it was the middle of summer, everywhere was parched, how was anybody supposed to get muddy feet in the first place? But even as he'd said it, his mind filled with a terrifying image of Meg Shelton, slowly tunnelling through the deep, dank earth, intent on clawing her way back to the surface.

But how could Alfie say anything about that? What would Dad think? So, he kept repeating the same thing.

'I'm as much in the dark about it as you, I promise!'

Anyway, Dad had discovered some cleaning materials stored under the bathroom sink, so they'd cleared up as best they could and then Dad headed back to his own room, but not before insisting that Alfie keep his door locked at all times, just in case some other muddy-footed intruder decided to wander in and mess the place up again.

'The door *was* locked,' Alfie assured him.

It was only then that another baffling thing occurred to Dad. 'What about the carpet?' he asked, pointing back into the bedroom.

'What about it?' asked Alfie.

'Well, how come there aren't any footprints in here?'

It was a disturbing question that Alfie didn't have an answer for.

It was only as Dad was leaving that Alfie thought to ask a question of his own. 'What made you come to my room in the first place?'

Dad gave him a look of disbelief. 'Are you kidding me?' he cried. 'All those weird noises you were making!'

'Noises? What noises?'

'Beats me. Sounded like you had a whole menagerie of animals in your room. Shrieks, squeaks . . . braying sounds. Never heard anything like it! You must have woken everyone in the building.' He frowned. 'You . . . you said something about a nightmare, right? What was it about?'

'I don't remember.'

'Well, whatever it was, you were doing farmyard impressions to accompany it.' He gave Alfie a stern look. 'This hasn't got off to the best start, has it?' he said. 'I was hoping to get a good night's kip, so I'd be nice and fresh in the morning. I really hope it's not going to be like this for the next month.' And with that, he'd gone back to his room.

Alfie had taken Dad's advice and turned the lock in the door – though even as he did it, it occurred to him that it would take a lot more than that to keep a witch out. It hadn't worked earlier.

Thankfully, there were no more disturbances that night and Alfie eventually managed to grab a few fitful hours of restless sleep.

But now he was tired and irritable. He studied the breakfast menu listlessly, not feeling in the least bit hungry.

'I think I'll have a fry up,' said Dad, desperately trying to lighten the mood. 'Since Blackwood & Phibes is paying for it, I may as well spoil myself.' He looked at Alfie. 'I wonder where everyone else is?' he said. 'Do you think it was something we said?'

'It *is* quiet,' said a voice, right beside them. Alfie nearly fell off his seat. Neither he nor Dad had noticed Selena's stealthy approach. She was standing right beside Dad, a notepad in one long-fingernailed hand and a pen poised to write. 'Tea or coffee?' she asked with that pained grimace that was supposed to pass for a smile.

'Coffee for me,' said Dad. 'Nice and strong.'

'Bad night's sleep?' asked Selena, arching her fake eyebrows. 'I didn't have a good one myself.' She threw a pointed look in Alfie's direction. 'I think somebody had the TV turned up a bit loud. Sounded like a wildlife documentary.'

'Not me,' Alfie assured her. 'Didn't even have it on. I'm not interested in the telly.'

'Hmm. That's very odd.' Selina looked unconvinced. 'Last time I heard noises like that was at Blackpool Zoo.'

'I think Alfie had a nightmare,' offered Dad. 'You know how it is. Strange bed and all that.'

'Strange?' Selina looked vaguely insulted. 'I'll have you know that's a Dunlopillo mattress!'

'Oh, not strange, exactly. I meant . . . unfamiliar.'

'I'm sure he'll soon feel right at home,' said Selina. She turned to look at Alfie. 'And what can I get for the young gentleman this morning?' she asked.

'Er . . . orange,' said Alfie. 'Please?' he added when she didn't respond.

The grimace deepened. 'Fresh or squash?' she asked.

'Er . . . fresh, please.'

'Excellent.' She scrawled the words 'fresh orange' carefully on to her pad. 'And what culinary delights may we tempt you with?' she wondered.

'I think I'll go for the full English breakfast,' said Dad. 'Busy day ahead. Need to keep my energy levels up.'

'Very good. And how would you like your eggs?'

'Poached, please.'

Selina frowned. 'We offer fried, boiled or scrambled. I'm afraid Malcolm doesn't really have the knack of poaching. Bit messy.'

'Ah, OK. Umm . . . fried then, please.'

'Excellent choice.' Selina wrote laboriously on the notepad, the tip of her tongue protruding from her lips. She turned to Alfie. 'And what will David Attenborough have?' she wondered.

Alfie stared at her for a moment, not getting it. Then he realised she'd made a poor attempt at a joke. 'Oh, right. The noises. Yes, very good. I'll just have some toast, please.'

Now Selina's face collapsed into a mask of disapproval, her lips compressed into a tiny 'O.' 'That's not very much to get a growing lad through the day,' she observed. 'Surely we can do better than that.' She looked towards Dad as though making

47

an appeal to him.

'Give him some scrambled eggs,' suggested Dad.

'I don't *want* scrambled eggs!' protested Alfie.

'Of course you do,' replied Dad. He turned to Selina. 'Of course he does. And er . . . maybe a rasher of bacon.'

'Very good, Mr Travers.' Selina seemed happier with the adjustment. She wrote on her pad, then looked at Alfie again. 'Brown or white?' she asked.

'Eggs?' gasped Alfie.

'Toast,' said Selina.

'Oh. Er . . . white, please.'

'Brown,' said Dad. 'For both of us.' He looked at Alfie. 'Healthier,' he explained.

Selina seemed satisfied. 'Well, you two just relax,' she said. 'I'll have this for you in a jiffy.' She turned and strode off towards the kitchen.

'I'd rather have it on a plate,' whispered Dad, with a grin, before registering the furious look on his son's face. 'What's wrong with you?' he asked.

'What's with all this, "give him some scrambled eggs" nonsense? I didn't *want* scrambled eggs. I just wanted toast.'

'Yes, well, I agree with Selina. That's not enough to see you through till lunch time. You'll only be buying sweets and stuff.'

Alfie glared at him. 'I don't even eat sweets!' he protested. 'How old do you think I am, nine?'

Dad ignored the question. 'So, what *are* you planning to do today?'

Alfie shrugged. 'Hadn't really thought about it,' he said.

Dad reached into his jacket and pulled out a bunch of leaflets. 'I got these from the foyer,' he said. He set them down on the table in front of Alfie, fanning them out as if expecting him to choose one. 'Local things you can visit,' he explained. 'Parks. Bird sanctuaries. Or head into Preston, if you prefer. There's a museum and an art gallery . . .'

'Yeah, well, I'll have a look later on,' said Alfie.

'It's no use just hanging around here. You've got some money, so why not choose one of these places and work out how to get there on public transport.'

'Yes, all right, I will. Stop nagging!'

Dad sighed. 'I'm not nagging. I just don't want you to be bored. Honestly, I really think it would have been less stressful for me if you'd stayed at home.'

'Oh thanks. That makes me feel welcome.'

Dad was about to say something else but just then, Selina hurried in with a tray carrying a cafetiere of coffee and what must have been the tiniest glass of orange juice on the planet. She set the things carefully down in front of her sole customers in a kind of awful silence, in which every clink of a teaspoon sounded like an alarm bell.

'That looks good,' said Dad, unnecessarily. 'I don't know

49

about you, but I'm barely human until I've had my first shot of caffeine.'

'I'm a tea drinker myself,' Selina told him and then leant closer, as if to confide a secret. 'Lapsang souchong,' she whispered and gave him a conspiratorial look. 'The good stuff. We've got fifteen different blends of tea in the kitchen, if you ever fancy something a bit more refined.' She swept up the tray and strode dramatically back out of the room.

'I'm not surprised nobody else wants to eat here,' muttered Alfie. He picked up the thimble full of orange juice and threw it back in one gulp. 'She's *weird*,' he added. He pulled his face into an approximation of Selina's. 'Fifteen different teas!' he trilled. 'The good stuff!'

'Oh, she's just . . . a bit of a character,' reasoned Dad, pouring coffee into a china cup. He added milk and sugar, lifted it to his lips and took an eager sip. His startled expression suggested it didn't taste as he'd expected it to. 'Bit strong,' he said, and heaped a couple more spoons of sugar into his cup. He tried again. 'Tastes . . . a bit . . . odd,' he decided. He set down his cup and appraised Alfie for a moment as though considering what to say next. 'We haven't really talked, have we?' he said. 'About what happened with Sophie.'

Alfie's spirit sagged. This was pretty much the last thing he needed. 'There's nothing *to* say, Dad. We split up. End of.'

'Yes, of course, but I know that she went with one of your

best friends, so —'

'Dad . . .'

'I just wanted to say . . . well, you're still very young and though it all seems like a big deal to you now, you'll look back at this and think maybe you had a close shave.'

Alfie looked at him in surprise. 'Are you saying you didn't like Sophie?'

'No, of course not! No, she was great . . . well, maybe not *great* exactly, but . . . nice, you know. Decent. But look – me and your mother, we didn't get together until I was in my thirties.'

'And split up when you were in your forties,' Alfie reminded him.

'Yes, thanks for that. But that's not the point I'm making.'

Alfie frowned. 'What *is* the point you're making?'

'What I'm saying is, don't be in a big hurry to tie yourself down. Have some fun, enjoy yourself . . . ' He seemed to rethink the last line. 'I mean, don't . . . don't be careless. You know, make sure you use some protection . . . '

'Dad, what are you babbling about? It's a bit late for a talk about the birds and the bees!'

'Yes, I appreciate that. I just —' Dad broke off in surprise. Alfie had reached across the table to set down his glass and the sleeve of his top had slipped back. 'Hey, Alfie, what have you done to your wrist?'

Alfie stared at it in dismay, realising that it looked much

worse than it had the night before. There was now a startling blue-black ring encircling the narrowest part of his arm.

'Oh, that's . . . nothing,' he said.

'What do you mean, "nothing"? That looks nasty. Does it hurt?' Dad reached out a finger and prodded the bruise. Alfie couldn't help wincing. 'How the hell have you done that to yourself?' persisted Dad. 'Do we need to get you to a doctor or something?'

'Don't be daft! It's just a bruise . . . I . . . bashed it against the door last night.'

'On purpose?'

'Of course not! Why would I do something like that?'

'I just . . . well, you hear about teenagers harming themselves all the time. I read something about it. About how when young people are down about something. When they're *depressed*. I'm . . . worried about you, that's all.'

You have every right to be. The thought flashed through Alfie's mind, but he couldn't bring himself to talk about what had really happened to his wrist. Not to Dad, anyway.

'Look,' he said. 'I'm not depressed about what happened with Sophie. All right? She made a choice and that choice was she wanted to be with Brendan. Yeah, I was cut up about it for a bit – and I really didn't want to be hanging around in Bristol, bumping into them every five minutes, you know. Seeing them together all loved up, well, that would have been really crap.

So when the chance came to spend some time here with you, I grabbed it.' He spread his hands. 'No mystery,' he said. 'I'm good, really.'

Except I'm being followed by a witch.

Again, the unbidden thought, flashing across his mind like a steel blade; and again, the realisation that he couldn't talk to Dad about it. Because what would he think? Especially when he got so worked up over a bruise. But then Alfie thought about Mia and wondered if perhaps she might be able to help him. After all, it was because of her that he was in this predicament in the first place. Kind of.

Selina bustled back into the room carrying two plates. 'Here we are,' she announced, grandly. She slid the respective plates in front of her two customers and then took a step back, grimacing proudly. Alfie and Dad regarded their food in stunned disbelief. Dad had got off most lightly, Alfie thought, because at least his meal was vaguely recognisable as what it was supposed to be. Those pink, glistening, flaccid streaks were the bacon, right? And the two black cylinders that looked as though they had been over-inflated until they burst, must surely be sausages. The two frazzled, black-fringed orange spheres had probably been eggs in a former life. But what was Alfie to make of the great mound of grey matter on his own plate, a vile looking sludge that had been haphazardly heaped on to two slices of charcoal black toast? Scrambled eggs? Really? How could anyone have got it so wrong?'

'Can I get either of you some ketchup?' offered Selina, looking slightly pained when both of them said, 'Yes, please!' very loudly and without hesitation.

'Very good.' She turned on her heels and stalked out of the room.

Dad lifted a fork and prodded experimentally at one of the egg yolks. The metal prongs barely made a dent in it. 'Well,' he said, quietly. 'This doesn't look like a winner on *Masterchef*.'

'It doesn't look *edible*,' muttered Alfie. 'I told you what Mia said. The food here is —'

'. . . absolutely delicious!' said Dad, a little too loudly as Selina prowled back in carrying a bottle of ketchup.

They watched as she set it down, waited until she'd gone back out of the door and then fought to be the first to douse their plate liberally with it.

'I can see we're going to have to rethink the dining arrangements,' said Dad, lifting a forkful of greasy bacon to his mouth and chewing with difficulty.

Alfie contented himself with moving his food around the plate, trying to make it look like there was less than there actually was. He slipped into an approximation of Selina's Lancashire accent. 'Imagine what Malcolm would do to a nice piece of halibut,' he said, and Dad nearly choked on his food.

'You'll have to buy yourself a sandwich from somewhere

later on,' he advised Alfie. 'And I'll see if I can make alternative arrangements for the rest of our stay.'

Alfie frowned. 'How will you break the news to Selina?' he wondered.

Dad frowned. 'Not sure,' he said. 'But we can't go on like this.'

CHAPTER FIVE

AN ALLY

Luigi's Cafe was right where Mia had said it would be and there was the name above the door in a fancy, swirly typeface. Alfie pushed the swing door open and peeped inside. He was five minutes early and there were no other customers seated at any of the tables. A lean, middle-aged man, wearing a red apron with the name 'Luigi' printed on it was slumped dejectedly behind a wooden counter. He was staring mournfully at a phone, but perked up visibly when Alfie stepped inside and made his way across the room.

'Good morning to you,' he said. Alfie had expected him to have an Italian accent, but his Lancashire tones were even broader than Selina's. 'What can I get you?'

'Er . . . Diet Coke, please,' said Alfie.

'And?'

'Just that for now,' Alfie told him. 'I'm meeting someone.'

The man looked somehow deflated. 'Right you are,' he said. 'A Diet Coke.' He indicated a glass cabinet on the counter that was liberally stuffed with cakes and biscuits of every shape and colour. 'I have some very good homemade desserts,' he said. 'My rocky road has won prizes!'

'Has it?' Alfie shrugged. 'Well, er . . . maybe later. When my friend gets here.'

'Take a seat,' said the man. 'Anywhere you like. I'm Giovanni, by the way.'

Alfie looked at him in surprise. 'Not Luigi?' he asked.

The man looked puzzled. 'Luigi?' he muttered.

'Well . . . I thought . . .' Alfie waved a hand towards the front window. 'You know, what with the name being over the door and everything.' He pointed. 'And on your apron.'

Giovanni seemed to ponder the matter for a moment, then a look of understanding dawned on his face. 'Oh, right. *That* Luigi.'

'I suppose a lot of people must ask you about it,' reasoned Alfie.

Giovanni shook his head. 'No,' he said. 'Nobody's ever mentioned it before. My Grandfather set this place up in the nineteen-fifties.'

'Ah. And *his* name was Luigi?' ventured Alfie.

Giovanni shook his head. 'He was called Bill,' he said. 'Not sure why he called it Luigi's. Italian-sounding, I suppose. Anyway, 'ave a seat. I'll bring your drink over to you.'

Alfie did as he was told. He sat down and looked around the deserted cafe, wondering if this was the general state of all eating establishments in the village. Where was everybody? Had something happened that nobody had told him about? Were they all gathered in the village square having a party? He pulled out his phone and looked at his messages, checking to see if Mia had added anything to her last one. She hadn't. He scrolled back a bit and read the trail of messages they'd sent back and forth earlier that morning, worried that he might have sounded like an idiot.

HI THERE!!! WE MET YESTERDAY
IN THE GRAVEYARD.
I WAS WONDERING IF WE COULD MEET UP LATER
TODAY IF IT'S NOT TOO MUCH TROUBLE

Her reply had come back within a few minutes.

You don't waste any time, do you

IT'S NOT WHAT YOU THINK

AN ALLY

I'M NOT HITTING ON YOU

Bummer!!!!
How can I help?

IT'S ABOUT YOUR MATE

My mate??????

MEG SHELTON

She's not my mate.
She's a dead witch.
What's the problem?

I THINK SHE WAS IN MY BATHROOM LAST NIGHT

There was a nine-minute pause before she replied to that one.

Not funny

NOT LAUGHING.
PLEASE CAN WE MEET?

Another break, four minutes this time, then:

Luigi's Cafe on the High Street.
I'll be there at 12

A one minute pause, then:

You're buying the drinks

And then:

Please don't be a weirdo

I'M NOT
SEE U LATER.

Alfie sighed and put down the phone. As far as he was aware, he wasn't a weirdo – but something weird was definitely happening to him and he needed to talk to somebody about it. After some deliberation, Mia seemed like the logical choice.

Giovanni ambled over with a can of coke and a glass. He glanced at Alfie's phone. 'Stood you up, has she?' he asked, setting the things down on the table.

'I don't think so,' said Alfie. 'I'm a bit early.'

Giovanni smiled sympathetically. He leant closer. 'Take my advice, son. Don't be early. Be late. Treat 'em mean, keep 'em keen.'

Alfie looked at him blankly. 'I'll ... er ... try and remember that,' he said.

Giovanni winked and wandered away. Just as he slipped back behind the counter, the door opened and there was Mia. She stood for a moment, framed in the doorway – silhouetted against the sunny street behind her. She was gazing thoughtfully towards Alfie, as though having serious doubts about getting any closer to him. Alfie thought she looked somehow different than the way she had the day before, though he couldn't say exactly how. Was her hair different, maybe?

Mia appeared to take a deep breath. She stepped inside and let the door swing shut behind her. Giovanni nodded as though he recognised her. 'The usual?' he asked.

She nodded and cautiously approached Alfie's table, where she stood for a moment looking down at him as though seriously thinking about turning on her heel and walking out. But then she seemed to come to a decision. She pulled out a chair and sat down opposite him.

'Well,' said Mia, 'as text conversations go, that has to be one of weirdest I've ever had.'

'I know,' Alfie replied. 'I'm sorry.'

'Don't be sorry. It's different, at least. So ... what exactly did you mean? Meg Shelton was in your bathroom last night. I'll be honest with you, it's not the best chat-up line I've ever heard.'

'It's not meant to be a chat-up line,' he assured her. 'It's what happened. She was there . . . and she left dirty footprints all over the floor. Bare footprints. No shoes.'

'Riiiight . . .'

'Don't say it like that!'

'How else am I going to say it? Where was this, exactly?'

'In my bathroom at The Excelsior. And that's not all.' He leant forward over the table and lowered his voice to a whisper. 'There were no footprints on the bedroom carpet.'

'Riiiiight . . .'

'Stop saying that! Maybe you can explain to me how somebody can get into an *en suite* bathroom without walking through the bedroom? You just tell me that.'

Mia frowned. 'Did anybody else see these . . . footprints?' she asked.

'My dad. He helped me clean them up. Of course, he thinks *I* made them.'

'I can see how he might jump to that conclusion. Instead of thinking, *hey, it was probably a dead witch that did it.*'

'Yeah, go on, make a joke of it. Here, see if you find this funny.' Alfie pulled back the sleeve of his top and showed her his wrist. 'What do you make of that?' he asked her.

'Repetitive strain injury?' she ventured. Then she waggled her eyebrows suggestively. 'I won't ask you how you got it.'

Alfie gave a snort of irritation. 'What if I told you I have the same thing on one of my ankles?' he asked her.

Mia frowned. 'Your ankle?' she murmured.

'Yes. You must remember. We were standing by Meg Shelton's grave yesterday and you made me say those words, three times . . .'

'I don't think I made you say anything,' Mia insisted. 'You *chose* to say them.'

'. . . and you said my face had gone white. Remember that?'

'Yeeees . . .'

'Well it went white because . . .' – he took a deep breath – 'because I'd just felt somebody grab hold of my leg!'

There was a deep silence. Then:

'Caramel latte,' said Giovanni, brightly, setting a mug down in front of Mia. 'Can I interest either of you in a slice of rocky road?'

The silence continued as Alfie and Mia sat there staring at each other.

'Yes, well . . . if you change your mind, just give me a shout,' said Giovanni. He turned on his heel and headed back to the counter. 'No, no,' he muttered under his breath. 'There's no need to thank me.'

The silence continued. Then Mia reached out, took a packet of brown sugar from a bowl, ripped the top off it and tipped the contents into her cup. She picked up a teaspoon and gave the latte a stir. 'You realise how that sounds?' she muttered.

'Of course I do! But trust me, it happened. I'll show you my ankle if you want.' He started to lean to one side in order to roll up the right leg of his jeans but Mia put a hand on his arm to stop him.

'No, that's all right,' she told him. 'I'll take your word for it.' She lifted her cup to her mouth and took a sip, then made an appreciative sound. 'Best caramel latte in the village,' she announced.

Alfie nodded impatiently. 'You'll excuse me if I don't get too excited about a cup of coffee,' he said. 'I've got other things on my mind right now.'

Mia indicated Alfie's wrist. 'And what about that?' she asked.

He looked down at it. 'What about it?'

'Did that happen at the same time? When your, er . . . leg was being pulled?'

'No. That was the cat.' Alfie registered her blank expression and continued. 'A cat followed me home from the graveyard yesterday. I mean, *all* the way home.'

'Uh huh.'

'Then last night, it woke me up, scratching on my bedroom windowsill with its claws.'

'Riiiight.'

'I opened the window and reached out to try and push it away and it . . . it grabbed my wrist.'

Mia put down her cup.

'The cat grabbed your wrist?'

'Yes, I know how that sounds!' protested Alfie. 'I made a point of not telling my dad for that very reason. Obviously, it wasn't really a cat, was it?'

'Oh, right.' Mia considered his words for a moment and added. 'So, what was it then?'

'It was *her*, wasn't it? Your mate, Meg Shelton.'

'Why do you keep saying she's my mate? It's not like I ever met her!'

'No, but you know more about her than I do. I'd never even heard about her until yesterday, when you fed me all that guff about her. And then you made me do that walking-round-the-grave-three-times thing and — '

'There you go again! I did not tell you to do that. In fact, I seem to remember, I asked you *not* to do it. But you were trying to impress me, so —'

'Oh, is that what I was doing? Sorry, I didn't realise!'

'I mean, obviously I can't blame you for that. If I were you and you were me, I'd probably be doing the same thing. I'm the sort of person boys like to impress.'

'Is that a fact?'

'Yeah, 'fraid so.'

They sat there glaring at each other in silence for a moment. Then Alfie picked up his can, poured Coke into his glass and took a gulp.

'Is that why you told me not to do it?' he asked her. 'Because you knew this was going to happen to me?'

'Of course not! It's like I told you. It's just one of those things you'd never do. You know, like walking under a ladder or . . . walking past a magpie without saying "good morning".'

Alfie stared at her. 'Who does that?' he asked.

'Lots of people,' she assured him. '*I* do. It's a superstition. Some people live their lives around them. Spilt some salt? Throw a bit over your shoulder. Black cat in the road? Don't let it cross your path from right to left . . . or is it left to right? I can never remember.' She frowned. 'The cat you mentioned, I don't suppose . . .'

'It was ginger,' he said.

'OK.' Mia took another sip of her coffee and then seemed to consider for a moment. 'Let's be rational,' she suggested. 'Maybe your imagination got the better of you. You heard the story about Meg and your mind started working overtime. You imagined that something grabbed your leg.'

'Then what about the bruise?'

'Hmm.' Mia pulled her phone from her pocket and tapped a few keys. She studied the screen for a few moments. 'OK,' she said. 'I put "unexplained bruising" into Google and this is the top hit.' She began to read aloud. '"Perpora, or phantom bruises, develop from damage to the vessels under the skin. This damage causes the blood vessels to leak blood. It can also be caused by a medicine such as aspirin or any blood thinners . . ."' She paused and looked at him. 'I don't suppose you took any aspirin?'

Alfie waved a hand in dismissal. 'No, I didn't. And what about the cat?'

She scowled. 'Maybe that's all it was. A cat. They *do* follow people sometimes, you know, especially when they're hungry. The thing you said about it grabbing your arm . . . when did that bit happen, exactly?'

'It was late last night. It woke me up, scratching at the window and . . . what?'

'You said it yourself. You were asleep. So maybe you only *thought* you woke up. Maybe you had a nightmare and you bashed your arm while you were dreaming.'

Alfie shook his head. 'You don't get it. You weren't there when I was in the shower.'

She grinned mischievously. 'No, perhaps I should have been!'

'Be serious. How do you explain the mud on the floor?' He thought for a moment and remembered something else. 'And when I woke up, my wrist was all muddy too. Right where the bruise came through later. That's why I got in the shower in the first place, to clean myself up.' He lowered his voice to a whisper. 'While I was in there, somebody came into the bathroom and stood watching me. I could sort of see them through the glass, but it was all steamed up. When I opened the door, there was nobody there – just the footprints.'

'All right, now you're actually giving me the creeps,' Mia told him.

She gave him a sympathetic look. 'Look, I can see that you really believe all this ... but there's a logical explanation for the footprints. Maybe your dad was playing a trick on you.'

'Trust me, he wouldn't do that.'

'Why not? Doesn't he like to play jokes on you?'

'No, he doesn't. Well, not that kind of joke, anyway.'

'All right. But what I really don't understand is why you called me.'

'You're the only person I know here. Obviously, I can't tell my dad about it.'

'Why not? Don't the two of you get on?'

'Of course we do, but ... well, he's just started this new job and he's already under quite a bit of stress, so I don't want to get him all mixed up in it. He wouldn't be able to cope. He's a *worrier*. And I thought, what with you being an expert and all ...'

Mia snorted. 'I'm not an expert on witches!' she protested.

'Well, you knew all about creepy Meg ... and the Tollpuddle witches or whatever you call them. The ones they hung.'

'The word is "hanged",' she corrected him. 'And it was the Pendle witches.'

'Whatever. So, you seemed like the right person to talk to about this.'

Mia sighed. She drained the last of her coffee and set her cup down with a clunk. 'Like I said, I'm not an expert. But I do know somebody who is. Listen, what are you doing today?'

'I don't have any plans,' he assured her.

'Good. We'll go and see Hannah.'

'Who's Hannah?'

'I'll tell you on the way.' She lifted her head and looked towards the counter. 'Giovanni, we'll have a couple of those rocky roads, to go. My friend will pay.'

The two of them got up from the table and started towards the counter. Halfway there, Mia stopped in her tracks, turned suddenly around and leaning forward, she kissed Alfie lightly on the lips. He stood there, stunned.

'What was that all about?' he gasped, as she pulled away.

'I thought it would save time,' she said. 'So we won't be all hung up and awkward about doing it later.' She reached into the pocket of her jeans and pulled out her phone. 'I need to make a call,' she said, heading for the door. 'See you outside.'

'Er . . . right . . .' Slightly dazed, Alfie wandered over to the counter, where Giovanni was wrapping up a couple of chunky chocolate-coloured slabs in paper serviettes. He handed them across to Alfie and gave him a sly wink. 'See,' he said. 'Treat 'em mean. Works every time. We'll call it a tenner, shall we?'

'Huh?'

'Latte, Coke, two rocky roads?'

'Oh, right.' Alfie fumbled in his pocket, found a folded banknote and handed it over. Giovanni rang up the amount on an old-fashioned till and slipped the money into the drawer. 'Nice one,' he said. 'See you again.'

'Probably,' murmured Alfie and, still slightly stunned, he headed for the door.

CHAPTER SIX

HANNAH

Hannah lived in the little village of Singleton, only a twenty-minute bus ride away. On the journey there, Alfie repeatedly asked Mia for more information about the mysterious person they were visiting, but she just kept telling him to be patient and that he'd find out when they got there. His attempts to learn more about Mia herself also fell on stoney ground. She didn't give much away. All he managed to discover about her was that she was an only child, that her mother was 'a bit odd' and that Mia was obsessed with the idea of being a fashion designer and perhaps, one day, 'some kind of artist'.

They sat on the top deck of the bus, looking down on views

of sun-parched fields and winding country lanes. As they rode, Alfie kept getting the distinct feeling that somebody was watching him, but whenever he turned his head to look to the back of the bus, he saw that he and Mia were the only people up there. He supposed that his recent experiences had unnerved him, but still he couldn't shake the conviction that he was being observed.

After a short ride, they got off and Mia led him along streets that were even more deserted than the ones he'd encountered in Woodplumpton. It was another hot afternoon and Alfie found himself thinking how packed Bristol would be on a day like this. There would be people dressed in shorts and summer dresses, eating ice creams and wandering around the various parks and attractions that dotted the city. Here, it was as though everybody else had just vanished into thin air – like he and Mia were the only people left in the entire world.

'Is it always as quiet as this?' Alfie asked.

Mia smiled. 'Sometimes it gets dead busy,' she told him.

'Oh yeah, when's that?' he asked her.

'When we capture one of those city types and take them to the village square to sacrifice them to the old gods.' She noted his shocked expression and grinned at him. 'Sorry,' she added, 'couldn't resist.'

As they continued walking, Mia shrugged. 'I think a lot of people are away on holiday at the moment. Most of my friends are. It's funny, really. I was only reading this morning that the temperatures here are hotter than the Costa del Sol and it's raining in Ibiza. Something to do with global warming.'

Alfie thought of his mates in their various holiday destinations, standing around glum-faced in the rain and felt vaguely cheered by the idea.

Mia finally came to a halt outside a small, white-painted cottage. It looked like something out of a fairy tale, with a lichen-encrusted roof almost low enough to climb on to. 'This is Hannah's place,' announced Mia. She led him through a wooden gate, along a short, flagged path to a red-painted door. The path was fringed with pots of carefully tended flowers, the brightly-coloured blooms looking resplendent in the sunshine. 'She's very proud of these,' added Mia, with a flourish. 'Spends hours on them. She knows all the names.'

'What if she's not in?' wondered Alfie.

'Oh, she's in all right. I phoned ahead to check.' Mia reached out and pressed a doorbell. They waited in silence for a few moments and then the door swung open. A small, plump, middle-aged woman with short grey hair stood on the doorstep, beaming out at them. The eyes that regarded them from behind tortoiseshell glasses were a vivid shade of blue.

'Mia, there you are, haven't seen you in ages! And this must be the young man you told me about.' Her eyes edged sideways to study Alfie for a moment, as though weighing him up, before moving back to Mia. 'I must say, it all sounded rather intriguing on the phone. Right up my street! Well, come in, come in, I'll pop the kettle on and we'll have a cup of tea. Everything's better with a nice cuppa, don't you think?' She led them inside, and they followed her along a short hallway, the rough-plastered walls adorned with old-fashioned prints and photographs. They entered a small, neat sitting room. Hannah ushered them to a sofa, found out how they took their drinks and then hurried out again. Alfie looked quizzically around the room, noticing that three entire walls were covered with bookshelves, each one of which was crammed to bursting point with a multitude of brightly-coloured volumes. Closer examination revealed that several books had been written by the same person – Hannah Morton. Alfie looked at Mia, and pointed to the books. 'Hannah Morton. Is that ... *her*?'

Mia smiled. 'You're a regular Sherlock Holmes, aren't you?' she observed.

Alfie got up from the sofa and walked over to the bookshelves. He scanned the nearest row of titles. *Folk Tales of Lancashire, A Short History of Witchcraft, A Dictionary of Demonology* ...

'She really *is* an expert on this stuff!' he observed.

'Of course. I told you she was! If anybody can explain what's going on with you, it's Auntie Hannah.'

'Auntie?'

'Yes, she's my mother's older sister. She worked at the Uni

in Preston for years. The books were just a sideline, then. She took early retirement a few years ago so she could do it full time.' Mia waved a hand at the rows of volumes. 'As you can see, she's been busy.'

'I don't think I've ever met a writer before,' said Alfie. He lowered his voice. 'Is she like really rich?'

'I wouldn't say so. She's not that kind of a writer. From what she tells me, not many writers make much money. But she seems to do all right out of it. Now, the book you're looking for is . . .' She scanned the shelves and pointed. '. . . third row down, fourth along.' Alfie looked where she'd directed him and came to a slim volume. He took it down from the shelf and studied the cover. '*Call Her Meg*,' he read aloud. He looked at Mia. 'Have you read this?' he asked her.

Mia looked awkward. 'No,' she admitted. 'I should have done. Hannah gave me a copy when it came out, but . . . well, you know how it is. Always meant to. But Hannah's told me stuff about her before now. I think she has a special interest in the story, what with Meg being local and all. She was actually born in this village.'

'No way!'

'It's true!' said Hannah, bustling into the room with a tray of tea and biscuits. 'Her family lived not more than a hundred yards from where you're standing. Imagine that!' She noticed Alfie hurriedly trying to replace the book. 'Oh no, that's all right, dear, you're welcome to look at any of my old scribblings. I think a book that's never picked up is a sad thing indeed, don't you?' She went over to the sofa and placed the tray on a low coffee table. 'Here, come and sit down and I'll pour you a drink. I've made some flapjacks too.'

Alfie returned to the sofa, taking the book with him. While Hannah poured the tea, he opened it to the first page and read the introduction.

Meg Shelton (or to use her birth name, Margery Hilton) was a woman from the little village of Singleton, near Preston. Poor all her life, and unmarried, she was widely accused by her neighbours of being a witch. Whenever something went wrong in the community – if milk turned sour or prize cows failed to produce offspring, if children were stillborn or a crop failed – the blame was inevitably laid at Meg's door.

We know very little about her actual life (not even her birth date) and what we do know of her exploits is based mostly on hearsay and rumour. To the citizens of Singleton and, later on, Woodplumpton, she was a dangerous creature with the ability to transform herself into a range of different guises – something she would do in order to carry out some kind of wicked trick on her neighbours. What is certain is that after her mysterious death in 1705, she was buried in the graveyard of

St Anne's Church in a manner that appears to flout all the laws of sanctity and decorum – and after her burial, those outlandish stories about her continued to flourish . . .

Alfie sighed. He closed the book as Hannah set a steaming mug of tea in front of him. She indicated the plate of flapjacks. 'Help yourself to those,' she suggested. 'Don't be too polite, now.' She appraised him for a moment with those piercing eyes. 'So, Mia tells me you've had a bit of an encounter with our Meg,' she murmured. 'Exciting stuff.' She settled herself into an armchair on the far side of the coffee table, then picked up her own cup and cradled it in her plump hands. Alfie looked back at her, trying to determine if she was taking the rise out of him but her expression appeared to be perfectly serious.

'Well,' he said. 'Yes. I think she . . . I think Meg, is haunting me. I know that sounds crazy . . .'

'Let's get rid of that word straight away,' Hannah urged him. 'I've heard a lot of very strange stories over the years. I would never dismiss any of them as "crazy", certainly not without first knowing all of the details. So, why don't you tell me everything that's happened to you? Take as long as you need and make sure you don't leave anything out.'

'Er . . . OK.' Alfie thought for a moment and then decided to start at the very beginning, the afternoon he'd met Mia in the graveyard. He told Hannah about the awful moment when he'd recited the incantation and had felt that invisible hand close briefly around his ankle. He continued from there, pausing only to show Hannah his bruised wrist and leg – recounting the scary incident of the previous night and briefly finishing up with his meeting with Mia earlier that morning. When he had finished, he picked up his mug of tea, sat back in his seat and took a gulp from it, while Hannah considered everything he'd told her.

'So,' she said at last. 'Let's look at it logically. The manifestations involving Meg herself have only occurred at night. Perhaps that's when she's at her strongest.'

'It was daylight when I saw the cat,' Alfie reminded her.

'Yes, but we can't be certain that's a supernatural occurrence,' said Hannah. 'As I'm sure you'll accept, that might just be a coincidence.'

'I told him that,' said Mia. 'I mean, if I had a fiver for every time a moggy has followed me . . .'

'Quite,' agreed Hannah. 'But the bruises . . . the footprints . . . they are very real phenomenon. And I can't think of any way a muddy-footed person could have walked through a bedroom without leaving evidence of their presence on the carpet. Can you?'

They both shook their heads.

'That suggests to me that Meg must have apparated in the bathroom itself.'

'Apparated?' echoed Alfie.

'Oh, that just means . . . to take form. It seems to me, Alfie, that she is homing in on you for some reason, I suppose because, well, you sort of invited her to.'

Alfie stared at her. 'Are you . . . are you saying you believe me?' he gasped. He realised that what he'd actually been hoping for was that Hannah would give him a convincing explanation for what had happened and thus set his mind at rest. The last thing he'd expected was that she would *agree* with him.

'I certainly believe these things have happened to you,' she told him. 'Not just in your mind, you understand, but in reality. Or at least, reality as you perceive it. Now, reason tells me that you cannot be the first person to walk three times around The Witching Stone and say those words – I would imagine that countless children must have done exactly that over the centuries – but I have never heard of anybody doing it and getting such a powerful reaction. So, we have to ask ourselves, what is it about you that acts as a conduit for Meg? What makes you so attractive to her?'

'Could be those dark eyes,' suggested Mia. 'Lots of women are a sucker for that.'

Hannah chuckled. 'I rather think it must be something more complicated,' she said. 'Tell me, Alfie, where are you from?'

'Bristol. I was born there.'

'You don't have any relatives in this part of the world?'

'Not that I know of. And what difference would it make if I did?'

'I don't know, dear. I'm just looking for possibilities. I'm trying to think if there's anything about you that might be an incentive for her to reach out to you.'

'Look, this feels weird,' said Alfie. 'You're talking about it as though it's just an everyday thing . . . like, I don't know . . . eating dinner.'

Hannah smiled. 'What else am I to do?' she asked him. 'I believe what you just told me. The only other explanation would be that you have inflicted those bruises on yourself and you've made up a story to try and scare us. But why would you do such a thing?'

'I wouldn't. I *haven't*,' Alfie told her. 'I promise you.'

'Well then, that's good enough for me. Until it's disproved, I believe that Meg Shelton is trying to make contact with you. It's quite exciting when you think about it.'

'Exciting?' Mia looked doubtful. 'More like creepy.'

'Well, yes, I'll give you that. But I tell you what, if I could swap places with you, Alfie, I would. There's so much more I want to know about that woman.' She gestured to the slim volume in Alfie's hands. 'The problem is, we know so little. I had to get that thing self-published. My regular publishers said there just wasn't enough there to warrant a proper release. They were right of course. I hate it when they're right. We wouldn't have sold enough copies to fill somebody's hat. It was more a labour of love, that one.'

Alfie looked intently at Hannah. 'What do you think she wants from me?' he asked her. 'I mean, the story that Mia told me . . . it was like, if you say those words three times, Meg Shelton will come after you. Do you think she means to harm me?'

'Oh, goodness no. Why would she want to do that? What have you ever done to her? Perhaps she's seeking your help.'

'Help with what?'

Hannah shrugged her tiny shoulders. 'That I cannot say.' She considered for a moment. 'But I see this as an opportunity. There's so much more to find out about her. When I was preparing the book, I read everything I could lay my hands on . . . ancient texts, eye-witness accounts, online anecdotes and what little historical evidence I could scrape together. There wasn't much to go on, but I was left with the overriding belief that Meg Shelton was a wronged woman.'

'In what way?' asked Mia.

'I think she was badly treated.'

'Buried head down with a boulder on top of her?' Alfie snorted. 'Yeah, I'd say so.'

'Yes, but I'm not referring to that.' Hannah looked thoughtful. 'The assumption that many people make is that Meg was an old woman when she died, but I happen to think that she might have been much younger than is generally assumed. We don't even have a birth date for her! Some people have also speculated that she might have been pregnant at the time of her death and that the father of the child was a powerful landowner in this area, a man of great wealth. Her death was highly suspicious. We're told that she was killed in her own home, crushed against a wall by a rolling barrel. Now, I don't know about you two, but I cannot for the life of me think of a convincing situation where such a thing might actually happen.'

'Are you saying that she might have been murdered?' asked Alfie.

'It seems like a distinct possibility,' said Hannah. 'And here's another strange thing. The house she lived in, which some people refer to as Cuckoo Hall, was given to her rent-free by an unknown person – possibly the same man who fathered her child. What if that man was married and was conducting a secret affair with Meg? What if he feared she might inform others of her condition and name the man who had got her into such a state? What if the landowner decided to silence her?' She sighed, shook her head. 'Again, with so few facts to go on, it's only conjecture on my part. And yet, the more I think about it, the more it seems to make sense. Why would anybody bury an alleged witch in consecrated ground? I know of no other place in the world where this has happened. Was somebody feeling guilty about her death?'

'You've really thought this over, haven't you?' observed Mia.

'It makes me angry when I think about her,' said Hannah. 'Remember, this happened at a time when one of the easiest ways to silence a difficult woman was to denounce her as a witch. When such a person dies, the whole community breathes a sigh of relief instead of coming together to investigate the cause of her death.' She pointed to the book in Alfie's hand. 'I have a spare copy of that I can lend you if you like,' she suggested. 'It won't take you long to read and it might just give you some ideas.'

'Thanks,' said Alfie. 'That would be great. I'll make sure I get it back to you.'

'Oh, there's no great hurry,' Hannah assured him. 'I'm not planning on going anywhere and it's not as if there's a whole queue of people clamouring to get hold of a copy.' She seemed to ponder for a moment. 'Of course, it's quite possible that it's all over now. Maybe you won't encounter any more strange goings-on. But if you should . . .'

'Yes?' murmured Alfie, leaning forward.

'Use it as an opportunity to find out what Meg wants.'

Alfie stared at her. 'How would I do that, exactly?'

'You might try asking her,' suggested Hannah. 'Just a thought.'

CHAPTER SEVEN

VISITATION

Alfie lay in bed, staring up at the darkened ceiling, totally unable to sleep. He had put off going to his room for as long as possible that night, sitting in the communal lounge of The Excelsior with Dad, the two of them nursing drinks. Alfie had assailed Dad with a torrent of questions about his first day at the new job. Dad had been pleased at first that his son was taking such an interest in his career, but as time wore on, and the questions became ever more random, he had finally drained the last of his pint and announced it was time for them to turn in.

Alfie had gone up to his room with the reluctance of a doomed man heading for the guillotine. He couldn't help remembering what Hannah had said. *'The manifestations involving Meg herself have only occurred at night. Perhaps that is when she is at her strongest.'*

Not a promising thought. But Hannah had also said that it might already be over, hadn't she? That it might just have been a passing thing. Alfie clung on to that notion in the desperate hope she'd been right. He really didn't want this to continue.

On the bus back to Woodplumpton, Mia had tried to reassure him. 'It probably isn't going to amount to anything,' she kept telling him. 'It'll be one of those unexplained things that happens once in a while. The ones you never find an explanation for.'

'Such as?' he muttered bleakly.

'Well, like the time I couldn't find my favourite beanie. I looked everywhere for it, but it was nowhere to be seen. Then the very next day, I looked in the drawer where I always keep it and there it was.'

Alfie frowned. 'That really doesn't feel quite as worrying,' he said.

'No, but ... it *is* a bit weird, right? *Unexplained.*' She gave him an encouraging smile. 'Anyway, if you feel you need help, you've got my phone number. Ring me if you need to talk. Any time.'

But what was he supposed to do now? Ring Mia and tell her that he was lying awake, unable to sleep? That he was scared to close his eyes in case a dead witch popped out of the woodwork? And what was Mia supposed to do then – hurry straight over and bang on the front door of The Excelsior until somebody let her in? To do what, exactly?

Alfie shook his head. He reached out to his bedside table for the glass of water he'd left there when he turned in and saw, in the gloom, that it was virtually empty. He drank what was left of it and then pushed back the covers and got out of bed. He took the glass to the bathroom, switched on the light and went over to the washbasin, relishing the cold touch of the tiles against his bare feet. He leant forward and turned on the tap, letting it run for a while to make sure it was suitably cold before filling the glass to the brim. He turned off the tap and raised his gaze to the mirror above the basin. His eyes widened.

Somebody was standing behind him, looking directly over his shoulder. The mirror reflected the image of a long, thin face caked in mud. Terror jolted through him like an electric shock and he span around, opening his mouth to let out a yell. But before he could make a sound, a hand clamped hard across his mouth – a powerful hand with a wet, earthy taste to it. The muddy woman used her other hand to wrench the glass of water he was still, holding, roughly from his grasp and raised it to her lips. She tilted it back and drained the contents in a single, noisy swallow. Alfie, pinned against the washbasin by the sheer power of her other hand and the weight of her body, could only stare in wide-eyed terror as she lowered the glass, then thrust it straight back at him.

'More!' she grunted.

He stared at her in disbelief, his body jolting with fear.

'MORE!' she said again, in a deep gravelly voice; and then added, 'If you make a sound, I'll break your neck.'

He nodded, and she finally released the pressure on him enough to allow him to turn back to the basin. Her powerful fingers closed now around the nape of his neck, her touch sending shivers down his spine. As he glanced at her reflection in the mirror, he noted that she was perhaps in her forties and that underneath that thick layer of dirt, she certainly wasn't the wizened crone he might have expected. He noticed too that the lower half of his own face was now marred by a dirty handprint. He bowed his head, turned on the tap and refilled the glass, though his hand was shaking so badly, he spilt most of the contents before he managed to turn slowly back to face her. Again, she grabbed the glass from him, as though her very life depended on it and she slugged the water down, before letting out a long sigh of relief. 'I was thirsty,' she told him.

Alfie opened his mouth to speak but she stilled him with a raised finger. 'Remember what I told you,' she hissed. 'Cry out and it'll be the last sound you ever make.'

So much for Hannah's claim that Meg meant him no harm, he thought. He tried to reply in a whisper but could hardly form words. 'Wh . . . who . . . wh . . .' He paused, gathered his resolve and tried again. 'Wh . . . what do you want?' he managed to say.

He was starting to take in more of her now – the tall gaunt shape of her, wrapped in rotting rags, her filthy hair falling in a matted tangle to her shoulders. And he was aware of the smell of her too, the powerful earthy stench filling his nostrils, almost making him retch. 'What do you want?' he asked again, fearing that she hadn't understood him the first time.

Her eyes narrowed for a moment and he noticed that they were a deep shade of green. 'I want your help,' she rasped. So, Hannah had been right about that much, at least.

'B . . . b . . . but why me?' stammered Alfie.

'Why do you think, you pup? You summoned me.'

'Oh.' He shook his head. 'Ah . . . now, see, that was . . . that was kind of a joke.'

Again, the eyes narrowed. 'A joke?' Her stern expression suggested that if she knew what a joke was, she wasn't finding this one funny.

'Yes, see, I was just messing around. And I . . . I really didn't think you'd . . . you know, turn up.'

She scowled as though his words didn't make any sense. 'Why summon me if you didn't want me to answer?' she croaked. She thrust the empty glass back into his hand and turning away, she looked quickly around the bathroom, as though trying to make sense of it. 'What is this place?' she asked him. She reached out a hand and prodded the white tiled wall experimentally with a long index finger. 'Is it a scullery?'

'Er . . . no. No, it's a bathroom.' He thought for a moment and then remembered something. 'You were here last night, weren't you? I know you were. You made a right mess . . .' He looked down and saw that there were new footprints all over the floor. He pointed to them and she studied her bare feet for a moment as though she'd never been aware of them before. Then she lifted her head and pointed to the shower cubicle. 'You were in the rain box,' she said. 'The last time I came here.'

'Rain box? You mean the shower?' Alfie's mind was racing. For the moment, stupidly, the thing that dominated his thoughts was to find a way to stop her from making any more mess in here, knowing full well that he would be the one tasked with the job of cleaning up after her. He moved quickly across to the cubicle and opened the door. He reached in and switched on the shower.

'You . . . you should go in here,' he said.

She grimaced. 'In there?' she hissed. 'Why?'

'We need to get you cleaned up!' he said. *And I'll have a chance to run away*, he thought.

She gave him an accusing look. 'You'd better not try!' she snapped. Had he just said that last bit out loud? He didn't think so.

'Er . . . yes, just step right in there. You can get all that mud off you.' *And maybe I can find a weapon.*

'I'm not your enemy,' Meg assured him. 'You won't need

a weapon.' She seemed to think for a moment. 'Or were you thinking of defending me with it?'

Alfie stared at her. 'Did you just read my mind?' he gasped.

But she seemed entranced by the shower now, noticing the clouds of steam that were rising from it. She shuffled closer and extended a hand into the cubicle, staring in open-mouthed astonishment as the muck dissolved under the flow and made shocking patterns on the white floor. 'It's hot!' she hissed. 'The rain is hot!'

'Yes. Keep your voice down! You'll wake my dad. I don't want . . . oh!'

He turned quickly away, aware of his face reddening, because now she was stripping off her ragged dress without a moment's hesitation. There was the soft slap of the filthy fabric hitting the tiled floor and then a long, ecstatic moan as Meg stepped into the flow of the water. 'Oh, it's good!' he heard her say. 'So good.'

'There's er . . . shower gel in the metal holder there,' Alfie told her. 'And shampoo. Just help yourself. Have a good scrub.' The absurdity of the situation suddenly overcame him. He was giving washing instructions to the sixteenth century witch who was currently taking a shower in his bathroom. Of course he was! He had lost his mind. There was no other explanation. He had completely taken leave of his senses. He looked quickly around. *Maybe*, he thought, *I could chance making a run for it.*

'Try it and I shall come after you,' growled a voice from the shower. He pictured himself being pursued down the landing by a naked woman and promptly abandoned the idea of fleeing. She had worked out how to use the shower gel.

'It smells of flowers!' he heard her gasp.

'Er . . . yes. Lavender and thyme, I think. Just help your —' Alfie broke off as he heard a polite knocking at his bedroom door. 'Alfie?' he heard Dad call. 'Are you all right in there?'

Oh no! Alfie started towards the door then froze in his tracks as a hiss came at him from the direction of the cubicle. He half-turned to see Meg's fierce expression regarding him from a halo of foam.

'If you tell him about me, I will kill him,' she said calmly. 'Understand?'

He gulped. 'Right,' he said. 'No problem. It's just my dad, please don't hurt him.'

'I'm warning you!'

'I'll get rid of him, I promise. I'm just going to close this door, OK? In case he sees you.'

'He won't see me.'

'Just the same, I'd better close the door.'

'No tricks, now.'

'I promise, I'll get rid of him.'

He stepped out of the bathroom, pushed the door shut and hurried across the bedroom to the outer door. He turned the lock and eased the door slightly open to reveal Dad's sleep-deprived features, peering blearily in at him. 'Alfie, what the hell is going on in there?' he asked. 'I thought I heard voices . . .'

'Just the telly,' Alfie assured him. 'I was watching a film. Sorry, I couldn't sleep.'

'Can't you use headphones? Selina's already complained about the noise you made last night . . .' Dad hesitated and listened for a moment. 'Can I hear water running?' he muttered.

'No . . .' Alfie saw Dad's doubtful expression and realised he needed to change tack. 'I mean, *yes* . . . yes, that is water. I was just about to take a quick shower. I'm a bit sweaty.'

'Alfie, it's one o'clock in the morning. Can't it wait?'

'Oh, I won't be long,' Alfie assured him. 'Or . . . or if you like, I'll switch it off now and wait till morning. Yes, probably a better idea. I don't want to cause any fuss.'

Dad looked weary. 'Alfie, are you all right?' he asked. 'You're acting very oddly.'

'I'm fine, Dad. Perfectly OK.' *Except there's a dead witch having a shower in my bathroom.* 'Really.'

'Just try and get some sleep,' said Dad. 'Please.'

'Sure. No problem. I'll do that. See you later.'

Dad opened his mouth to say something else, but Alfie promptly slammed the door in his face and turned the key. He waited for a moment, listening intently, until he heard Dad's footsteps moving slowly away along the landing. Alfie took a deep breath, turned and headed back to the bathroom. He opened the door and Meg was standing in front of him, stark naked.

'Whoa!' he gasped, turning hastily away. He waved a hand in the general direction of the towel rack. 'Would you maybe, like to . . . cover yourself up?' he suggested.

He waited a respectable amount of time and then cautiously turned to look. He saw to his relief that she had draped a white bath sheet across her body, one that had the words 'Excelsior Guest House' embroidered on it. *A surreal touch*, he thought. He saw that the new, cleaned-up version of Meg Shelton looked a lot less frightening than her former incarnation. Her long straight hair was now a rich shade of auburn and the face that studied him, though not exactly beautiful, was somehow rather striking – with high cheekbones and a straight, proud nose. She turned to survey the clump of rags on the floor beside her. 'My dress,' she murmured thoughtfully.

He followed her gaze and could see her point entirely. 'You can't put that back on,' he murmured. 'It's rank.' Alfie thought for a moment. 'Follow me,' he suggested and led the way back into his bedroom. He tried not to giggle like a mad person. After all, wasn't it perfectly natural after you'd helped a dead witch to clean herself up to then find her something to wear? But what did he have that might possibly fit her? He rooted through the suitcase he still hadn't got around to unpacking and after some indecision, pulled out a grey sweatshirt and a pair of loose-fitting plaid pyjama pants. 'Try these,' he suggested, handing them to her; and had to turn promptly away again as she dropped the towel and examined the clothes, working out how to get them on. It took Meg quite a while, but eventually, she was decently covered, even if the legs of the pyjamas did finish half way up her slender shins. She walked around a little, looking down at herself, clearly perplexed by his choices.

'These are men's clothes,' she decided at last.

'They're all I have,' Alfie assured her.

'And what of my dress?'

'I'll . . . get rid of it,' he told her. 'I'd say it's past saving, don't you think? I suppose that's because it's been . . . in the ground?' Saying that made him feel distinctly uncomfortable. He sat down on his bed and motioned Meg to the room's single armchair. 'Sit down,' he said. 'We need to discuss what to do about you.'

She followed his advice, settling herself awkwardly into the chair. 'Soft,' she murmured as she patted the multi-coloured upholstery with one hand. 'This chair is soft. Where I'm from, chairs are made of wood.'

'Uh huh. Yes, well, some chairs still are. That's what you call a comfy chair. Now look,' Alfie continued, 'I'm not being funny but, well, you need to go back.'

'Back?' The witch stared at him, as though unfamiliar with the word. 'Back where?'

'Back to wherever you were,' he said. 'Before you came here.'

She shook her head. 'I cannot go back,' she told him.

'I was afraid you were going to say that,' Alfie murmured. 'But look, you have to. I didn't mean to call you here. It was an accident. Like I said, I was just trying to impress Mia ...'

'Mia?'

'This girl I met beside your grave. She told me about you. And she said if I walked around The Witching Stone three times and said "I don't believe in witches —"'

Meg's green eyes seemed to blaze. 'I'm no witch!' she snarled, through gritted teeth. 'They only said that because they wanted rid of me. Oh yes, I had powers, but I never used them for evil purposes, only to heal. Now you have summoned me —'

'Look, I really didn't!'

'You have summoned me,' she continued, 'to come and take my revenge on them!'

'Take revenge on who?' murmured Alfie, startled.

'The people of Woodplumpton,' said Meg. 'Who else?'

'Oh, but ... well, that doesn't seem fair. I mean, it's not the people who are here *now* that did that to you, is it? It's the people of the ... the seventeen-hundreds.'

Meg gave him a searching look. 'What do you mean?' she snapped. She looked around again, studying the wallpaper and the furnishings, as though noticing for the first time how different things looked. She turned back to look at him. 'What year is it now?' she asked. 'I have been away for some time, I think.'

'Er . . . yes.' He looked at her apprehensively. 'Don't freak out or anything —'

'Freak out?'

'Yes, well, it has been quite a while. It's two thousand and twenty.'

She stared at him, uncomprehending. 'What do you mean?' she asked.

'I mean what I said. It's the year two thousand and twenty.' He spoke the sentence slowly, as though explaining to a child. 'That's . . .' – he did a quick sum in his head – '. . . around three hundred and twenty years since you . . . since you were buried.'

Meg sat there looking at him, an expression of shock on her face; and then her eyes suddenly filled with fat tears that ran trickling down her newly scrubbed face. 'How is such a thing possible?' she whimpered.

'I really don't know. But what I'm saying is, the people you want to get revenge on, they're long gone.'

'Gone? Gone where?'

'Well, I mean they . . . they've died. Obviously.'

'But their ancestors remain?'

'Oh, I wouldn't know about that. I'm not from round here. Maybe.' He shook his head, not knowing quite what to tell her. 'So, you see, I think the best thing for everyone would be for you to just, you know, go back.'

She was beginning to look annoyed. 'I already told you,

I cannot go back,' she snarled. 'I *will* not. Not until I have had my revenge. And you . . .' She pointed a finger at him. 'You will assist me.'

He stared at her. 'Oh, I really don't think I can do that,' he protested. 'This isn't my fight.'

'But you summoned me!'

'You keep saying that, but I didn't mean to. It was a mistake.'

'But you did it. Which means you are my apprentice.'

'I . . . I can't be! I haven't got time. I . . . I've got schoolwork to revise for!'

'Pah!' She leant sideways and spat on the carpet.

Alfie looked down at the blob of phlegm disapprovingly. 'I really would prefer it if you didn't do that,' he said.

She studied him intently for a moment. 'I'll leave you to think about it,' she told him. 'I'll be back tomorrow night.'

'There really isn't any p —'

And she was gone. No flash of light, no puff of smoke. One moment she was there, the next . . . just the empty chair – though Alfie could see a damp patch on the back of it where her wet hair had trailed. He looked slowly around his room, wanting to be sure that she wasn't still lurking somewhere waiting to pop out again, but he appeared to be alone. He got up from his bed and walked over to the bathroom doorway. He stood there looking in. There was no doubting the array of muddy footprints on the floor, nor the dark stains that were still pooled ominously in the shower cubicle. He sighed, realising that he was going to have to get all traces of her cleaned up before he could even think about getting some sleep. Not that he imagined he'd be able to.

He walked over to the cabinet and opened the doors beneath the wash basin, taking out a bottle of cleaner and a packet of cloths that were stored there. He found a roll of black bin bags and tore one off, then picked up Meg's tattered dress between thumb and forefinger, wrinkling his nose at the awful smell. He dropped it into the bag and tied a knot in it. He was about to drop it in the litter bin but decided to hang on to it, telling himself that it might be needed as evidence.

Then he went to work, cleaning up the mess and trying very hard not to think about Meg Shelton's next visit.

CHAPTER EIGHT

ANOTHER BREAKFAST

Alfie trudged into the dining room of The Excelsior, to find Dad already sitting at a table. He looked red-eyed and poorly shaven after another interrupted night's sleep. On the far side of the room, a middle-aged couple were seated at a table, the man engrossed in a newspaper, the woman glumly studying her phone. *Holidaymakers*, Alfie supposed, though their miserable demeanours didn't exactly suggest they were having a great time. Dad looked up from his own phone as Alfie slid into the seat across from him.

'Ah, here he is,' muttered Dad, tonelessly. 'Mr Noisy.'

'Very funny,' muttered Alfie.

Dad leant closer and lowered his voice. 'No, actually, not

funny at all,' he hissed. 'I've already had Selina making some very pointed comments about the noise you were making last night. If you go on at this rate, they'll end up turfing us out of here.'

'I'm sorry,' said Alfie, adopting a contrite look. 'I couldn't sleep.'

Dad grimaced. 'I, on the other hand, was sleeping like a baby . . . until you started kicking up a rumpus next door. What were you watching, anyway? All I could hear was some woman screeching about something being hot!'

'Er . . . yeah, it was . . .' Alfie struggled to think of something convincing. 'A film. A film set in . . . South America.'

'Oh yeah?' Dad gave Alfie a suspicious look. 'What channel was that on?'

'I don't know. I just switched the telly on and there it was.'

Dad looked suddenly worried. 'Alfie, it wasn't one of those *special* channels, was it? You know, the 'Adult Only' ones. Because we have to pay for those.'

'No, of course not!' said Alfie. 'I wouldn't be interested in anything like that. No, it was just these two people on holiday and the woman was complaining that she was too hot.' He shrugged his shoulders. 'I was only half watching it.'

'At maximum volume,' Dad reminded him.

Alfie grabbed a menu and pretended to study it. 'So, what's for breakfast?' he asked, trying to sound enthusiastic. 'I don't suppose you want to risk the full English again?'

Dad shook his head. 'I've been thinking about that,' he murmured. 'We need to order something that even Malcolm can't spoil.'

'Well, he managed to burn my toast yesterday, so . . .'

Alfie broke off as Selina cruised into the room and made a beeline for their table. 'And how are my two best customers feeling this morning?' she asked, brightly.

Dad actually looked around the room, as if to make sure she hadn't been referring to somebody else and then smiled at her. 'You're very kind,' he said. 'We're fine, aren't we, Alfie? Well-rested and raring to go.'

Selina directed a withering look at Alfie. 'I wish I could say the same,' she told them. 'But something woke me up in the night. Again. Voices.'

'Yes, I've already had a word with Alfie about that,' Dad assured her. 'It won't happen a third time. But, well, you know how it is. Strange room, strange bed. He's finding it hard to get to sleep. I'm sure he'll soon settle in.'

Not if Meg comes visiting every night, thought Alfie, ruefully.

'So, what can I get for you gentlemen?' asked Selina, raising her notepad. She looked at Dad. 'I seem to remember you're a coffee man, isn't that right?'

'Usually,' admitted Dad. 'But . . . I also remember you mentioning your vast array of teas, yesterday. So, I believe I'd like a pot of English Breakfast, please.'

'Certainly. Excellent choice. And for the young sir?'

'Orange,' said Alfie. 'Fresh. Please,' he added hastily.

'Very good. And to eat?'

Dad tapped the menu. 'I'm just in the mood for a nice bowl of cereal,' he said. 'Something healthy . . . ah, right there. Swiss muesli. Perfect.'

'Good choice,' said Selina. 'It's chock-full of dates and seeds and banana chips – all that stuff. Everybody says it's really good for you.'

'Just the job,' said Dad.

'With milk?'

'Yes, please. Skimmed, if you have it.'

Selina nodded. Dad looked at his son with a forced smile. 'Alfie?'

'Just white bread and butter, please. Definitely no scrambled egg.'

Selina pursed her lips into a tight pout of disapproval. 'Very good,' she said. 'White bread and butter it shall be.' She scribbled furiously on her notepad, turned on her heel and stalked out. Alfie looked at Dad with eyebrows raised. 'Muesli?' he muttered.

'Well, like I said, even Malcolm can't muck that up. It comes straight out of a box and into a bowl and he just has to pour some milk on it. What could go wrong?' He leant back in his chair looking pleased with himself and studied Alfie. 'So, what have you got planned for today?'

Alfie was prepared for this. 'Oh, I thought I'd go out and have a look around. Get to know the area a bit better. Mia knows all the local places of interest, so . . .'

'Mia again.' Dad gave Alfie a certain look. 'I hope you're not getting in too deep, son. After everything that happened with —'

'Please don't say her name again,' hissed Alfie. 'And it's nothing like that. Mia and me, we're friends. That's all there is to it. And, like I say, she knows all the places to go.'

Dad seemed appeased. 'Well, it's good that you're taking an interest,' he said. 'And only fitting, really, when you think our family roots are from around here.'

That line hit Alfie like a punch to the gut. He glared across the table.

'What are you talking about?' he gasped.

'Just what I said. Our family are —'

'. . . from round here? No way! We're from Bristol!'

Dad smiled at his outraged expression. 'Well, the last couple of generations are, certainly. But we haven't always been there. I remember quite clearly my mum telling me that my great grandmother came from a little village in Lancashire, somewhere near here.' He frowned, trying to remember. 'What was it called, though? It was a long time ago. Something . . . could it have been something beginning with S?'

Alfie felt his heart thump in his chest. 'Not Singleton?' he murmured.

Dad looked amazed. 'Yes, I actually think it *was*! That's amazing. How did you know that?'

'Oh, it's just, I was there yesterday,' whispered Alfie. His face must have betrayed his anxiety, because Dad looked amused.

'It wasn't that bad, was it? I'm sure Mum said it was a charming little village.'

'It was,' said Alfie. *It was also the birthplace of Meg Bloody Shelton!* He couldn't prevent the thought from flashing, unbidden, through his mind. Hannah had asked him if he had any family in this area and he'd said no. How could he have known any different?

'What's the matter with you?' asked Dad. 'You look like you've seen a ghost.'

Alfie shook his head. 'I'm just hungry,' he muttered. 'Bit of a sugar dip. How come you never mentioned this to me before?'

'I don't know. I didn't think it was important.'

'Of course it's important! What if I've got relatives around here?'

Dad looked bewildered. 'Maybe you have,' he said. 'What's the big deal? It would be nice to discover a few new faces, wouldn't it?'

At that moment, Selina bustled into the room, carrying two English breakfasts which she took to the other diners and set down in front of them. They sat there, looking down at their respective plates in silence.

Dad winked at Alfie, slyly. 'Wait for it . . .' he whispered.

'Could we have some ketchup?' asked the man.

'And some brown sauce,' suggested the woman.

'And some mustard,' added the man.

Selina nodded and went out of the room.

'Priceless,' whispered Dad. 'They need something to hide the taste. Clearly yesterday wasn't a fluke. Perhaps we should chip in and book Malcolm some cookery lessons.'

Alfie studied Dad for a moment. 'Never mind about that. Tell me about Singleton,' he said. 'What was your grandmother doing there?'

'My *great* grandmother,' Dad corrected him. He shrugged his shoulders. 'I don't know. I never met her, or my great grandfather, for that matter. I believe they both died before I was born.' He furrowed his brow. 'I seem to remember hearing that he was a carpenter of some kind, but what she did, is anybody's guess.' He spread his hands and then seemed to have an idea. 'Hey, there's a summer project for you,' he said. 'Exploring our family tree! It'd be like *Who Do You Think You Are!* I'd be fascinated to know more about it.'

But Alfie was thinking that he really didn't want to go poking around in the past. What if it turned out that he and Meg Shelton were somehow related? He was about to say something else when the woman at the next table made a kind of retching noise, and spat something back on to her plate, just as Selina reappeared carrying the bottles of sauce. The man was staring at his wife's food and he made a kind of gasping sound. Selina moved closer until she was standing beside the woman. She too inspected the plate. 'Oh, my goodness,' she said. 'I'm so sorry. I've no idea how *that* got there.' She set the bottles of sauce down on the table. 'Perhaps I can bring you something else?' she offered.

The woman jumped suddenly up from her seat, almost knocking Selina over in her urgency. 'That is absolutely disgusting!' she said, pointing at the plate. 'I had that in my mouth.' She looked at her husband. 'Alfred, get your stuff together. We're not staying here a moment longer.'

The man threw down his serviette and got to his feet. He took his phone from his back pocket, leant forward and took a photograph of the plate. 'That's going on *Tripadvisor*,' he snarled. 'We'll have you closed down.' Then he stepped past Selina, took his wife by the arm and marched her out of the room. Selina stood there, staring open-mouthed at the woman's plate, as though she couldn't believe her eyes.

'Er . . . is everything OK?' asked Dad, awkwardly and Selina snapped out of her funk and went into autopilot. She grabbed the two plates and ferried them towards the exit. 'Everything's fine!' she said in a bright, but unconvincing tone. 'Not a problem!' She moved quickly out of sight and Dad and Alfie heard her voice menacingly intoning one word.

ANOTHER BREAKFAST

'MALCOLM!'

Dad winced. He looked at Alfie. 'I wonder what that was about?' he muttered.

Alfie wasn't remotely interested. 'Look, you must remember something more about them!' he insisted.

'About *who*?'

'Your great grandparents!'

'I really don't. I barely heard more than a mention of them when I was a kid. Who remembers that kind of stuff? But like I was saying—'

He broke off at a sudden noise coming from the direction of the kitchen – what sounded very much like crockery smashing. It was followed by a shriek from a female voice, almost certainly Selina, and then a muffled crash, as though something heavier had tipped over. There was a short silence and then a male voice shouted something that sounded distinctly like, 'It's alive!'

'What the hell is going on?' asked Dad, mystified. 'Sounds like World War Three in there.'

'I'll tell you what's going on,' said Alfie, irritably. 'I'm asking you questions and you're ignoring them.'

'I can't give you answers I don't have,' insisted Dad. 'Like I said, maybe you could—'

He broke off, as Selina reeled into the room doing her very best to look calm, despite the fact that her formally immaculate white blouse had a big, eggy smear down the front of it.

Her hair was in disarray – a long lock of it hanging into her eyes, which Alfie couldn't help noticing, were filled with tears and trailing two trickles of black mascara down her face. She was carrying a silver tray on which a teapot and a glass of orange rested. She set them down very carefully, because her hands were shaking.

'Is everything all right?' Dad asked her. He waved a hand towards the other table. 'Those people seemed angry about something.'

'Their meal wasn't quite as they wanted it,' she said, making a real attempt to keep her voice calm. 'The matter has been dealt with and normal service has been restored.' She gave them a pained grimace that was probably intended to be a confident smile. 'I'll just pop and get your food,' she added. Before Dad could say anything else, she turned on her heel and hurried out of the room. Dad gazed after her for a moment. 'Something's not right,' he said. 'She looked as though she was about to explode.' He turned back, lifted the tea pot and poured himself a cup of tea, then added a generous slosh of milk. 'This surely can't be worse than the coffee,' he told Alfie and raising the cup to his lips, he took a generous gulp. His eyes widened for an instant and then he spat the entire mouthful on to the pristine white tablecloth.

'Dad!' cried Alfie. 'That's gross.'

Dad pulled a face. 'The milk,' he said. 'It's really off. Sour as anything.'

If milk turned sour . . . the blame was inevitably laid at Meg's door . . .

The words from Hannah's book came to Alfie as though he could see them printed out in front of him. Without thinking, he raised his glass of juice to his lips and took a mouthful – then he too was spraying it from his mouth in absolute disgust. It tasted as though it had been made from rotten fruit. Unfortunately, he did it just as Selina reappeared, carrying a bowl and a plate. She hurried forward, set the things down on the table and looked at the two of them in distress. 'Is something wrong?' she asked them.

Dad immediately tried to downplay the incident. 'It's just . . . I think perhaps Malcolm didn't check the milk before he served it. It's a little . . . er . . . ripe.'

Selina lifted the jug to her nose and took a sniff. Her expression twisted into a look of disgust. 'I'm so sorry,' she said. 'I don't understand. That milk was fresh from the dairy this morning. Something weird is going on here. Those people just —' She broke off as she saw that Alfie's gaze was now fixed to Dad's breakfast bowl. She followed his gaze and took a deep breath. The thick muesli was in motion. Alfie realised that the dark shapes that he had first taken to be sliced dates, actually had legs – legs that were moving frantically about as the creatures tried to manoeuvre their way through the thick, milky substance that surrounded them. They were little frogs, he decided, or, judging by their warty backs, tiny toads. And there were scores of them.

'Bloody hell,' said Dad, in astonishment.

Then Selina started screaming, fit to lift the roof off the building. After a few moments, there was the sound of frantically running feet and a big, brawny man wearing a dirty apron, came running into the room. He had a crew cut and his muscular arms were decorated with crudely rendered tattoos. 'Selina?' he gasped. 'What's wrong, my darling?'

She pointed an elegantly manicured finger at the bowl, and then screamed again.

Now the 'dates' were clambering over the edge of the bowl and hopping frantically about on the tablecloth.

CHAPTER NINE

EVIDENCE

lfie pushed open the door of Luigi's Cafe to find that, once again, there were no other customers. Giovanni was sitting in his customary spot behind the counter and was once again thumbing morosely through pages on his phone. He glanced up and smiled. 'You again,' he said. It was perhaps intended to be welcoming, but sounded somehow more like an accusation. *Well*, Alfie thought, *it* was twice in two days. He tucked the black bin bag he was carrying under one arm and approached the counter.

'Morning,' he said.

'And another lovely one it is,' said Giovanni. 'Meeting your girlfriend again?'

'Yes. She's not my girlfriend, though. Just a friend.'

'Who happens to be a girl,' Giovanni reminded him, with a wink. 'You don't have to make excuses, pal. I know how these things go. Hey, how were those rocky roads, by the way?'

'Er . . . very nice,' said Alfie, trying not to look guilty. He was all too aware that they'd been forgotten about and that his portion was still squashed in his jacket pocket, wrapped in a serviette.

'And what can I get for you today?'

'Diet Coke, please.'

'A man of regular habits,' Giovanni replied. 'Anything to eat with that? I've just put out a freshly baked Victoria sponge with buttercream.'

'No, thanks. Maybe later.'

Giovanni waved a hand. 'Take a seat. I'll bring your drink over.'

Alfie wandered across to the same table he'd occupied yesterday and put the bin bag down on a vacant chair, before sitting next to it. He took out his phone and checked his messages, wanting to be sure that Mia hadn't sent him anything since her last one. But there was nothing new. The message thread had been shorter than last time.

HI. ME AGAIN
SOZ CAN YOU MEET ME
SOMETHING IMPORTANT TO TELL YOU

EVIDENCE

You're keen

NO I'M NOT

Soz

CAN WE MEET

OK. Same time same place
Coffees on you AGAIN

ALSO – I HAVE SOMETHING TO TELL YOU!!!!!!!

He didn't have very long to wait. The door swung open and Mia stepped into the cafe, looking entirely different to the way she had yesterday. This morning she was dressed completely in black. She'd whitened her face with some kind of make-up and her lips were painted a very dark red. She was wearing a pair of vintage shades, which she removed and tucked into the neckline of her T-shirt. She looked at Giovanni.

'The usual?' he asked her.

Mia nodded. She strolled across to the table where Alfie was waiting for her. Her gaze fell inevitably on the bin bag. 'What's that?' she asked him, smiling. 'Please tell me you've bought me a ridiculously expensive present.'

He shook his head. 'Afraid not,' he said. 'That's evidence. For what happened last night.'

She sank into a chair opposite him, looking worried. 'What *did* happen last night?' she asked him. 'Oh wait, don't tell me. More muddy footprints.'

'Worse than that,' he assured her. He lowered his voice. 'Muddy witch. *Entire* muddy witch. In my bathroom.'

She studied him, warily. 'Riiiight,' she said. 'Awkward.'

'Don't say it like that,' he snapped.

'How else would you like me to say it?' she asked him. 'I mean, it's a bit . . . out there, isn't it? Footprints, that's one thing, but . . . Meg Shelton, apparating in your bathroom?'

'She did more than just apparate! She spoke to me.'

'Did she now? What did you talk about?'

'Lots of things. And then she had a shower!'

Mia leant back in her seat. 'See, it's when you say things like that, it's hard to take you seriously. I mean, you have to admit, it does sound a bit . . .'

'Trust me, I know how it sounds,' he assured her 'The fact is —'

He broke off as he heard a grunt of exasperation from Giovanni. They both turned to look at him.

'Everything all right?' Mia asked him.

Giovanni was holding a mug in front of him and staring into it in disbelief. 'The milk's off!' he cried.

'Off? What do you mean, "off"?'

'He means it's sour,' said Alfie. 'We had the same problem at The Excelsior this morning,' he told Giovanni. 'It was rancid.'

'But . . . that doesn't make sense,' muttered Giovanni. 'I drank a glass of this only ten minutes ago and it was fine then. How could it go off so suddenly?' Giovanni moved to the sink and emptied the contents of the mug into it. 'Let me check the rest of my stock in the big fridge,' he suggested. He opened the door to his stockroom and went inside.

'There's no point,' said Alfie. 'It'll all be bad.'

Mia gave him a baffled look. 'How could you possibly know that?' she whispered.

'Why do you think?'

She looked confused. 'Is it . . . something to do with the hot weather?' she ventured.

'No! It's something to do with Meg Shelton. Look . . .' He reached into his jacket pocket and pulled out the book that Hannah had lent him. He opened it to the page he'd marked earlier and showed her the sentence he was referring to.

If milk turned sour . . . the blame was inevitably laid at Meg's door . . .

Mia read the line and then lifted her gaze to Alfie's face. 'Oh, you're surely not saying —'

'Mia, you should have been at The Excelsior this morning! It wasn't just the milk that was weird. My dad ordered a bowl of muesli and it had —'

He broke off as Giovanni emerged from the stockroom looking distraught. 'All of it!' he cried. 'Every bottle stinks! What am I going to do?'

'Phone the dairy?' suggested Mia.

'Yes, good idea! Sorry Princess, I'll bring you something else in a minute. Might have to be a black coffee this morning . . .'

'I hope there's no milk in any of your cakes,' said Alfie and Giovanni's face registered panic. He moved to the glass display, took out a large Victoria sponge and sniffed at it. 'This was fresh out this morning,' he said. 'I only put a couple of teaspoons in it, but —' He broke off in surprise and stared at the cake. Even from their seat at the table, Alfie and Mia could see that the white icing on the surface was beginning to move. 'Maggots!' shrieked Giovanni. He grabbed the plate, swung around and flung the entire thing into a swing top bin. 'What the hell's going on here?' he cried. 'That cake only came out of the oven fifteen minutes ago!' He threw an accusing look at Alfie, as though suspecting it might be his fault. 'You said something about The Excelsior having the same problems?'

'Er . . .'

'*And* you said there was something wrong with the muesli,' Mia prompted him.

'Yeah, that was off too,' said Alfie vaguely.

'What am I going to do?' cried Giovanni. 'Today's always one of my busiest.'

Alfie looked around in disbelief. 'Really?' he murmured.

'Yes. All the mums come in after the school run. Look, you kids keep an eye on the place, will you? I'll pop to the corner shop and buy a few pints to keep me going.' He pulled out his phone. 'And on the way I'll phone my cousin's cafe in my hometown and see if they've had any problems there.'

'Your hometown?' murmured Alfie. 'That would be. . .?'

'Leeds,' said Giovanni, and went out of the door at speed. It slammed shut behind him.

'He's wasting his time,' said Alfie. 'I reckon the milk at the shop will be off too.'

'You can't know that.'

'Yes, I can. Because Meg is doing this. She told me she wanted revenge on the people of the village, and this is how she's going about it. You saw what it said in the book. Milk goes sour. It's what witches *do*. And that muesli I was telling you about? It wasn't just off. It was full of these little toads . . .' He registered Mia's incredulous expression. 'Please stop giving me that look,' he told her.

'It's because you keep running away with yourself,' she said. 'Tell me from the beginning, exactly what happened.'

'What, you mean breakfast?'

'No, I mean Meg!'

'Oh, right. OK. Well, I woke up in the night —'

'Ah right, so you were dreaming again!'

'This wasn't a dream. Let's get that straight. I was wide awake – and please stop interrupting!'

'Sorry. Go on.'

'I woke up and went to the bathroom for a glass of water. I was standing at the sink and the next thing I knew, she was right behind me, looking over my shoulder. Scared the hell out of me.'

'I expect it did!'

'She wasn't a pretty sight. I mean, she was covered in mud, from head to foot. Filthy. That's why I made her get in the shower.'

Mia winced. 'There,' she said. 'Right there. That bit.'

'What?'

'A dead witch appears in front of you and you make her get in the shower?'

'Well, she was making a mess of the bathroom! I . . . I turned on the shower and told her that she needed to take her dress off —'

Mia raised her eyebrows. 'Whoa! Are you sure you want to say any more about this?' she asked him. 'Only it's in danger of getting a little saucy.'

'Don't talk daft! It wasn't in the least bit saucy. Terrifying, is what it was. And, obviously, she wasn't going to take a shower with her clothes on, was she?'

Mia was trying hard not to smile. 'I suppose not,' she

admitted. 'No, that wouldn't make any sense at all.' She made an effort to compose herself. 'So . . . what's she like? Is she all old and warty?'

'No! She's . . . middle-aged, I guess. Not bad looking really, once the mud was off her. And she loved that shower. Called it a rain box. Kept saying that the rain was hot . . . I expect that probably seemed like magic to her, right? Look, you're grinning again. This is deadly serious!'

'Sorry, I'm trying to keep it together but honestly, if you listened back to this . . .' She cleared her throat. 'OK, so Meg's scrubbing herself down with the shower gel. Where are you when this is happening? Ew, you're not watching, are you?'

'No! I wasn't going to stand there staring at her!'

'Good.'

That's when my dad turned up and I had to get rid of him. Meg said if I didn't, she was going to kill him.'

Mia grimaced. 'Well, that's definitely not funny,' she admitted. She looked at him hopefully. 'Your dad saw her, did he? He witnessed this?'

'No. But he *heard* her. That's why he came to my room in the first place, because she was shouting about the hot water being so good and everything. I told him it was a TV show I was watching . . .' He thought for a moment. 'Actually, that's a point. When I said to her I was going to close the door in case Dad saw her taking a shower, she said, "he won't see me". Maybe that means I'm the only one that *can* see her.'

'Very convenient,' observed Mia, giving him a sly look.

'Well, yes, I suppose it is – but in her place, I reckon I'd be the same. I wouldn't want to show myself to everybody – only to certain people. Maybe just to the person that summoned me – she said that was me and now I was kind of . . . responsible for her.'

Mia snorted. 'And how many kids do you suppose have done exactly what you did, over the years? Saying that line and walking three times around the Witching Stone. Must be thousands!'

'Yes, I get that. And I've been wondering the same. You know, why me?'

'Seems like a fair question.'

'Well, listen to this. You know I told Hannah that I was from Bristol and that my family had always lived there?'

'Yes . . .'

'Turns out, that's not true at all. Where do you think my great-grandparents actually came from?'

Mia shrugged her shoulders. 'Mars?' she suggested.

He ignored the taunt. 'Singleton!' he said.

'Aw, Alfie, come on!'

'I know how it sounds, but I swear it's true! My dad told me this morning.' He studied her incredulous look. 'I had no idea!' he assured her. 'Really. It just came up in conversation. Dad was suggesting I should look into the family tree as a summer project. But now I'm scared to. What if there's a connection?

What if that's the reason she heard my voice?'

'Oh, come on, that's a bit —'

'What?'

'A bit of a coincidence, don't you think? You coming here, meeting me by Meg's grave . . . and then me taking you to Singleton yesterday . . .'

'It *is* a coincidence,' admitted Alfie. 'But coincidences happen, don't they? You read about incredible coincidences all the time.' He thought for a moment. 'Or maybe it isn't a coincidence at all. Maybe she fixed it so I came here. Maybe she . . . lured me.'

Mia shook her head. 'Every line you say makes it weirder,' she complained. 'As if it wasn't weird enough to start with.'

He frowned. 'OK, prepare to eat humble pie,' he told her dramatically. He reached over, picked up the bin bag and handed it across the table to her. 'Just have a look at that,' he said, 'and *then* tell me I've imagined it all.'

She took it from him with evident reluctance.

'What is it?' she asked him nervously.

'It's hard evidence,' he said. 'That's the dress Meg was wearing.'

'Oh right. The dress you made her take off before she got in the shower . . .' Mia's eyes widened suddenly. 'Oh my God,' she said. 'What's she wearing now? Please don't tell me she's walking around Woodplumpton stark naked!'

Alfie snorted. 'Of course not. She's wearing one of my sweatshirts and some pyjama pants.'

'Oh, right, naturally.' Mia started to pick at the knot that Alfie had tied in the bag. 'So, did you wash her dress or anything?'

'No, I didn't. Some evidence that would be, all nicely laundered! No, that's exactly as it looked when she ... apparated.'

Mia opened the bag warily and peeped inside. She took a deep breath. 'So, this is what your well-dressed witch about town wears, is it?' she murmured.

'I guess so. I've never met one before. I mean, look at the state of it. That's ...' He hesitated. Mia was smiling again. 'What's so funny?' he asked her.

'Well, I have to hand it to you,' she said. 'I mean, you've worked this routine pretty successfully for a couple of days now, and you had me fooled for a while, but I guess this is the punch line, right? This is the bit where you say, "April Fool!" Except, of course, it's not April.' She reached into the bag and pulled out a crumpled white bath towel with the words 'Excelsior Guest House' embroidered on it. Alfie stared at it in dismay, his mouth falling open.

'No,' he said. 'No way.' He shook his head. 'That's not ... that's not what she was wearing.'

'You don't say?' Mia threw the towel at him and he caught it awkwardly. 'You actually had me going there for a while,' she said. 'You really did.'

Alfie was turning the towel over and over in his hands, as though expecting it to turn into something else. 'This isn't what I put in there,' he protested. 'I swear. Look, it still has some muddy stains on it . . .'

'Oh, does it really? That's not proof, is it?' said Mia flatly. 'The mud could have come from anywhere. It could have come from you after a game of football.'

'Somebody's changed it,' insisted Alfie. 'You have to believe me. I hid it at the back of the bathroom cabinet, so nobody could have known it was there. Only Meg. *She* did this.'

'Alfie . . .' said Mia. She sounded weary. 'A joke's a joke, and you've done pretty well with this one, but don't you think you've taken it a bit too far? I mean, I don't mind you fooling *me*, but I took you to meet Hannah and everything. It wasn't fair to drag her into it. She's serious about this stuff. She *believed* you.'

'You don't understand,' he told her. 'Meg told me that she wanted revenge on the people of Woodplumpton . . . and that she was going to use me to help her get it. But she's really clever, don't you see? She'll do anything to make sure that nobody believes me.' He glared at her. 'Even you. I thought I could count on you.'

'Hey, stop trying to do the guilt trip thing on me! Can you blame me for not believing this nonsense? I mean, come on, it *is* a bit far-fetched.'

'Fine.' Anger jolted through him, making him react. He stood upright, so suddenly that the chair behind him fell over with a clatter. 'I'll sort it out myself,' he said. 'No need for you to get involved.'

'Hey, wait, it's just . . .'

But Alfie had already turned on his heel and was striding towards the door, the towel still clutched in one hand. At that moment, the door burst open and Giovanni appeared carrying a couple of carrier bags stuffed with cartons of milk.

'I'm saved!' he announced dramatically. 'Joe at the corner shop says he's had no problems.' He held up a small container with the top already off. 'I even tried some, just to be certain,' he added. And then, as if to reassure himself, he took a quick swig of the contents. His eyes bulged and he spat the mouthful on to the floor at Alfie's feet. He stared down at it. 'No!' he gasped. 'It can't be. It was fine a moment ago. And it's six days within its sell-by date.' He lifted his gaze to Alfie. 'It . . . it must be something to do with *you*!' he gasped.

Alfie stepped past him without another word. He went out of the open door and into the glare of the sunlight. He stood there blinking for a moment, then started walking, his head down, not really caring where he was going – too angry to stop and think about what he was doing. Two elderly women approached from the other direction and he barely registered them, obliging them to get out of his way to let him pass. They stared after him in silent indignation. He realised he should have turned back and apologised, but his anger wouldn't allow him to slow his pace. He had gone only a short distance when he became dimly aware of footsteps running after him and then a hand grabbed his wrist and pulled him back. He turned, his mouth open to shout something abusive, and Mia's arms were around him, holding him close against her. He struggled to pull away, but she held on more tightly.

'Hey,' she said. 'Calm down. Take a deep breath.'

'I'm not making it up,' he hissed, into her ear. 'I'm not, I promise you I'm not.'

'OK,' she murmured. 'I hear you. Let's . . . let's just take a moment, shall we?'

He held himself rigid for a few moments longer, aware of his heart thudding in his chest like a drumbeat and then, with an effort, he allowed his body to relax a little.

'I'm sorry,' he said. 'I hate it when somebody doesn't believe me.'

'I get that,' she said. 'I'm the same. But you can understand how unlikely it all sounds, right? You must know it's bonkers.'

He nodded. 'Of course,' he said. 'I probably wouldn't believe it either.'

'OK,' she said. 'So, I'm going to let you go now. Promise me you won't run off.'

'I won't,' he assured her.

'Good.' She released him and they stepped away from each other. They stood on the sun blasted street, gazing at each other.

'Here's where I am with this,' said Mia gently. 'I believe that you believe this thing is actually happening to you. I haven't decided if it's for real or if it's just in your head, but whatever it is, it's real to you – and I shouldn't have said what I did back there. I should have cut you some slack, because it can't be easy to talk about something like that.' She seemed to take a moment to mentally go over what she'd just said, as though checking she'd covered everything. 'That's the closest I can get to an apology right now,' she concluded. 'Is that enough?'

Alfie nodded. 'It'll do,' he said.

'Good. Now, listen. You know I said I had some news for you? Well, I have.'

He frowned. 'What's that, then?' he asked her.

'Well, I can't be sure, but . . . you know all those mentions about Meg living in a place called Cuckoo Hall?'

He nodded.

'And you know how in all the books and articles, nobody ever seemed to know where it was?'

Again, he nodded.

Mia smiled. 'It's a bit of a long shot,' she said, 'but I think I know where it is. And I was going to suggest maybe the two of us could go there and have a look around?'

'Great,' he said. 'That's fantastic. We'll go now, shall we?'

EVIDENCE

Mia smiled. 'Maybe we should head back to Luigi's first,' she suggested. 'We need to make sure Giovanni hasn't had a nervous breakdown.'

CHAPTER TEN

CUCKOO HALL

The bus dropped them on a quiet stretch of country road. Mia, after a quick look at the map on her phone, led Alfie across the street and along a narrow lane that was bordered by high, privet hedges. They walked for a few hundred metres and then emerged on to a wide stretch of moorland, across which a dirt track led up a gentle incline to a ridge. They crested it and then descended steeply into the valley beyond. They walked for about twenty minutes and then came to an area of dense woodland that stretched across their path like a barrier – but as they drew nearer, they could see that the track led in between ranks of tall, tightly-packed conifers. As they stepped into the shade of the trees, the temperature seemed to plunge and the sound of birdsong they had heard on the open moorland ceased as abruptly as if a switch had been thrown. Now there was only the rhythmic crunching of their feet on the litter of fallen branches that covered the track, which offered them just enough room to walk side by side. Alfie gazed uneasily around, looking into the narrow, dark avenues between the trees.

'What is this place?' he muttered. 'It's dead creepy.'

'It doesn't seem to have a name,' Mia told him. 'It's just the place where my grandma used to play when she was little.'

'Your grandma?'

'Yes. She was called Flora.' Mia smiled, as if remembering something. 'She lived just up the road from here. Been gone nearly a year now, but everybody loved Flora to bits. My grandad, Albert, died in his seventies but my grandma lived for years after that. She was well into her nineties when she finally passed. I miss her.'

'So, what does this have to do with Cuckoo Hall?'

'Well, look, I can't be absolutely sure she was right about this but . . . well, I remembered that one day the two of us were talking about Meg Shelton. This was around the time that Hannah published the book about her, and that's how it came up. I happened to mention Cuckoo Hall and Flora smiled and said she knew the place very well. I told her she must be mistaken, because Hannah had said that nobody knew where it was and she'd done the research. But Flora insisted that she and her mates used to play around in it when they were little. They used to dare each other to go in there, because they all thought it was haunted.'

Alfie snorted. 'Must have been a long time ago,' he said. 'What made her think it was Cuckoo Hall? In Hannah's book, it says —'

'Yeah, I know what it says. But you see, Flora had a pretty good reason for thinking this was the place.'

'Oh yeah? What was that.'

Mia gave him a look. 'I'm not saying. Just in case it's not true.'

'OK. And did you tell Hannah what your grandma said?'

Mia nodded. 'I did, actually. Hannah even said the two of us would have to go and check it out some time. But then she had a fall and sprained her ankle, so it got put off. And then it was winter, and I suppose we just forgot about it. It didn't feel so important then. Now it really does. Anyway, it can't do any harm to have a look at the place, can it?'

'I guess not.' Alfie frowned. 'You don't believe in any of this, do you?' he muttered.

She looked at him quizzically. 'What do you mean?'

'You think Meg's just in my head.'

'I never said that.'

'You didn't have to say it. I can see it in your eyes, every time I mention her. Like you can't decide whether to just nod and smile or run away screaming.'

Mia smiled. 'Let's just say I'm keeping my options open,' she assured him.

'What do you think about what Giovanni said?'

'What, about the sour milk being something to do with you? Oh, he didn't mean that, he was just freaking out.'

'Yes, but think about it, Mia! He bought the milk in the corner shop and it was fine. Ten minutes later, he gets back to where I am and it's suddenly rancid. And I've been thinking about The Excelsior this morning. If I hadn't been there, maybe breakfast would have been just the same as usual.'

'You're saying your superpower might be the ability to make milk go sour?'

They looked at each other for a moment and then both started laughing – but they quickly stopped when they heard the weird echoes of their laughter ringing off the surrounding trees.

The track led onwards, for what seemed miles, into the forest and then, quite suddenly, the conifers gave way to tightly-packed deciduous trees, lush and green in their summer foliage.

'This is the oldest part of the woods,' Mia told him. 'Flora mentioned it. She said it's been here for hundreds of years. It used to be much bigger than this but over time it's been cut back. The house is in here somewhere, and this track is supposed to lead right to it. I don't know what kind of state it will be in. Flora told me it was nearly falling down when *she* used to go there.'

They moved into the older woodland and it grew darker still, the thick canopy above blocking out the sunlight. Alfie had somehow expected the bird song to resume, but it didn't. It was eerily silent here, as though only the trees had survived.

'We could be wasting our time,' muttered Alfie dismally. 'They could have demolished the place. Maybe we should —'

He broke off as something loomed into view up ahead of them. It was the remains of an old two-storey cottage, built of dark grey stone. The roof was mostly gone, and rotting black beams lay exposed to the elements. As they came slowly closer, they could see that the cottage was virtually enclosed by tree trunks – indeed, in one place, a tree had somehow managed to entwine itself around the very fabric of the building, a greenish brown branch plunging in through a broken window, as though attempting to embrace the building and claim it as its own. Alfie and Mia moved round to the front of the cottage, clambering and squeezing their way through the tightly-packed trunks in order to do so. Finally, they got to the main entrance and saw the remains of an ancient door, hanging lop-sided in its frame and pushed half open to reveal a dark, forbidding interior.

'Now then . . . Mia was examining the door carefully. 'If Flora was right about this place, there should be something . . . ah! There!' She pointed at a shape carved into the wood just above the rusted remains of an old door knocker. Alfie stepped closer to peer at it. It was half obliterated by patches of lichen, and he had to reach up and scrub some of them away with his fingertips in order to fully reveal what lay beneath. But it was, unmistakably, the crudely carved outline of a bird in flight.

'Is that a cuckoo?' asked Alfie doubtfully. 'I've no idea what one even looks like.'

In answer, Mia tapped her phone and held it out for him to see. 'I downloaded this last night,' she told him. She lifted the screen until it was next to the carving. The photo showed a deep-chested grey bird with a long tail and a tufted head. It was impossible to be sure, but the carving wasn't a million miles away in shape.

'Wow,' whispered Alfie. 'Maybe Flora was right about this place.'

Mia nodded. She switched on her torch and directed the beam through the gap in the doorway and into the cottage. Alfie fumbled for his own phone and followed her example, adding his light to hers. They found themselves looking into a small, bare room – the floor covered with a thick layer of fallen leaves. There was something horribly forbidding about the room, as though nobody had stepped inside there for a very long time.

'Come on,' suggested Mia and she led the way inside, placing her feet with care on the uncertain flooring. Alfie went after her. Once fully inside, they swept their torch beams around the room, picking out the shape of a rusted cast iron fireplace and, in one corner, what looked like the remains of a broken rocking chair. On the rotting plaster of one wall, somebody had used spray paint to write a brief message in big, black letters.

Get out now if you want to live!!!

Alfie swallowed. 'Charming,' he said, and the echoey sound of his own voice almost made him panic. 'I don't like this place much,' he whispered, noticing as he did so that his breath was clouding in the light of the torch.

'Me neither,' said Mia. 'Maybe we should —'

She gasped in surprise as something fast and lithe leapt suddenly down from an alcove in the wall off to their left. Whatever it was went racing away from them, flinging dry leaves in all directions, before plunging through a doorway at the far end of the room. Mia swung her torch round but was too late to pinpoint whatever had made the noise.

'What the hell was that?' cried Alfie, trying not to panic.

'A cat, I think. We must have startled it.'

'I'm the one who's startled!' He thought for a moment. 'It . . . it wasn't a ginger cat, was it?'

'Don't know. It moved too quickly to tell what colour it was. Why?'

'Meg has a cat like that.'

She stared at him for a moment and then seemed to make an effort to compose herself. 'All right,' she said. 'Let's go and have a look.'

They concentrated their twin beams on the doorway through which the cat had fled and saw that it led to a small rough-plastered hall. Alfie and Mia glanced at each other in the gloom and nodded. They moved forward, Alfie taking the lead this time, horribly aware of the dry leaves rustling around his ankles as he walked. Halfway along the hall, a set of blackened wooden steps lead upwards into darkness. They looked rotten and incapable of supporting any weight and Alfie contented himself by directing his torch beam up them, realising that the climb was completely blocked by fallen debris a few feet higher up. There was no way either of them could get up there.

He turned back to look along the hall, his eyes straining for signs of movement. He told himself that a cat couldn't hurt him, and yet there was something about that ginger creature that really scared him. Further on, another doorway beckoned – there were less dead leaves now, and, looking up, Alfie could see that this end of the building still had some vestiges of a roof over it. A heavy wooden door hung ajar in its rotting frame. Alfie swallowed nervously, reached out a hand and pushed it open. The ancient hinges made a loud, grating sound that set his nerves jangling but he steeled himself, took a deep breath and stepped decisively into the room. He could see, straight ahead of him, the outline of an old bedstead, a wooden frame and a jumble of rusted springs. He opened his mouth to tell Mia to follow him, but with a suddenness that made his heart jolt in his chest, the door swung shut behind him making a crash that echoed throughout the building. There was a moment of shocked silence and then Alfie heard Mia shout something on the other side of the door. The old metal handle began to twist frantically back and forth as she tried to force her way in, but her efforts seemed to have no effect whatsoever.

'Alfie?' he heard her call. 'Help me with it.'

He reached up to lend his efforts to the task but then froze as he became aware of something moving above him. He stepped back from the door, swung the torch beam upwards to the ceiling and saw what had made the noise. He let out a yelp of terror, sharp and high-pitched.

Meg was splayed on her back against the rotting roof beams, staring down at Alfie with an expression of malevolent anger. She had somehow traded the sweatshirt and pyjama pants for a long green dress that seemed to billow around her as though stirred by the wind. She opened her mouth and let out a long hiss of displeasure. 'You!' she sneered. 'What are you doing here?'

He opened his mouth to reply but the words seemed to die in his throat. He could only stare up at her, as she began to drift slowly downwards from the beams, defying gravity, her arms outstretched on either side. She swung herself round into an upright position and came gently down to rest on her bare feet a few steps in front of him. She stood there, still glowering at him, as though expecting an answer.

'Speak, pup!' she urged him. 'How did you find me?'

CHAPTER ELEVEN

A CONVERSATION

lfie tried to answer Meg's question, but for the moment at least, he couldn't manage to find enough words.

'I . . . I just . . .'

'Alfie! Are you OK in there?' Mia's fist hammered urgently on the other side of the jammed door, making him jump. Meg took a moment to lift her gaze towards the source of the sound.

'Who is that?' she growled.

'J . . . just a friend,' stammered Alfie.

'Get rid of her,' snarled Meg. She looked at Alfie. 'Now!' she snapped. 'Or it shall be the worse for her.'

He didn't dare disobey. He turned back to the door and

shouted a warning. 'Mia! Stop knocking. I'm OK. Just . . . wait for me outside. Please.'

A pause then: 'What's happening in there?'

'I'm all right, really. I can't explain right now. Please, just go.'

Another long pause – then finally the sound of Mia's footsteps moving slowly back across the room towards the front door.

'You told somebody about me,' said Meg. It wasn't a question, but a statement.

'Yes. I . . . I don't think she believes me though.'

Meg lifted a hand to shield her face and Alfie realised he was still aiming the torch beam straight at her. 'However you're doing that,' she growled, 'stop it now.'

He killed the torch and slipped it back into his pocket. The ensuing gloom was hard to bear, but his eyes gradually adjusted to the meagre light spilling in through a tiny dust-grimed window. Now he noticed that the ginger cat was sitting on the sill, silhouetted against the glass. It was licking one of its front paws and watching Alfie with interest.

'Now tell me,' murmured Meg. 'How did you find me?'

'It was just . . . Mia's grandmother used to play here when she was little, so . . . How are you even here?' he managed to ask. 'I thought you could only come out at night.'

Her thin lips twisted into a smirk. 'Whatever gave you that idea?' she asked him.

'Well, Hannah thought . . .'

'Hannah?'

He winced. 'Just somebody I . . . spoke to.'

'About me?' Now she looked furious. 'How many people have you blabbed to?'

'Oh, nobody else, I promise! I talked to Hannah because she knows all about you. She's an expert. She wrote a book about you.'

Meg's expression took on a look of astonishment. 'Somebody wrote a book about me?' she murmured. 'What do you mean?'

'Well, it's just that you're a big deal in Woodplumpton these days. The grave and everything. They tell the tourists all about you.'

Now she looked puzzled. 'What are . . . tourists?'

'You know. Visitors?'

Meg seemed doubtful. 'And what does this Hannah say about me?'

'She says, well, that you were probably murdered.'

Meg snorted. 'Probably? Definitely!' She moved a step closer to Alfie and he took an instinctive step back, his shoulders slamming against the closed door. 'And does this Hannah say who was responsible for my death?'

Alfie shook his head. 'I . . . I don't think so. I haven't really had time to read the whole book.' He fumbled in his jacket pocket and then held the book out for Meg's inspection. 'Here,' he said. 'Hannah lent me a copy.' Meg took it from him, held it to her face and sniffed at it. Then she lowered the book and stared blankly at the cover.

'What does it say?' she asked him.

'Oh, I'm sorry, can't you . . .?' He paused, not wanting to make her angry again. 'It says, "Call Her Meg". That's the title of the book.'

'Hmm. "Call Her Meg" . . . "Call Her Meg" . . .' She seemed to mull the words over for a few moments, before smiling. 'I like this title,' she concluded. 'And I would very much like to meet Hannah.'

'I expect she'd *love* to meet you,' said Alfie. 'She'd have plenty of questions.'

Meg scowled and thrust the book back at him. 'Of course, it won't be possible,' she said. 'Only you can see and hear me.'

Alfie nodded. 'Ah, right, I figured that was how it worked,' he said. He slipped the book back into his pocket and thought for a moment. 'So . . . do you know who did it?' he asked her. 'The . . . murder.'

Meg shook her head. 'I did not recognise the men who killed me. They were strangers to my eyes. But I know who must have ordered it. It was Blackwood. Lord Vincent Blackwood.'

For some reason, the surname rang a bell with Alfie. It was one he had heard somewhere recently, he thought, but he couldn't place it.

'What else does this Hannah say about me in her book?' asked Meg. 'Bad things?'

'Oh, no . . .' Alfie wracked his brains to try and remember what Hannah had told him when they had met. 'She said she thought you might have been, er . . . pregnant when you died.'

Meg gave a short laugh. 'She was wrong there,' she snapped. 'I'd had my baby two months by the time they killed me. He was just a babe in arms. But they stole him away from me. The last thing I remember seeing was them taking him from his crib . . . there.' She pointed across the room into one corner and Alfie was shocked to see that there were indeed the remains of something heaped on the floor – some blackened lengths of wood tossed into an untidy pile, and what looked like a few scraps of mouldy fabric. 'I still don't know what happened to my boy,' she said. She turned back to look at Alfie. 'You are going to help me find out.'

Alfie stared at her. 'How do you expect me to do that?' he protested.

'You have a tongue in your head, don't you?' she asked him. 'Well, I would suggest you start using it to ask the right questions. Otherwise, I might just decide to pluck it out and make it into a garter for my stockings.'

Alfie swallowed. 'Oh no, look, that's not fair. I never asked you to —'

Meg lunged suddenly forwards and clamped a hand around his throat. She lifted him effortlessly from the ground, as though he weighed no more than a bundle of twigs, and pinned him up against the door. 'I would advise you not to question me,' she told him. 'My patience is short. I have waited a very long time for this opportunity. Far too long. Now tell me, boy, what are you going to do?'

'Use . . . my . . . tongue,' he rasped, through gritted teeth.

'Good. See that you do.' She turned abruptly away, allowing him to drop to the floor in an untidy heap. He slumped there, gasping, trying to get his breath back to something approaching normal.

The cat made a sudden mewing sound and leapt down from his place on the sill. Meg moved towards the dirty window and Alfie was horrified to see the indistinct outline of a head appearing on the other side of the glass like an apparition. Mia must have made her way around to the back of the house. She was staring into the room.

'Alfie!' she shouted. 'What's going on in there?' She sounded impatient.

'What did I tell you before?' snarled Meg. 'I said to get rid of her.'

Alfie struggled to clear his throat. 'She's my friend,' he croaked. 'She's worried about me.'

'She'll have something else to worry about in a moment. Perhaps I'll blind her . . . or afflict her with a plague of boils . . .'

'No, please, don't do that!' Alfie scrambled upright and moved to the window. He pressed his face to the glass. 'Mia, please go away,' he shouted. 'She says she'll hurt you if you don't!'

'She? Alfie, do you mean Meg? Is she in there with you?' The face pressed up against the glass. 'I . . . I can't see anyone but you.'

'Just trust me. Please! Go away!'

There was silence and then Mia's outline backed slowly off. 'If you're not out in ten minutes, I'm calling the police!' she shouted. 'You hear me?'

'Don't call anyone. I'm fine, really.' Alfie turned back to Meg. 'All right,' he said hastily. 'She's going. There's no need to harm her, she only wants to help.' He made an effort to gather his scrambled wits. He needed to find out as much as he could. 'OK, so the people that killed you stole your baby. Is that right?'

Meg nodded.

'And what was his name?'

'Edgar. His name was Edgar.'

'OK. And why would somebody want to take him?'

She scowled and turned away from the window. She paced around for a moment, evidently agitated. 'Blackwood wanted an heir. His wife was barren and could not give him a child. So, he stole mine. And because he knew I would come after him, he had his hirelings silence me.'

Alfie nodded. 'And this Blackwood character, he was . . .?'

'What?'

'He was Edgar's father?'

'Aye.'

'But you said he had a wife.'

She looked at him scornfully. 'Of course he did. He took me as his paramour.'

'His what?'

'His moll, his fancy woman, his bit of fluff! Call it what you like. And he gave me this place to live, rent free.' She gestured around at the derelict building and scowled. 'Ah, but it was a fine little dwelling then,' she added. 'The only home in the area that had windows.' She moved back to the window and traced a fingertip across the dusty glass. 'And remote enough that he could call on me whenever the fancy for female company took him. Which was often, because, like most men, he was lustful and fond of his ale. But then I fell pregnant. And he knew I would never give up my son, no matter how much money he offered me. So, he took Edgar by force and had me killed.' She leant over and spat on the floor. 'I need to find out what happened to my boy. I need to stand at his grave and mourn him. And meanwhile, I will take my revenge on the people of Woodplumpton.'

'Ah yes, I was going to talk to you about that. The sour milk . . . the toads in the muesli . . .'

'The what?'

'It's a breakfast cereal. It's like nuts and oats and . . . never mind about that. But it's you, isn't it . . . making it happen?'

Meg smiled with pride. 'Just reconnecting with my old abilities,' she said. 'Rediscovering my powers and exercising them. It's funny how quickly it all comes back to you.'

'But I thought witches didn't have any real powers?'

'Most don't. But I am special.'

'It's all a bit unfair though, isn't it?'

She glared at him. 'What do you mean?' she hissed.

'Well, it's like I said before. The people in the village now, they don't have anything to do with what happened to you. That was all hundreds of years ago before they were even born! Take Giovanni, in the café – you've really messed up his business. It'll cost him a fortune in lost sales.'

Meg shrugged. 'You think I care?' she snapped. 'I am enjoying using my old skills and until my thirst for vengeance is satisfied, the chaos will continue.'

'So, you're saying that if you can find where your son's buried, you'll stop disrupting everything?'

Meg seemed to contemplate the idea for a while before she replied. 'I'll certainly consider it,' she said. 'I only want to be allowed to mourn as a mother should. It's not very much to ask is it?'

'I . . . I suppose not . . .' Alfie hesitated before asking the next question. He reallydidn't want to make her angry again, but he had to ask it just the same. 'And is there . . . is there any reason why you can't just . . . find the grave yourself?'

There was a long silence then. She looked at him as though he was some kind of simpleton.

'What do you think is happening here, boy?' she cried.

'How can I possibly do it? I need an anchor in the world of the living. You are that anchor. You are the conduit that allows me to emerge from the darkness and exercise my powers. Oh, I have the ability to influence things —'

'How do you mean?' Alfie interrupted, and promptly wished he hadn't, as she made a suddengesture at him and he felt a blow hit him in the chest and push him back against the door with a force that threatened to make the wood buckle beneath him.

'You're . . . you're hurting me!' he gasped.

Meg waved her hand in dismissal and the pressure was instantly released. 'As I said, you are the conduit for my power. And I do not recognise this world,' she continued. 'Everything has changed. Many of my old haunts are gone forever.' She looked mournfully around. 'At least this place is still standing,' she said. 'At least I can come here when I need to.'

She moved back to the window and peered again through the misted glass.

Alfie tried to get his breathing back to normal. 'How did they do it?' he asked.

She turned and looked at him. 'How did they do what?'

'How did they . . . kill you.'

She shrugged. 'It was easy enough,' she said. 'They lay in wait for me and took me by surprise before I had time to marshal my powers. One man held me down, while his companion jumped up and down on my chest until the life was squeezed out of me. He was a heavy man. It did not take long.' She snapped her fingers, scowling. 'Easy enough to end a life in such a way. Is that how it is remembered in the book?'

Alfie shook his head. 'I think there's a story about you being crushed against a wall by a rolling barrel. Here, in your house.'

Meg snorted. 'And they believed that?' she cried.

'Well, I don't know if they believed it. It's just what they were told. Hannah said it didn't really make any sense.' Alfie pondered for a moment. 'Why me?' he asked her.

'Hmm?'

'Why did you come to me when I pulled that stunt in the graveyard? Mia said there must have been thousands of kids over the years that have tried it. But you answered me. Why?'

'Because you're the first voice I heard.'

'That's it? There must be some reason you came to me and not the others!'

'Who can say? I heard your voice and I responded to your invitation.' She sighed, lifted a hand to her temples. 'I grow tired. It wears me out making myself visible like this. You should go. You have work to do on my behalf.'

Something in Alfie rebelled at her certainty. 'What if I said I won't help you?' he asked her. 'What if I said I'm too busy to do your dirty work?'

Meg studied him in silence for a moment, a contemptuous sneer on her face. 'You cannot afford to make me impatient,' she warned him. 'I can hurt you. You have already experienced that. Even worse for you, I can hurt those you care about.' She pointed towards the window. 'The girl who waits outside. What is her name? Ah yes, Mia! It would be a shame, wouldn't it, if some misfortune befell her? And there are so many things that could happen to a young girl like that. Bad things.' She tilted her head to one side. 'And I also seem to remember a man that came to the room when I first appeared to you. Your father, I believe. I could stop his heart with a finger click.'

'But that's not fair!' protested Alfie. 'What's any of this got to do with them?'

'You care for them,' murmured Meg. 'And now it has everything to do with them. Be warned boy, I'm not one for making idle threats.' She made a dismissive gesture with one hand. 'Now get to your work and do not give me cause for impatience. I shall call on you again, very soon, and I will expect to see progress.'

Alfie opened his mouth to tell her not to bother, but quite suddenly, he was alone in the room. He turned to look at the door and saw to his surprise that it was standing open again, just as it had been when he'd first seen it. He pulled it back, the hinges making that hideous creaking sound and he retraced his steps down the hall and through the leaf-littered front room. He emerged into the light, blinking, and Mia came scrambling through the trees to throw her arms around him. She hugged him tightly then pulled away to study his face. 'What the hell happened in there?' she asked him.

'I talked to Meg,' he told her. 'And there's something she wants me to do.' He took her hand and led her back towards the track. 'We need to go,' he said. 'I'll tell you the rest on the way. She wants me to —'

He stopped in his tracks, his mouth open. 'Oh my God,' he said.

Mia stared at him. 'What's wrong?' she asked.

'Blackwood,' he said. He had just remembered where he'd heard that name before.

CHAPTER TWELVE

QUESTIONS

Dad looked at Alfie in amazement. 'Come again?' he said. 'You . . . you want to come to work with me?' They were sitting at their usual breakfast table in the otherwise-deserted dining room of The Excelsior. Dad had been so surprised by Alfie's suggestion, he'd actually stopped looking at his phone for a moment. 'Seriously?'

'Yes,' said Alfie, trying to make himself look as sincere as possible. 'I just thought it was time I took an interest in your work. I mean, you go off every morning to Blackwood and Phibes and I don't have a clue what you get up to there. Which, when you think about it, is crazy, right?'

Dad frowned. 'Erm . . . well, I suppose so.'

'I mean, it won't be very long before I'm thinking about a career myself,' added Alfie. 'And, well, what if I decide to follow you into . . . whatever it is you do?'

Dad switched off his phone and set it down on the table. 'It just seems odd that you've never expressed any interest in it before,' he said. 'Not a peep. In fact, I seem to remember you saying once that you wouldn't do my job if they offered you a million pounds an hour.'

Alfie laughed and hoped it sounded more convincing to Dad than it did to him. 'Oh yeah, but that was years ago!' he protested.

Dad shook his head. 'It was actually last month,' he said.

'Well, er . . . maybe I've seen the error of my ways.' Alfie didn't like the way Dad was staring at him, so he studied the menu in front of him, noting the large sticky note on the front of it with the words: Apologies! No milk or dairy products! 'Are we *really* going to eat here?' he whispered fearfully. 'Nobody else is risking it.'

'I feel sorry for them,' said Dad. 'It can't be easy. And Malcolm told me they've had the pest control people in, so there shouldn't be any repetition of what happened yesterday.' He looked thoughtful. 'I've never seen such tiny frogs,' he muttered.

'I think they were toads,' Alfie corrected him.

'Zoology was never my strong point,' admitted Dad. 'Anyway, I think we owe it to Selina and Malcolm to give it one more try.'

Selena came in with her order pad and attempted to give them a cheerful smile. Alfie tried not to stare at her, and he felt Dad tense beside him. There was something dramatically different about Selina this morning. Her features were marred by a particularly nasty outbreak of boils. She'd obviously attempted to cover them with make-up, but they looked really awful – great pus-filled hillocks that covered just about every part of her face. To add to her troubles, her eyes were rimmed with red, as though she'd spent much of the previous night crying, and her usually elegantly-coiffed hair hung in greasy straggles.

'Good morning, Selina,' ventured Dad. 'How . . . are you?'

She made a faint gesture towards her face. 'Not at my best, I'm afraid, as you can see. They came up in the night,' she said, sounding apologetic. 'No idea what's caused them. I've always maintained a spotless complexion. Spotless! I won awards for my clean looks when I was a teenager! I've got an emergency appointment with the doctor this afternoon, to see if he can shed any light on the matter.'

Dad did a fairly convincing double take, trying to pretend that he hadn't noticed the problem at first glance. 'Oh, yes, the . . . acne,' he murmured. 'Perhaps an allergic reaction to something? I wouldn't worry, they're barely noticeable.'

'You're being kind, but I know I look an absolute fright. Came up in a matter of minutes, they did! I looked in my mirror and I nearly screamed the house down! It's a wonder you didn't hear me. Honestly, with everything that's been happening lately, I'm beginning to wonder if we're not the victims of some kind of evil curse.'

'Ha! Like that could happen,' said Alfie, studying his menu intently. He couldn't bring himself to look Selina in the face, and not just because there was one particularly nasty yellow boil on the tip of her nose that might pop at any moment.

'I'm sure now you've had the pest controller in, everything will be back to normal,' said Dad soothingly. 'Did they have any ideas about the, er . . . frogs?'

'Toads,' murmured Alfie.

'He seemed to think they were a South American species. Tropical variety. Thought they might have come in on a consignment of bananas. How they found their way into a sealed box of Swedish muesli is anybody's guess.'

Dad nodded, understandingly. 'I'm sure it's all sorted now.'

'Oh, I do hope so,' said Selina. 'I keep asking myself, what could go wrong next?' She shook her head as if trying to dispel bad thoughts. 'Now, gentlemen, what can I get you from our somewhat depleted offerings?'

Dad studied the menu hopefully. 'Well now, what would you recommend?'

'As you know, dairy is off the menu,' said Selena, gravely. 'And Malcolm decided to take eggs off too after that unfortunate incident with those guests yesterday . . .'

'Oh yes, what was that about?' asked Alfie, and quickly wished he hadn't.

'Well, it was bewildering,' said Selina. 'That's all I can say about it. A fried egg, for goodness' sake! What could possibly go wrong with that? But curled up inside it was this . . . this . . .' Selina struggled to describe it and then shook her head. 'I can't even say it,' she concluded. 'It was too disgusting!' She arranged her spotty face into an expression of revulsion. 'Well, that was enough for them, wasn't it? They checked out immediately. And the photograph went straight on to *TripAdvisor*.' She turned her mournful gaze on Dad. 'I don't mind telling you, Mr Travers, that you are now our sole guests. If something doesn't change soon, we are going to be ruined. Ruined!'

'I'm so sorry to hear that,' said Dad. He fished in the pocket of his jacket and found a handkerchief. He gave it a quick check for cleanliness and handed it to Selina, who dabbed furiously at her brimming eyes.

'I only wish all our customers were as understanding as you,' she whispered. 'The business with the milk . . . I simply don't understand it. We use the same dairy as everybody else in the village and we're the only ones that seem to have had a problem with it.'

'Oh, no, it happened at Luigi's too,' Alfie told her. 'Yesterday.'

Both Selina and Dad gave him questioning looks.

'The little cafe on Market Street?' asked Selina.

'Er . . . yeah,' said Alfie. 'Giovanni's place.'

'What were you doing there?' asked Dad.

'Oh, just meeting up with Mia for a bit of a chat. Anyway, his milk was off, every last drop of it. And there were maggots in his Victoria sponge.'

'Ew.' Selina's face was a mixture of disgust and relief. 'So, we're not the only ones! But it's very strange, because I've spoken to the proprietors of most of the hotels and guest houses in the area and they've all got business as usual. Why just us and Giovanni?'

Because I was at both places, thought Alfie gloomily. It seemed the only logical answer. He thought about what Meg had told him yesterday – that he was a conduit for her powers. Was that it? She could only exercise her dark magic on people that had some connection with him? Did that mean that he was in danger of carrying these terrible afflictions to every place he visited?

'Anyway, gentlemen, what will it be this morning?' asked Selina, making a valiant attempt to change the direction of the conversation.

'I'll take a black coffee,' said Dad. 'And a couple of buttered crumpets with jam.'

Selina looked apologetic. 'It will be margarine, I'm afraid. We don't want to risk trying the butter. Dairy, you see. I'm sorry, I usually hate margarine, but . . .'

'Not at all,' Dad assured her. 'That'll be fine. Alfie?'

'Er . . . bread and margarine for me,' he said. 'And tap water to drink.'

For a moment, Selina looked as though she was about to object but she must have realised that she was on very sticky ground. 'Coming right up,' she said. She handed Dad's handkerchief back to him and took herself off to the kitchen. Dad gazed after her. 'Poor Selina,' he said. 'I don't know why, but I feel kind of guilty about what's happening.'

Alfie stared at him. 'Why should you?' he asked. 'It's nothing to do with us!'

'Well, of course not. And I know it doesn't make any sense, but . . . well, it all seems to have gone wrong for her and Malcolm since we arrived. Almost as though we're unlucky in some way.'

'Don't talk daft,' said Alfie, and hoped he'd managed a convincing tone. He turned his thoughts to more pressing matters. 'So, tell me about work,' he suggested. 'What's it like at Blackwood and Phibes?'

'It's all right. You know, typical family business. Been doing things their own way since time immemorial and therefore a bit reluctant to change, but I'm managing to make inroads.'

'An old family business, you reckon?

'I suppose . . . '

'So, it's been handed down for generations, right?'

Dad frowned. 'I really don't know about that . . .'

'And what are Mr Blackwood and Mr Phibes like?'

'Mr Phibes doesn't exist any more. The last one died a few years back. But they kept the name, because it was so well known around the area. And Ralph seems like a decent bloke.'

'Ralph?'

'Yes, Ralph Blackwood, the Managing Director.'

'So there's still a Mr Blackwood?' In his excitement, Alfie nearly shouted it out. 'What's he like? I suppose he must have quite a history.'

Dad looked baffled. 'I've really no idea. I've only been there a couple of days. But as I said, he's a friendly enough chap. He works in the office, most days, so . . . Alfie, what's going on?'

'Nothing's going on. But it would be very handy if I could talk to Ralph . . . er, Mr Blackwood.'

'Talk to him?' Dad looked alarmed. 'What about?'

'Well . . .' It was time to do some urgent improvisation and Alfie could only give it his best shot. '. . . it's just my . . . my homework project. I've been told to put together a project about . . . roots. Family roots. It's for English language.'

Dad looked puzzled. 'I thought you told me that schools don't do those kinds of projects any more,' he said.

'No. Apart from Mr Davidson. He's very old-fashioned.'

'Is he really?'

'Yes. He said it might be a good idea to concentrate on a family business, one that goes back a few generations. I'm to try and find out the history of one. And this sounds like the perfect place to start. The fact that you're already working there makes it even sweeter.'

'Hmm.' Dad looked as though he was pondering the matter. 'So how come this is the first I've heard of it?'

Alfie shrugged. 'I guess I forgot about it until now. But, well, I don't want to go back to school with nothing to show, do I? That wouldn't go down very well. And, er . . . this *is* going to count towards my final exams.'

'Really?' Now Dad looked annoyed. 'Why didn't the school think to share that information with me?' He looked at his phone. 'I've a good mind to ring them and give them a piece of my mind.'

'They won't be there,' Alfie assured him. 'Teachers have holidays, too, you know. And now I think about it, they did give us some paperwork to pass on to you, ages ago, but . . . I forgot all about it.'

'Alfie!'

'But, hey! You know now, and there's still plenty of time to get something sorted out, so . . . if I just go in to work with you today, I can ask Mr Blackwood a few questions and make some notes.'

'Whoa, hang on a minute! I can't just go waltzing in there with you tagging along like my flipping shadow! I'd need to clear it with somebody first.'

'Yes, of course. I get that. I expect you can give Ralph a call and see what he thinks.'

Dad shook his head. 'I'm not doing that!'

'Aw, Dad . . .'

'Maybe I'll raise the subject with him over lunch,' he said. 'And we'll see how he's fixed. He's a busy man, you know. He isn't going to come running to do your bidding at five minutes' notice.'

'I guess not.'

'But I'll sound him out.'

'Thanks, Dad!'

'And Alfie . . .'

'Yes?'

'I hope I don't have to tell you that this job is very important to me . . . to us. I don't want you going in there and getting his back up about something.'

Alfie affected a wounded look. 'How would I do that?'

'I don't know. By asking him difficult questions, I suppose.'

'I'm not going to do that!'

'OK. All I'm saying is, assuming he agrees to talk to you, just watch what you say to him.'

'Don't worry, Dad. I'm just going to ask him about his ancestors and so forth. Most people are proud of that stuff, aren't they?'

'The truth is, most people don't know much about them. Look at when you asked me about my great-grandparents.'

Selina appeared, carrying a tray. She set down coffee, water, a plate of crumpets, a fresh jar of strawberry jam and a helping of bread and margarine. She studied it all carefully for a moment as though reassuring herself that everything was in order. Then she smiled, turned on her heel and walked away. Dad lifted the coffee cup to his mouth and took an exploratory sip. He set it down, added a couple of spoonfuls of sugar and tried again. He nodded. 'Well, that tastes slightly less disgusting than the tea did yesterday,' he admitted. 'Which is a start.'

Alfie picked up a slice of bread and tried a bite of that. It didn't really taste of anything, but at least it was edible. 'If we go on at this rate, we'll be like a couple of skeletons by the time we head home,' he observed.

Dad nodded. 'I know.' He lowered his voice to a whisper. 'I was thinking, it might be time to try The Fatted Calf again. For dinner.'

Alfie smiled. 'I thought you said you felt sorry for Selina.'

'I do, but . . . eating here is unpredictable to say the very least.' He unscrewed the lid of the jam and peered apprehensively inside. 'I think this is OK,' he murmured. He got a teaspoon and pulled a blob out for closer inspection, before depositing it on a crumpet and spreading it with a knife. He lifted the crumpet to his mouth and chewed slowly, before deciding it tasted fine and taking a bigger, more enthusiastic, bite. 'Decent jam,' he observed. 'You want some?'

'I'll stick with what I've got,' said Alfie. 'So, you'll ask Mr Blackwood? Today?'

'Yes, yes, all right. Honestly, what's the big hurry? You've got the whole of the holidays in front of you.'

And I've got Meg waiting in the wings, wondering what's keeping me, thought Alfie. But he just smiled and took another mouthful of his bread – then watched in horrified fascination as Dad raised the remains of his crumpet to his mouth. There was something black stuck in the jam – a large fat spider, its legs wriggling frantically.

Alfie opened his mouth to say something, but it was too late. Dad's teeth closed on the crumpet and he chewed noisily, the contents of his mouth crunching unpleasantly.

He made a face. 'There's almost too much fruit in this jam,' he muttered – and then noticed Alfie's horrified expression. He swallowed the mouthful and gave his son a questioning look.

'Something wrong?' he asked.

Alfie shook his head. 'I'm fine,' he murmured wearily. 'But Dad, you won't forget, will you? Mr Blackwood. Ask him today. It's really important.'

CHAPTER THIRTEEN

INTERLUDE

A lfie opened his eyes and was momentarily astonished to realise that it was night – though not as astonished as he was to realise that he was walking barefoot along a muddy track that led over a familiar-looking ridge and down into a valley. He looked around and tried to place exactly where he was. It looked very like the track that he and Mia had followed to get to Cuckoo Hall; but the trees that stretched across his path some distance ahead were not conifers, but the rambling deciduous trees of the deeper forest.

Mia's words came back to him. *'This is the oldest part of the woods. It's been here for hundreds of years. It used to be much bigger than this but over time it's been cut back.'*

Alfie made an effort to gather his scrambled wits. How the hell had he wound up here? The last thing he remembered was seeing Dad off to work and then going up to his room to await a call from him . . . but it had been early morning then. Where had the rest of the day gone?

Meanwhile, he kept walking, covering the ground at an urgent pace, as though hurrying to get to an appointment. All too soon, he was moving into the forest, the light of the moon abruptly extinguished by the overhanging canopy of summer foliage. He was dimly aware of sounds around him – the fluttering of birds amongst the branches high above, the hooting of an owl somewhere off in the deep woods and once he thought he glimpsed the fleeting shape of a fox prowling between the tree trunks. But though he kept telling himself that it really wasn't a good idea to keep on going in this direction, the compulsion to keep placing one foot in front of the other was overpowering.

All right, he told himself, trying to stay calm. *So, this is a dream. It's the only explanation.*

Sure, that was it. He'd settled down to wait for Dad's call and that string of restless nights had finally caught up with him. He'd drifted off and was doubtless slumped on his hotel bed, right now, locked in a deep and restless sleep – so whatever happened here couldn't affect him. There was no need to be afraid. In a few moments, he'd wake up and everything would be the same as it had been before he'd succumbed to exhaustion . . .

But meanwhile his bare feet were carrying him deeper and deeper into the woods and he was aware of rough stones and fallen twigs under the soles of his feet. As he walked, he thought about the lack of conifers. Did that mean this dream was taking place back in the day, long before the coniferous forest had even been planted, when the original woods had covered a much bigger area? It seemed to make sense.

After a while, he wasn't entirely surprised to see Cuckoo Hall looming out of the darkness ahead of him, but that too was quite different to the dilapidated ruin he and Mia had visited. The doors and windows were in good order and the thatched roof intact. A plume of smoke rose from the stone chimney and a soft glow of light showed through one of the front windows. Furthermore, the woods had not encroached upon the building as they had in the modern day. There was a proper path to the door and even a simple wooden fence that bordered a stretch of land to the front and sides of the cottage. Even in this uncertain light, Alfie could see that the area was liberally planted with flowers and herbs.

He slowed to a halt and stared. He could see now that two cloaked figures had just stepped furtively out from the cover of the trees ahead of him and were quietly letting themselves in at the garden gate. They walked slowly up to the door and paused to look around. Alfie resisted the impulse to throw himself into cover, but though the men's gazes swept over the spot where he was standing, they didn't seem to register him. They turned back to the door and one of the men lifted a gloved hand to do something to the handle. He fiddled for a moment and then the door swung silently open. The men let themselves inside.

Alfie started walking again, until he was at the open gate. He really didn't want to go any closer than this, but his feet would not allow him to stay where he was. They took him closer and closer to the front door. He reached it and peeked cautiously inside. The room beyond was illuminated by a solitary oil lamp and Alfie could see that the place was in good repair, the walls smoothly plastered, a low fire burning in the iron grate; but of the men, there was no sign. Alfie stepped inside, hardly daring to breathe. He gazed across the room to the short stretch of hallway that he remembered from before – the one that led to the back room. He was about to take another step when a sudden scream echoed throughout the house – a woman's scream, the shrillness of it making Alfie's heart jump in his chest. There was the sound of a heavy impact and the scream was abruptly cut off, mutating into a low groan of agony. Alfie remembered what Meg had told him about her death and he could hold back no longer. He launched himself forward, ran along the hallway and burst through the open door of the room beyond.

There was a lantern in here too, and it lit the scene in ghastly detail. One of the men had Meg stretched out on her back and was holding her down by her shoulders. His companion, a big thick-set bearded man was just climbing off her shattered chest, but her eyes were wide open, her face arranged into a malevolent grimace. She began to utter a breathless jumble of words, which might have been some kind of curse, but the big man turned back to her and launched himself up on to her chest for a second time.

Alfie had to look away, but he heard the brittle snapping of bones and the hideous squelch of crushed organs. Meg's words were abruptly silenced and when Alfie dared to look again, he saw that though her eyes were still wide open, her chest was a crushed and bloody pulp. The fingers of her outstretched hands wriggled in a last convulsion and then were still.

The first man released her shoulders, got up and moved across to the wooden cot in the corner of the room. He leant over it, reached in and extracted a bundled shape. The baby, wrenched rudely from sleep, gave an indignant squawk. The second man hesitated by Meg's body, gazing intently down at it as if wanting to be sure there was no life left in her. He even extended a foot to kick at her, but there was no reaction. At length, he nodded, seemingly satisfied with his night's work. 'Sleep well, witch,' he muttered.

The first man moved towards him, the stolen baby mostly covered by his cloak, and he said something to his companion. The man nodded and they both turned to the door, where Alfie still stood, open-mouthed in horror – but again, they did not seem to register his presence. They started towards the door and Alfie could not prevent himself from stepping aside to let them pass. They went out of the room and he heard their heavy footsteps clumping along the hallway. He didn't follow them, but went instead to Meg's sprawled body and dropped to his knees beside her. He couldn't help thinking that perhaps if he'd hurried, he could have overtaken the men. He could have prevented this from happening. He reached out a hand and stroked her cheek, but the heat was already fading from it.

'I'm sorry,' he whispered.

'You will be,' she said.

Her eyes came suddenly into focus and stared at him in cold accusation.

He awoke with a yelp and was relieved to find that, sure enough, he *was* lying on his bed in The Excelsior, exactly where he had known he would be the whole time.

He lay on his back for a moment, allowing his breathing to settle back to something approaching normal, and he wondered what it was that had woken him. As his senses gradually returned, he became aware of something odd. His feet felt . . . wrong. He sat up a little and stared towards the end of the bed. He was shocked to see that his feet were bare and plastered with dirt. Worse still, they were sore. He sat up, reached out a hand and brought one foot closer so he could inspect the sole.

He snatched in a breath. It was scratched and bloody, as though he had been walking for miles across woodland.

'No!' He shook his head. 'No way.' He examined the other foot and it was in the same sorry condition, but when he turned to look at the window, bright sunlight was spilling into the room. It had been night-time when he walked to Cuckoo Hall, so it must have been a dream. But how did you scratch your feet in a dream? He got off the bed, noticing as he did so how the previously spotless coverlet was now blotched and stained. How the hell was he going to explain this one away?

He stood for a moment, unsure of what to do, then walked across to the bathroom door and threw it open, telling himself that whatever else happened, he needed to get cleaned up. He went to the shower cubicle and switched on the flow of the water. He stripped off his clothes, flinging them carelessly aside, and climbed into the shower, closing the door behind him. The powerful spray of hot water made the scratches sting even more. He took some shower gel, worked it to a lather in his hands and then, wincing with the pain of it, he stooped and began to scrub his feet clean. He stood there in the spray of hot water, steam rising in clouds around him as he frantically scrubbed the mud and blood away, watching it pool on the white shower floor and run in streams down the trap.

He straightened up, allowing the water to cascade over his head. He was vaguely aware of a rush of cold air behind him as the shower door swung open and his heart seemed to momentarily stop beating.

A sharp-nailed finger tapped him on the shoulder and a woman's voice, right beside his ear whispered, 'Wake up, boy.'

He opened his eyes with a gasp of terror to realise that, once again, he was lying on his bed at The Excelsior. He sat up in a panic and saw, to his relief, that this time his socks were on, the coverlet was unspoilt and, as far as he could tell, his feet were perfectly fine. A shrill noise was drilling itself repeatedly into his senses and it took his fuddled senses some time to recognise his own phone's ring tone. He turned his head and looked blearily towards the bedside cabinet and sure enough, there was the phone. He hesitated a moment longer and then reached out to pick it up. The display told him that Mia was calling. He groaned, shook the fuzziness out of his head and answered. 'Hello?' he murmured.

'Hey, Alfie. I've been ringing for ages. You OK?'

'Er . . . uh . . . yeah, I think so.'

'I didn't wake you up, did I? You sound half asleep.'

He pulled himself together. 'No, don't be daft. What would I be doing sleeping at . . .' He glanced at his watch, '. . . twelve twenty-three in the afternoon? No, I'm just sitting here waiting for my dad to call.'

'All right. Well, I've been going through your text —'

'My text?' He remembered that he'd fired a rambling message off to Mia just after Dad had left. 'Oh, yeah, of course.'

'I'm about to phone Hannah, so I wanted to check a few points with you to make sure I've got everything right.'

'I thought I put it all in there,' complained Alfie.

'Yes, but spelling isn't your strong point. And some of this sounds a bit weird.' A pause. 'So, what I've got here . . . you're saying you want Hannah to find out anything she can about somebody called Vincent Blackwood, right?'

'*Lord* Vincent Blackwood, yes.'

'And you're saying he's the one who killed Meg's baby?'

'No, he *stole* the baby and had Meg killed. The baby was called Edgar and he was two months old when he was taken.'

'Yeah, got that.'

'And I don't expect he was still a baby when he died. So, most likely, Hannah needs to look for stuff about a man called Edgar Shelton or maybe Edgar Blackwood.'

'Hmm.' A brief silence. 'I'm not being funny, but you have tried Googling the name, I suppose?'

'Yes, I've done loads of searches, but nothing comes up. I've found other famous Blackwoods – one of them is a character in a Sherlock Holmes book – but nothing about a Vincent. I just thought Hannah might have a better way of going about it.'

'And you say here that Meg wants to visit her son's grave?'

'Yeah. Well, that's what she told me, anyway. I just need to let her know where it is, so she'll stop pestering me and causing so much havoc.' He shook his head. 'Mia, do you think I've gone crazy?'

An uncomfortably long silence. Then: 'Of course not.'

'Yeah, but you hesitated, didn't you? You had to think about it.' He took a deep breath. 'Mia, I just saw Meg's murder.'

'What do you mean? How could you . . .?'

'It was a dream, I suppose.'

'You just said you weren't asleep when I rang!'

'Yeah, I know I said that, and . . . well, I'm still not sure if I *was* asleep. But I was there at Cuckoo Hall, back before it was all falling to bits. It was night-time and I saw what happened to her, Mia. This big guy just . . . jumped up and down on her. It was horrible!'

'It sounds it! But Alfie, it *was* a dream. It must have been.'

'Well, that's what I keep telling myself. Only then, I woke up and my feet were all scratched and covered in mud.'

'How come?'

'Well, because for some reason, I was barefoot . . . in the dream, I mean . . . Anyway, I went straight to the shower to clean them and the next thing I knew . . .'

An alarm pinged on Alfie's phone. He looked at the screen. 'Mia, I've got to go. Dad's on the other line. Wait for me!'

'But . . .'

'Just wait a minute.'

He tapped the screen. 'Hey, Dad. You OK?'

'You took your time,' said Dad. 'You weren't asleep, were you?'

'Don't you start! No, I was just in the bathroom.'

'OK. Anyway, I can't quite believe this but against all the odds, Ralph says he's happy to have a chat with you. He's quite clued-up on his family history as it happens.'

'Oh, that's great!'

'So, if you can get over here for, say, two o'clock, he's got a gap in his schedule.'

'Brilliant. Thanks Dad. I owe you one.'

'You owe me lots! But listen to me, Alfie. This is important. I don't want you to upset him.'

'How would I do that?'

'Oh, if there's a way, you'll find it.'

'Dad, have a bit of faith in me.'

'What, like the time you managed to tell your headmaster exactly what I thought of the school's new website? Telling him I thought it looked amateurish?'

'I thought I might drum up a bit of business for you!'

'Hmm. Well, they weren't impressed.'

'That was years ago! And don't worry, I only want to ask Ralph a few questions about his family history.'

'It's Mr Blackwood to you! Don't call him Ralph, you're not his best mate! Just be respectful. Say please and thank you. Remember, he *is* my boss. You rub him up the wrong way, and we could be heading back to Bristol.'

'No worries. I'll be there at two. Now, I've got to go, I've got Mia waiting on the other line.'

'Mia? Alfie, I hope you aren't –'

Alfie cut Dad off and switched back to the other line. 'Hey,' he said. 'I'm heading up to Blackwood and Phibes at two. You got everything you need?'

Silence.

'Mia? Are you still there?'

Again, nothing.

'Mia, I know you're there. I can hear you breathing.'

A long, harsh hissing sound and then a woman's voice, all too familiar.

'Make sure you ask the right questions, boy!'

'Meg?' He stared at the phone in astonishment. 'How the hell did you . . .?'

The line went dead.

CHAPTER FOURTEEN

BLACKWOOD & PHIBES

Alfie got to the estate agents at five minutes to two. He'd brought a lined notebook and a pen along with him, in an attempt to look as though he meant business. He'd changed into his smartest shirt and a clean pair of black jeans, which was about as presentable as he could make himself. He went through the swing doors and found himself standing at a reception desk. A plump, middle-aged woman, seated behind the desk, directed a dazzling grin at him. She had permed blonde hair, artfully applied make-up and was wearing a neat little lapel badge with the name 'Sandra' printed on it. 'Good afternoon,' she said. 'Welcome to Blackwood and Phibes. How may I assist you?' Sandra spoke in a weird sing-song fashion, enunciating every word clearly and sounding rather delighted with herself.

Alfie nodded. 'Hi there. I'm Alfie Travers. I'm here to —'

'Oh, of course, you're Michael's son, aren't you? Should have known, you look just like him. You've got the same nose.'

Alfie didn't know quite what to say to that. Nobody had ever remarked on his nose before. 'Er, well . . . it's not the same one,' he said. 'Or we'd be sharing it, wouldn't we?'

Sandra seemed to consider the comment for a moment and then she beamed delightedly. 'Oh yes, I suppose you would!' She let out a laugh, a kind of prolonged high-pitched cackle. 'That's very amusing,' she observed. 'Michael's got a sharp sense of humour too, hasn't he? Is that where you get it from?'

Alfie could only shrug. 'I'm not sure. Maybe? So . . . er, I'm here to see Ralph, I mean, Mr Blackwood?'

'Oh yes, of course. Michael said you'd be dropping by this afternoon. How lovely! A research project, I believe. Now, if I can just ask you to wait there for one moment, I'll pop through and check that Mr Blackwood is available at this time.' She got to her feet and trotted towards a door, set into the wall behind her. She tapped politely, waited for a response and then went inside, closing the door behind her. Alfie took the opportunity to look around the large open-plan office, visible through glass screens to his right. He saw Dad sitting at a computer and chatting earnestly to a skinny young man, wearing glasses.

Dad was pointing at the screen and was clearly explaining something complicated and the other man was nodding, gravely. Dad glanced up, saw Alfie standing in reception and raised a hand to wave. His stern expression said, quite clearly, 'Don't mess this up.'

Alfie waved back and then turned, as Sandra emerged from the office, still grinning furiously. 'Mr Blackwood says you can go straight in. I'm fetching him a latte, can I get something for you, while I'm there?'

'Er . . . no, I'm fine, thanks.'

'Are you absolutely sure? I've got fizzy drinks!'

'Yes, thank you.'

'Haven't you got lovely manners? Well, in you pop and I'll be back presently. Go on, don't be shy! He doesn't bite.' She stepped aside and ushered him into a small inner office. Ralph Blackwood was sitting behind a desk, looking at a computer. He glanced up as Alfie entered and beamed a welcome.

'Ah, come along in and take a seat,' he said. 'Michael's told me all about you.' He was a portly man in his mid-fifties, dressed in an expensive-looking grey suit. His reddish hair was slicked back on his head and he had a podgy, rather red face. Alfie took one of the two seats opposite Mr Blackwood and gave him a nod.

'Thank you for seeing me,' he said.

'Not at all, not at all! Glad to be of help. So, Michael said you have a bit of a project on the go.'

'Yes, for school. It's all about family history, so I thought —'

'Well, you've come to the right place, I don't mind telling you that!'

Alfie smiled. 'Is that so?' he murmured.

'Oh, yes! As it happens, Blackwood and Phibes has a long and illustrious history in Woodplumpton and the surrounding area. Here, I took the opportunity of printing you off a bit of information, something I had commissioned several years ago. I always knew it would come in useful one day!' He handed over a slim sheath of papers with a flourish. Alfie took them and had a cursory glance at them. He registered several sheets packed with tiny print and a couple of old, black and white photographs.

'Oh, well that's . . . really useful,' he said. 'Thank you for taking the trouble.'

'Not at all. My pleasure.'

'So, your family's always lived in this area, has it?'

Mr Blackwood chuckled and held his hands up. 'You've got me bang to rights!' he said. 'Yes, I'm afraid I'm a local lad, born and bred and, as far as I'm aware, my lot have never travelled much further than the next couple of villages. You hear about families, don't you, who've crossed the oceans and explored exotic lands? Not my lot! They hunkered down and stayed in one place and that's how they prospered.'

Alfie nodded. This was exactly what he'd been hoping to hear.

'Right, well, the ancestor I'm most interested in talking

about is —'

'Thomas Blackwood, of course! Yes, dear old Thomas. The man who started it all. My great, great, great . . .' He considered for a moment. 'I'm never entirely sure at such times, how many 'greats' to put in front of 'grandfather', but suffice to say, he started the operation back in eighteen thirty-four and we've been in the property business ever since.' He pointed to the papers in Alfie's hand. 'You'll find it all spelt out in there. Thomas was originally a weaver by trade, but he saw an opportunity for getting into property and decided to seize it with both hands. So, he got together with his best friend, Montague Phibes, and the two of them pooled their resources. Without them, all this . . .' He gestured proudly around his little office, '. . . none of this would exist.'

Alfie tried not to look disappointed. 'Oh, right. That's very interesting,' he said. He opened his notepad and pretended to make a few scribbles on a blank page. 'The only thing is, I was . . . well, I was interested in going back at bit further than that,' he said.

'Oh yes?' Mr Blackwood looked puzzled. 'I assumed you were interested in the history of the *business*,' he said.

'Er, well, I am, sure, but . . . there must have been Blackwoods around here before Thomas, surely? I don't expect he started the business when he was a baby, did he?'

'Oh no, of course not. No, I believe he was in his thirties.'

'Right, so . . . so he must have had parents, mustn't he? And the people before them must have had parents, and so on. What I need to know is, who were the Blackwoods in this area before Thomas came on the scene?'

Mr Blackwood looked bemused.

'Now you're asking,' he said. 'I'm afraid before then, it's all a bit hazy.'

'Hazy?' Alfie stared at him. 'You surely must have some idea?'

There was a polite tap on the door. 'Come,' said Mr Blackwood grandly, and Sandra entered carrying a mug of coffee. She came around the desk and placed it reverentially in front of her boss. 'One latte,' she trilled, 'as requested.' She looked at Alfie. 'Are you *sure* I can't get you anything?' she asked. 'I have some very nice tropical fruit cordial in the fridge.'

'Oh, no, thank you,' said Alfie, eyeing Mr Blackwood's drink, nervously. He thought he knew what was coming next.

'You don't know what you're missing,' said Mr Blackwood. 'Sandra does make the best latte in the village.'

Sandra giggled. 'He always says that!' she told Alfie, and gave him a wink.

'Only because it happens to be true,' said Mr Blackwood. He raised the mug to his lips and took a sip. His eyes widened. He grimaced and then had to stop himself from heaving. He looked reproachfully at Sandra. 'Oh, Sandra, I think . . . I think there's something wrong with that,' he murmured, setting the mug down. 'It tastes a bit off.'

'Off?' Sandra looked mortified. She lifted the mug and took a delicate sniff of the contents. She too made a face. 'Oh, I'm so sorry,' she said. 'I don't understand. That milk was bought fresh this morning'

'Probably something to do with the hot weather,' said Mr Blackwood.

'I'll pop straight across to the corner shop and get a new bottle,' offered Sandra.

'I wouldn't bother,' muttered Alfie, mournfully and they both looked at him.

'Why do you say that?' asked Mr Blackwood.

'Oh, only because I've heard there's a problem, with . . . with the local dairy.' Alfie shrugged his shoulders. 'We've had the same thing at our guest house. Dodgy milk.' He shrugged his shoulders in a 'what can you do?' gesture.

Mr Blackwood and Sandra exchanged looks. 'Shall I bring you something else?' asked Sandra, who looked as though she might burst into tears at any moment.

'No, no, that's fine,' Mr Blackwood assured her. 'Not a problem. Thanks, anyway.'

Sandra took the offending latte out of the room, carrying it in front of her as though it might somehow infect her with its sourness. She closed the door behind her.

There was an uncomfortable silence. 'How peculiar,' said

Mr Blackwood. 'So . . . I'm sorry, you were saying . . .'

'That I really need to go back further than the eighteen-hundreds,' persisted Alfie. 'A hundred years earlier than that, in fact. The man I'm particularly interested in is Lord Vincent Blackwood.'

Now Mr Blackwood looked completely baffled. 'Who?' he said.

'Erm . . . Lord Vincent Blackwood? This would have been in the seventeen-hundreds. He was a big landowner back then – a very important man.'

'Was he really?' Mr Blackwood shook his head. 'I'm sorry, I'm afraid I've never heard of him. Have you tried Googling the name?'

'Yes, I have, and it keeps coming back with nothing.'

Mr Blackwood frowned. 'And you're sure you've got that right? Vincent is quite a distinctive name – I'm sure I'd remember it.'

'I've had it from a very good source,' Alfie assured him.

'Well, I'm sorry I can't be of more help. Of course, if it's the family business you need to know more about, I'd be more than happy to –'

'I've got plenty about the business,' said Alfie, irritably, waving the sheath of papers. 'But this is more important. I need to know about Lord Vincent. Are you sure . . . you're not just *pretending* you don't know who he is?'

'Pretending?' murmured Mr Blackwood. 'Why on earth would I do that?'

'Well, because of what he *did*.'

Now Mr Blackwood was staring at him and his genial smile had vanished. 'Whatever do you mean?' he asked.

'Well, I do get it. I mean, it's not the kind of thing you'd want to boast about, is it?'

'I'm sorry, I'm afraid you've completely lost me.'

'I mean, just because he was mixed up with Meg Shelton.'

Mr Blackwood's eyes widened. 'Meg Shelton?' he gasped. 'You mean . . . the witch?'

'The *alleged* witch,' Alfie corrected him. 'Most people think she was an innocent victim.'

'You mean that tourist invention that they bang on about at the church? The woman that's supposed to be buried under a stone?'

'That's no invention!' Alfie assured him. 'Oh no, she was a real person, I can tell you that much. And Lord Vincent Blackwood had her murdered and stole her baby. Fact. So, I'd understand if you did know about him but didn't want to admit it. But honestly, you can tell me, I'll keep it to myself.'

Mr Blackwood's mouth fell open. 'I don't know who you've been talking to,' he said, 'but that's absolute nonsense! You're suggesting that one of my ancestors . . . was a murderer?' He shook his head and gestured at the sheaf of papers that Alfie was holding. 'That's everything I know about my family history, right there. You're quite welcome to take that away with you and use it for your project. But I'm afraid I've never heard of the person you mentioned and, from the sound of it, I don't *want* to. *If* he even existed, which I very much doubt, he sounds like a thoroughly bad lot. A school project, you say? What kind of a school do you go to?'

'It's just a normal school,' insisted Alfie. 'Really.'

'Well, they want to be careful what they encourage their pupils to do. Your father didn't mention that you'd be coming here making *accusations*.'

'Oh, I'm not accusing you of anything!' he protested. 'Honestly!'

'That's something to be grateful for, I suppose. Now, if you don't mind, I have some work to get on with.'

He turned his attention back to his computer and tapped a key.

'I'm not finished!' insisted Alfie, shocked by how loud his own voice sounded.

Mr Blackwood stared at him open-mouthed. 'I beg your pardon?' he gasped.

Alfie got up from his seat. 'I need answers!' he yelled.

There was a sudden brief whooshing sound and quite suddenly, the computer in front of Mr Blackwood flared with an intense burst of brilliant light and then exploded, flinging debris in all directions. Mr Blackwood lurched back in his chair with a yell of terror and sat there staring at the computer, which was now billowing thick clouds of black smoke. A trickle of bright red blood pulsed from a wound on his cheek.

There was a brief silence and then an alarm started to squeal at ear-splitting volume. Above their heads there was a metallic click. A sprinkler system kicked into life and started to deluge the entire office with water. The computer hissed and sparked. Alfie and Mr Blackwood sat there staring at each other across a desk that was now being soaked with spray – all of Mr Blackwood's files rapidly being reduced to sodden rags. The door of the office burst open and Sandra stood there, mouth open, staring helplessly in at the chaos. Alfie couldn't help but notice that Dad was standing right behind her, looking over her shoulder, an expression of total disbelief on his face. Then he was gesticulating to Alfie and Mr Blackwood to vacate the room.

Alfie reacted instinctively. He ran around the desk, helped Mr Blackwood out of his chair and guided him towards the door, thinking as he did so that this really hadn't gone as smoothly as he'd hoped. Mr Blackwood was looking back at the chaotic scene that had only moments ago been his pride and joy.

'Alfie?' Dad was staring at him imploringly. 'What happened?'

It was a good question and one that Alfie didn't have the first idea how to answer.

CHAPTER FIFTEEN

AFTERMATH

'I'll ask you again,' said Dad, who was clearly making an almost superhuman effort to remain calm and patient. 'What happened in there?'

Alfie was sitting on a wooden chair that somebody had placed on the pavement outside Blackwood and Phibes. A thick blanket was draped around his wet shoulders. Inside the building, members of the fire brigade were working to make sure that there was no danger of any of the equipment in Mr Blackwood's devastated office catching alight again, though this seemed unlikely given how drenched everything was. As for Mr Blackwood himself, he'd been whisked away in an ambulance to have a rather nasty cut on his cheek attended to. The other staff members of Blackwood and Phibes were standing around in animated huddles, chatting anxiously to each other, as they waited for the all clear. Alfie was horribly aware of Sandra, standing with another couple of women and flinging suspicious glances in his direction at regular intervals.

'I'm *waiting*,' Dad reminded him.

Alfie could only shake his head. 'I don't know what happened,' he said. 'One minute we were chatting and the next thing I knew, his computer just kind of . . . blew up. It went off with a bang.'

Alfie said this as calmly as he could, but deep inside he knew that there had been more to it than that. He couldn't stop thinking about the last thing he'd said before the computer had gone up in smoke. Perhaps 'shouted' would be a better description. 'I need answers!' It hadn't sounded like his own voice at all. It had been all too recognisable as Meg's voice, as though she'd somehow spoken through him, using his mouth to shape the words. *A conduit.* Isn't that what she'd called him? And Alfie had no doubt in his mind that Meg, in her anger, had caused the explosion too.

'I've been working with computers for thirty years,' muttered Dad. 'And I've never heard of such a thing happening before. Never! Did one of you spill liquid on it? Did you maybe yank the wires out?'

Alfie shook his head miserably. 'I wasn't anywhere near it,' he insisted. 'I think, Ralph . . . er, Mr Blackwood, touched the keyboard. And then, boom! Up it went.'

Dad shook his head and then gave his son another stern look. 'And what was that he was saying, just before the paramedic led him away? Something about you making weird accusations about his family?'

Alfie shrugged his shoulders and grimaced. 'Search me,' he said. 'I think he was a bit confused, you know, what with the computer going up like that. Probably in shock. That cut on his face looked nasty . . .'

'The paramedics didn't seem too worried about it,' said Dad. 'They just wanted to be sure there was no chance of it getting infected.'

'I was only asking stuff about his family tree,' continued Alfie. He frowned. 'It's a shame the sprinklers had to come on. I expect everything in the office must be ruined.'

'Thousands of pounds worth of damage,' murmured Dad. 'I expect it'll all be insured, but it certainly doesn't help me with what I'm trying to do.'

'You . . . you won't get fired, will you?' asked Alfie fearfully, and Dad gave him a strange look.

'Why should I?' he asked. 'It's nothing to do with me, is it?'

'Yes, but what if they *blame* me? What if they think it's my fault? And you're the one who got me in there, so . . .'

'How could they blame you? It's not as if you made it happen, is it?

'Well, no . . . of course not. But —'

'It's just one of those million-to-one things. Faulty wiring, I expect, causing a short circuit. But it is odd, isn't it?'

'What's odd?'

'That it has to happen on the one occasion when you're in the office? It's almost like . . . it's like you're a jinx or something. A modern-day Job.'

'Who's Job?'

'Never mind.' Dad seemed to consider for a moment, then shook his head again as if to dispel any last doubts. 'Anyway, look, I'll have to get back in there as soon as they give the all-clear and see what's to be done about all the damage. Will you be all right to get yourself home so you can change your clothes?'

Alfie nodded. 'I guess so. Dad?'

'What?'

'I'm sorry about what happened.'

Dad sighed. 'Well, like you said, it's not as if you caused it, is it?'

'Erm . . . no. Course not.'

'Did you get what you were after?'

'Hmm?'

'For the school project.'

'Oh, er . . . not really. We'd only just started to talk.'

'Well, I don't know when Ralph will be up to having you back, so . . .'

Alfie waved a hand. 'Don't worry, I'll find somebody else.'

Dad nodded. 'I'll go and check if it's all right for you to leave,' he said, and wandered across to the solitary firefighter who'd been left with the engine. Alfie risked a glance in Sandra's direction and saw, to his dismay, that she was now making her way determinedly towards him. Alfie pulled the sodden sheaf of notes that Mr Blackwood had given him from his jacket pocket and tried to look as though he was engrossed in them, even though the printed letters had dissolved into a dirty smear.

'What happened in there?' demanded Sandra, and Alfie couldn't help noticing that her former sing-song tones had been replaced by a flat Lancashire accent.

He shook his head. 'I was just telling Dad,' he said. 'I haven't a clue.'

'Something went on,' announced Sandra. 'Something fishy.' I heard you raising your voice, just before it happened.'

Alfie tried not to look guilty. 'Oh, I . . . don't think so,' he said.

'Yes, you did. I heard you quite clearly. You shouted at Mr Blackwood. Something about wanting answers.'

'Oh, that, yes, I *did* say that. Not loudly though, just . . . normally.'

'It didn't sound normal to me,' said Sandra. 'Aggressive, is how I would describe it.' She leant closer. 'And what was that business with the milk?'

Alfie stared at her. 'The milk?' he whispered.

'Yes, the milk! Don't give me that look! It was as fresh as a daisy until the moment you turned up.'

Dad came wandering back and caught the note of tension in Sandra's tone. 'Everything all right?' he asked her.

She directed a withering glance at him. 'Something here doesn't make sense, Mr Travers,' she growled. 'I took a latte in to Mr Blackwood and the milk was sour. How do you account for that? It was bought from the corner shop this morning and placed straight in the fridge. It was fine until your son turned up.'

Dad furrowed his brow, trying to follow her logic. 'You're saying . . . that Alfie made the milk go sour?' he murmured.

'I'm saying it's funny,' muttered Sandra. 'That's all. And questions should be asked about it. We'll leave it there.' And with that, she turned on her heel and stalked back to her huddle of friends.

Dad looked at Alfie enquiringly. 'Any idea what she's on about?' he asked.

Alfie shook his head. 'Not a clue,' he said. He leant closer. 'I think there's something odd about her,' he whispered. 'When I was in reception, she kept grinning at me like a lunatic and talking in a funny high-pitched voice.'

'That's just how she talks,' Dad assured him. 'But she seemed to think you did something to the milk . . .'

Alfie held his hands out to either side of him. 'Well, that's nothing new, is it?' he reasoned. 'It's the same as The Excelsior.

AFTERMATH

Must be something to do with the weather.'

Dad seemed to accept this. He shrugged. 'Anyway, the
firefighter said you can head home if you're feeling OK. Don't
take too long about it though. You need to change straight out
of those wet things and hang them up to dry. I'll see you tonight,
once I know what's what.'

Alfie took the blanket from his shoulders and draped it over
the chair. He nodded to Dad and walked away. As he moved past
Sandra and her friends, he distinctly heard her say, 'Something
here just doesn't *smell* right'. He kept his head down and
moved on along the street, his wet trainers squelching gently
under his tread. Luckily it was a warm day and he wasn't too
uncomfortable, though he did get some odd looks from passers-
by, no doubt wondering how he'd managed to get himself
caught in a rainstorm on a sunny day like this.

That was exactly what Selina thought when he walked
through the reception of The Excelsior fifteen minutes later.

'Don't tell me it's raining out there!' she cried. 'The forecast
was for sunshine!'

Alfie turned to look at her. The boils on her face had turned
to a collection of bright red scabs and Alfie wondered how she
resisted tearing at them with her fingernails.

'No,' he assured her. 'No, I got caught out by a sprinkler system.'

'On a lawn?' she asked him.

'In an office,' he corrected her.

Her face moved through a series of expressions, ranging from surprise to bewilderment, before settling on her habitual attempt at a smile, which looked even more bizarre on her scabby face. 'I won't even ask how that happened,' she said. 'The things that have been occurring here lately, it's probably only to be expected.' She leant across the counter as if to confide a secret. 'I was telling Malcolm, only this morning,' she said. 'It's as if we're the victims of a curse. As though we've offended somebody without knowing it and they're taking some kind of horrible revenge on us.'

'Oh, no, I don't think —'

'Let me tell you the latest thing,' she whispered. 'If I hadn't seen it with my own eyes, I wouldn't have believed it.'

'I really need to go and —'

'Malcolm was in the kitchen, cooking up a bowl of stock for soups and so forth. We've learnt not to use any milk or other dairy products, so this was just a plain and simple vegetable stock. I mean, I ask you, what could go wrong with that?'

Alfie shook his head, to indicate that he hadn't the faintest idea.

'So, Malcolm is using a wooden spoon to stir it, as you do and all of a sudden, he feels the spoon being gripped by some powerful force. He lets go of the handle and he calls me in and we both stand there, looking as the spoon begins to spin round and round . . . and then it begins to sink slowly straight down into the pan, as though the stock is much deeper than it looks. It keeps on going until the handle is completely gone. Dissolved.

Not a trace of it.' She stared at Alfie, wide-eyed. 'What do you make of that?' she gasped.

'I . . . I really don't know what to make of it,' admitted Alfie.

'I know what you're thinking! You think I've lost my marbles, don't you? But we both saw it – we didn't imagine it. Of course, we had to throw the stock away. There was no way we could risk using it! What if we poisoned somebody? What if somebody got wooden splinters in their throat?' She reached suddenly across the counter and grabbed Alfie by the wrist, the power in her hand actually hurting him. 'Where's it going to end?' she gasped. 'I feel like I'm losing my mind!' Her eyes brimmed with helpless tears and Alfie felt sorry for her, but he didn't have the first idea how he might help.

'I need to go and change my clothes,' he murmured. 'I'm sorry.' He managed to detach her hand from his arm and headed for the stairs. He went up them at speed, unlocked the door of his room and went inside, slamming the door behind him. He paced around for a moment, then peeled off his wet jacket and went to the door of the bathroom. He hesitated, aware of the sound of running water coming from within. He took a breath, pushed the door slightly open and peered cautiously inside. She was in the shower again, scrubbing furiously at herself, her skinny body covered in lather. Alfie sighed, closed the door. He went to his suitcase, pulled out a fresh T-shirt and a pair of jeans and dressed himself. Then he sat down on the bed and waited.

After a short time, the bathroom door opened and Meg came out, draped in a bath towel. She scowled at Alfie, as though thoroughly displeased with him.

'What do you call that?' she snarled. 'What a waste of time that was. That idiot claimed he'd never even heard of Lord Vincent!'

'I did notice,' said Alfie. 'But did you have to go off on one and blow his computer to bits?'

'I was annoyed,' said Meg.

'You don't say! Well look, that kind of thing doesn't help at all. Not one bit. How do you expect me to get anywhere if you start sticking your oar in?' He waved a hand towards the bathroom door. 'And what's with using my shower whenever you fancy it?'

'It relaxes me,' said Meg.

'Oh, does it really? And what about me? Because I'm not feeling very relaxed right now.'

'Never mind how you feel. You've got a job to do and a pretty poor show you're making of it.'

Alfie glared at her. 'Well look, if this is going to work, we need to set a few ground rules, otherwise I'm not going to be able to find out anything. D'you hear me? You need to give me a chance to sort things out on my own.'

'I saw you trying to do that,' said Meg. 'You let that idiot run rings around you. If I'd had a chance, I'd have got the truth out of him. I'd have twisted his arm until it snapped.'

'Well then, maybe it's a good job you're not able to do it

yourself!' Alfie told her. 'I think he was telling the truth. He doesn't know anything about Lord Vincent. He's never heard of him. Lots of people don't know anything about their ancestors and anyway, it doesn't necessarily follow that he's from the same line of Blackwoods. But don't worry, I've got somebody working on it – somebody who's good at finding out stuff from the past. I just need a bit more time, that's all.'

'I grow impatient.' Meg got up off the bed and started pacing agitatedly about.

'Well, you've waited hundreds of years, surely a few more days can't make much difference,' reasoned Alfie. He frowned. 'And another thing,' he said. 'You're going to have to lay off all this mischief-making. It's too much.'

She stopped pacing and studied him for a moment.

'I have to have some fun,' she said.

'You've got a strange idea of fun,' Alfie told her. 'All this business with turning milk sour. It has to stop. It's happening everywhere I go, and people are beginning to put two and two together. That Sandra at the office, she thinks I'm involved.'

'I *like* the milk tricks,' muttered Meg. 'It's one of my best spells.'

'That may be so, but it's just making things harder for me . . .' He gathered his courage. 'Also . . . you need to lay off Selina and Malcolm.'

'What, the idiots who run this stink hole?'

'Well, that's charming! *You* seem fond enough of it, using

that shower all the time! I bet it's a lot nicer than you were used to back in the old days. And it's just not fair, what you're doing to them. The boils, the frogs or toads . . . whatever was in that woman's breakfast. What have they ever done to you?'

'Well, nothing . . . but that's hardly the point.'

'I'll tell you what will happen if you carry on down this road. Selina and Malcolm will go out of business and this place will have to close down.'

'You think I care about that?'

'Probably not. But think about it. If The Excelsior closes down, Dad and I will have nowhere to live. We'll have to head back to Bristol. And how is that going to help you? Who is going to look for Edgar's grave then?'

Her expression hardened. 'Are you telling me what to do?' she murmured.

'Not exactly. I'm just saying, I can't help you if . . . *oh*!'

She was pointing a finger at him. He felt a sudden pushing sensation in his chest, and he went down on to the bed. Then he began to slide backwards, at speed, across the duvet. His head bumped against the wooden headboard and then he was lifted upwards into a sitting position. 'Stop!' he gasped. 'Don't . . .' His body kept on going. It rose through the air and his shoulders slammed hard against the wall above the bed. He kept moving until his head bumped against the ceiling. Then he hung there, helpless, staring down at her. She was studying him, as she might study an insect before she brought her foot down on it. 'Let's get something straight,' she told him. 'I am in control of you. If I say raise your arm . . .' She snapped her fingers and his right arm shot above his head, the knuckles slamming hard against the ceiling. 'If I say bend your leg . . .' Again, she snapped her fingers, and his left leg lifted up and stuck out in front of him. 'You see how much control you have? None! So, if I were you, boy, I'd moderate your tone when you speak to me.'

Alfie struggled to form words. 'Listen . . . to me,' he gasped. 'I want to . . . help you . . . I'm *trying* to! But I can't do that if . . . you won't help yourself. You've got to stop playing tricks on people. It's just . . . getting in the way. Please . . . give me some space . . . let me do my job.'

She stared at him a moment longer and then made a dismissive flourish with her hand. The powerful restraint came off him and he fell in an ungainly sprawl back on to the bed, the impact nearly breaking the frame. He lay on his back, gasping for breath, and Meg came closer to sit on the bed beside him. She lifted a hand and almost tenderly, she reached out and tousled his hair. He shrank from the cold, clammy feel of her fingers.

'Let's say we set a deadline?' she murmured. 'How about I give you – let's be generous here – forty-eight hours? During that time, I'll declare an amnesty. No more tricks. No more bad milk. No warts, no boils, no frogs and toads. How does that sound?'

'It sounds pretty good,' said Alfie suspiciously.

'But hear my words, boy. If at the end of that time, you have still not found my son's grave . . .'

Alfie started to sit up, but she waved her hand and he was pushed flat again.

'If after that time, I am still left wanting, then you shall pay the ultimate price.'

'Wh . . . what does that mean?'

She leant over him, smiling dangerously. 'All that you love. All that you care for. All that you hope for. All that you cherish. Will founder and sink. Will crumble like dust. You shall watch it destroyed. You shall weep bitter tears.' She made a strange complicated gesture with her hands and then nodded her head. 'There,' she said. 'It is done. A witch's promise.'

'Was that some kind of spell?' he asked her.

She just continued to smile at him.

'What does it mean, Meg? What does it mean?'

But she was fading now, right in front of his eyes. He could see right through her. The towel she was wearing seemed to tumble in on itself and then it lay discarded on the bed, still damp from the shower. Alfie looked helplessly around the room. 'Come back!' he called. 'Come back and tell me what that meant. Meg! Please, come back.'

But she did not return.

Not that day, at any rate.

CHAPTER SIXTEEN

MEETING OF MINDS

Alfie got to the graveyard a little ahead of schedule. There was no sign of Mia yet. He took out his phone and once again, went over the exchange of text messages from earlier that morning

MIA IT'S ME. I NEED TO SEE YOU. SOON AS

OK! Luigi's?

NO. I THINK THE MILK THING MIGHT BE OK NOW
BUT BETTER NOT RISK IT

Where then?

GRAVEYARD B THERE AT 5.30
I NEED TO TRY SOMETHING

K

Alfie walked along the path until he got to Meg's grave. He stood for a moment, gazing down at the big grey boulder. Then he glanced quickly around. There was nobody else in sight – the place seemed completely deserted. If he was going to try this thing, he told himself, now was as good a time as any. He felt vaguely foolish for even considering what he was about to do, but figured he might as well give it a shot. What was the worst that could happen?

'Right,' he murmured. He reminded himself that last time, he'd walked around the boulder in a clockwise direction, so it seemed to make sense to do it in reverse this time. He moved around the grave slowly, stopping at the same point each time and saying, aloud, 'I believe in witches!' As he said it for the third time, he closed his eyes and concentrated, hoping that he'd feel something like he had on the previous occasion – but there was nothing, no phantom hand gripping his ankle, no cold sensation rippling through his body, just a vague sense of embarrassment. He sighed.

'That's a curious thing to witness,' said a voice right beside him and he nearly jumped out of his skin. The elderly priest seemed to have appeared from out of nowhere. He was standing on the path just a few steps away, a couple of books tucked under one arm. He wore a smart black suit and a pristine white dog collar. His thinning grey locks were slicked back on his head. 'You're doing it wrong, by the way,' he added.

Alfie stared at him. 'Sorry?' he muttered.

If memory serves me correctly, you're supposed to say that you don't believe in witches. That's how I remember it from my childhood, anyway.'

Alfie nodded and smiled bitterly. 'I already did it that way,' he admitted. 'Now I'm trying to *undo* the spell.'

'Are you indeed?' The priest smiled as though amused by the idea. 'And what happened when you tried it the proper way? Did old Meg pay you a visit?'

Alfie frowned. 'She did, actually. Yeah. Big time. Problem is, now she's here I can't seem to get rid of her.'

The priest's smile faded and was replaced with a look of concern. 'I'm hoping you're pulling my leg' he said.

Part of Alfie wanted to tell him the truth, to explain that there were things in this world that the old man's religion couldn't begin to explain, but at the last moment his resolve buckled. 'Of course, I am,' he said, and attempted what he hoped was a convincing smile. 'Sorry, couldn't resist.'

The priest seemed reassured. He moved closer and extended a hand to shake. 'I'm Father Aymler,' he said.

'I'm Alfie Travers.' They shook hands.

'I don't think I've seen you around here before,' said Father Aymler.

'No, I'm new. And I'm only visiting. Do you . . . belong to this church?' asked Alfie, waving a hand at the huge building behind him. 'I mean, do you work here?'

'No, like you, I'm just visiting. A colleague works here. I'm from St Anthony's, the Roman Catholic church. But I *was* raised in this village.' He looked down at the boulder. 'So, of course, I know all about dear old Meg. I was one of those children who was dared many a time to walk around this stone and say the forbidden words.'

Alfie nodded. 'And did you? Say them, I mean.'

Father Aymler looked thoughtful for a moment as if trying to remember. Then he shook his head. 'I was too scared at the time,' he admitted. 'I didn't have my faith back then, you see. And I suppose I actually believed those crazy stories about her.'

'And now?'

Father Aymler shrugged. 'Now I know better. Now I know that she's just the product of an old folk tale, something conjured from the gossip of locals. A minor tourist attraction, of course, but totally fabricated.' He pointed a finger at the grave. 'Trust me,' he said. 'There's nothing under that boulder but earth.'

Alfie studied him with interest.

'How can you be so sure?' he murmured. 'Have you ever dug down there?'

'No, not personally. But a few years back, some students from the university came here with special equipment. GPR, I believe it's called. Ground Penetrating Radar. It uses electronic pulses to search for buried things deep in the soil – I suppose they sensed the opportunity for a sensational story. They found nothing down there, of course – no bones, no coffin, *nada*. They informed everyone at the church of their results, but it was decided to, er . . . say nothing about them.' He gave Alfie a sly wink. 'Well, why spoil a good story? And it *does* bring in a few tourists.'

There was something in the old man's certainty that irritated Alfie. 'What if I told you that she *is* down there?' he asked. 'What if I told you that she's real – that she's been wandering around this village making all the milk go sour? And that she's been using me as her conduit? What would you say to that?'

Father Aymler looked delighted at the idea. 'I'd say you've a pretty fanciful imagination and perhaps you should consider becoming a writer of popular fiction!' He studied Alfie for a moment and when he got no response, his expression hardened a little. 'Listen, my son, if there's something troubling you, I'd be more than happy to talk to you about it, any time you like.'

Before Alfie could reply, they were interrupted by the sound of somebody clearing her throat. Alfie glanced up to see Mia standing a short distance away.

'Oh, hi,' murmured Alfie.

Father Aymler had turned and was now smiling at Mia. 'Hello,' he said. 'It's Mia Waterston, isn't it? I haven't seen you for ages. How are you?'

'I'm fine thanks.' Mia was studying her black boots as though not entirely pleased to see the old man. 'Just here to meet Alfie.'

'I see. And how's your mother? Still the same?'

Mia looked uncomfortable, but she nodded her head. 'Pretty much,' she whispered.

'Oh, well, do give her my best wishes, won't you? And tell her I'm still hoping to see her back in my congregation one of these days.' He turned back to Alfie. 'Well, must get on,' he said. 'Good day to you, Alfie.' He half-turned towards the boulder and inclined his head slightly, a smirk on his lips. 'Meg,' he murmured, and then he continued on along the path and went in at the open door of the church. Alfie and Mia gazed after him in silence for a moment.

'What were you doing talking to him?' asked Mia quietly.

'Oh, he just turned up as I was trying to take the curse off,' said Alfie.

She looked at him. 'You were trying to do *what*?' she gasped.

'I know it sounds daft, but I thought it was worth a try. I walked around three times in the other direction and said I *did* believe in witches. The reverse, see? Don't think it changed anything, though.'

Mia gave him a disparaging look. 'When I arrived, it sounded like you were telling Father Aymler all about Meg,' she said.

'I kind of was,' admitted Alfie. 'But I chickened out from giving him the full story.'

'You don't want to go telling him that kind of thing,' she warned him. 'Seriously. He's not just a priest. He's a psychiatrist too. There's nothing he likes more than talking to people with strange ideas. He'd have a field day with you.'

Alfie frowned. 'What was that he said about your mother?' he asked.

'Nothing.' The reply was a little too fast, a little too flat, to be entirely convincing.

'He said something like, "is she still the same?" What did he mean by that?'

Mia shrugged. 'How would I know? Is she still five foot three, does she still have curly hair? That kind of thing, I suppose.' Alfie remained unconvinced by the explanation. 'But you said, "pretty much", like you knew what he was on about, so —'

'Look, I don't want to be pushy but I abandoned a pretty good tie-dying session to come here and meet you, so this had better be good. What's going on?'

Alfie indicated a wooden bench a short distance away. 'Let's sit down over there,' he suggested. 'I've got quite a lot to tell you.'

***

'Forty-eight hours?' cried Mia. 'Really?'

'Well, quite a bit less than that by now. This happened around four-thirty, so I don't know how strict she's being about the deadline. But that's what she said. If I don't have answers for her soon, well . . .' He spread his hands. 'All bets are off.'

'And you're sure about the wording?'

'Absolutely sure. It's not the kind of thing you'd forget in a hurry.' He thought about the cold, clammy touch of her hand on his head and suppressed a shudder.

'You're saying it's some kind of threat against you?'

'Well, no, not against *me* so much.' He thought for a moment, recalling the exact words. 'All that you love. All that you care for. All that you hope for. All that you cherish . . . that's not a threat to me, but to others. To Dad and . . . to you?'

She seemed to perk up at this. She regarded him slyly. 'All that you *love*?' she ventured.

He felt his face reddening. 'Er . . . well, you know what I mean. Love as in "care about." I mean, we're mates now, aren't we?'

She looked disappointed. 'Just mates?' she murmured.

'Well, I mean . . . maybe a bit more than that.' He squirmed. He'd never been very good at this kind of thing.

There was a long, uncomfortable silence and then she said quietly. 'If you were thinking of leaning in for a kiss, now would be a good time.'

He didn't need telling twice. They moved together and sat

there in the stillness of the graveyard, their lips touching, and it seemed to Alfie that the birdsong in the surrounding trees and bushes increased steadily in volume until his head felt it would burst with the sound. They held the position for quite a few momentsand then, as if by mutual agreement, they moved apart.

'Well,' said Mia. 'Now I'm glad I decided to abandon that tie-dying session.'

'What, you're saying the kiss was better?'

'Oh yes, much more fun. Maybe we should give it another go . . .' She started to lean closer.

'Thing is,' said Alfie. 'What are we going to do about finding that grave?'

She swayed back and gave him a reproachful look. 'Did anyone ever tell you, you're great at killing the atmosphere?' asked Mia, but when he didn't have an answer for that, she sighed. 'Well, Mr Fun-Sponge, I have news on that front. I got a text from Hannah on the way here. She wants us to meet her in Preston tomorrow.'

'Tomorrow? That's ages away! Doesn't she know we haven't got a lot of time to spare?'

Mia looked aggrieved. 'I did tell her it was urgent. And, to be fair to her, she couldn't have got on to it much faster. She's planning to do a long session at the Harris Library in the morning. To use the local and family history archive, you need to give a day's notice. She says she should have something for us at two o'clock.'

'Doesn't she want us to help her with the research?'

'No, thank God! Trust me, I *did* try and help her out once before and you've no idea how dull it is in there. The stuff she looks at is all written in this old English style you can't make head nor tail of. And you can't even speak to each other! If you clear your throat, they all look at you as if you've just taken a dump on the floor. No, best we leave it to the expert.'

'But she thinks she'll find information about Lord Vincent Blackwood?'

'Well, if anyone can do it, Hannah's your best bet. She knows exactly where to look. I told her we'd meet her there at two o'clock.' She gave him a look. 'Unless, of course, you have something more important to attend to?'

He shook his head. 'No,' he said. 'Suddenly this seems very important.' He studied her for a moment. 'And Mia, since we're in this together . . .'

'Yes.'

'We need to be straight with each other. Tell me about your mum. I know there's something.'

She looked uncomfortable, shook her head. 'You really don't want to know.'

'Yes, I do. Go on.' He looked at her intently. 'Please,' he added.

She sighed. 'It's just that she . . .' Mia sat there looking at her feet, so Alfie put out a hand and held one of hers, tightly.

'Just tell me,' he urged her. 'How bad can it be?'

'It's not bad, so much as . . . sad, I suppose. Tragic.' She took a breath. 'My dad ran out on us a few years back,' she said. 'I was fourteen when he left and to be honest, I didn't much care. The two of us had never really got on. I think he would have preferred a boy . . . someone he could play football with, and all that crap.' She shrugged her shoulders. 'I always thought of him as one of the most selfish people I ever knew.'

'Selfish, how?'

'It was always about what he wanted out of life. He never let anything get in the way of that. So when he saw somebody he liked more than Mum, well, he just went for it, didn't he?'

'It happens,' admitted Alfie. 'My parents split up a long time ago, but it was . . . what do they call it? Amicable?'

Mia grimaced. 'This wasn't amicable,' she said. 'There were fights, rows, things being smashed, people yelling at each other at all hours of the day and night. And then, one morning, he just packed a bag and walked away from it. But my mum still loved him, more than anything else in the world. They were childhood sweethearts – there had never been anyone else for her. So, when he left, she . . . didn't handle it very well. Spent too many nights on her own, brooding over a glass of wine. She stopped talking, stopped caring about how she looked and came a little bit unstuck in her head, I suppose. She got so she didn't want to go out any more. Couldn't make herself do it. Agoraphobia, it's called. I suppose you've heard of it?'

Alfie nodded. 'That must have been hard to deal with,' he said.

'Still is. Oh, we get some help, but it's mostly me that runs the house – you know, washing the clothes, doing the shopping, cooking the meals, that kind of stuff. I think that's how I turned out the way I am.'

'What do you mean?'

'Oh, you know. Trying to organise everyone.'

Alfie smiled. 'That's not a crime,' he said. 'Does your dad know what's happening . . . to your mum, I mean?'

'Oh yeah. Not that he cares. He has a new life now. New partner, new house, a baby on the way. He sends me a card at Christmas with a tenner in it and I think he sees that as doing his bit.' She laughed bitterly. 'Anyway, the way I see it, it's his loss. My mum's a lovely person and I'm totally amazing, obviously.'

Alfie chuckled. 'Yes,' he said. 'I agree with that bit.'

She looked at him for a moment, and for the first time he saw the vulnerability in her – the sensitive girl that hid behind that assured persona. They moved together again, and this time there was no hesitation between them. Their lips found each other as if by instinct and their mouths explored.

But even in the midst of their kiss, Alfie was painfully aware of the time ticking all-too-quickly away and he told himself that he couldn't let anything happen to Mia and Dad; that he would do everything in his power to ensure their safety. Out of the corner of his eye, he could see Meg's grave and the huge stone that marked it.

CHAPTER SEVENTEEN

PAGES FROM HISTORY

'Something's different,' said Dad. He and Alfie had just taken their seats at their usual table in the dining room of The Excelsior. The morning sunshine was streaming in through the windows, giving the place a fresh, clean look. For once, it was busy with guests – holidaying couples dressed in summer clothes, all chatting happily, and apparently perfectly content with their breakfasts. Nobody appeared to have made a horrible discovery in their cereal bowl and none of the guests weremarching towards the exit in a strop, threatening to contact TripAdvisor. It all looked disconcertingly normal.

Alfie regarded it all through heavy-lidded eyes. He had spent much of the previous night on his laptop, browsing the internet, trying to find something that might give him a clue to where he should look for Edgar Blackwood's grave. He had found other Blackwoods on there – lots of them. As well as the villain in a Sherlock Holmes adventure, there was an up-and-coming pop star, someone who had been the founder of the long-lived literary magazine that was named after him, amongst others – but none had been any relation to the Blackwoods he was searching for. He had finally given up in the small hours of the morning and drifted off into a troubled sleep, haunted by bad dreams in which Meg Shelton returned to find that Alfie had no answers for him and was very quick to take her revenge. The final image before he woke was of Mia's terrified expression, as an ear-shattering scream spilt out of her.

As tired as he was, Alfie could see what Dad was getting at. He had never experienced The Excelsior running quite as smoothly as this. It really did seem as if Meg was keeping her end of the bargain – but for how long? Alfie glanced at his watch, painfully aware that his forty-eight-hour grace period was already down to thirty-one.

Selina appeared, and she too seemed transformed. The unsightly scabs had completely disappeared from her face, and her hair and make-up were immaculate. Even her welcoming smile was less of a grimace than usual. 'Ah, good morning, gentlemen!' she trilled. 'And what a lovely one it is. What can I get for you?'

'You seem to be in good spirits,' observed Dad.

'Do you know what, I believe I am!' she admitted. She gestured at her pristine features. 'The doctor gave me some cream which seemed to clear my complexion up like *magic* and we've had a whole bunch of new bookings since yesterday. I said to Malcolm, it's like a black cloud has been lifted off us. Like we've been struggling through a dark forest and we've suddenly stepped out into the sunshine.' She leant closer. 'We've even put dairy back on the menu,' she whispered, 'and so far, so good.'

'In that case, I'll start with a latte,' said Dad encouragingly. 'And I'll go for the full English.'

'Very good. Malcolm's even managed to get his poached eggs up to scratch,' said Selina. 'If that's what you'd like?'

'Fabulous.' Dad looked expectantly at Alfie.

'Oh, er, I'll have . . . a Diet Coke and um . . . beans on toast, please.' To be honest, right now, food was the last thing on Alfie's mind. He was all too aware that there were hours to kill before he and Mia had their appointment with Hannah in Preston. How was he supposed to fill the time?

'Excellent choice!' Selina scribbled on her pad and almost danced out of the room. Dad watched her go and then smiled at Alfie. 'Well, how's that for a change of mood?' he murmured. He noticed Alfie's red-rimmed eyes and frowned. 'What's up with you?' he asked. 'Bad night?'

'I didn't sleep too well,' admitted Alfie.

'I hope you weren't surfing the internet till all hours,' said Dad.

Alfie could have told him that yes, he *had* been on the internet and for a very good reason, but he didn't want to start down that road. He could imagine Dad's eyes getting wider and wider as the story spilt out and anyway, Dad had enough on his plate right now. He'd got back late from work the previous evening and hadn't been in the right frame of mind to talk about it then.

'How are things at Blackwood and Phibes?' asked Alfie cautiously.

'Oh, everything's under control,' said Dad. 'I spent a lot of time on the phone after you left, getting things straightened out. The insurance people haven't put up a protest about paying for the damage to the office. They sent somebody straight out to have a look.'

'Oh, that's good. Did they . . . work out what caused the explosion?'

'A power surge, they think. Must have been a big one, because the circuit board of that computer was fried. Never seen anything quite like it.'

'Hmm."

'And then Ralph came back from the hospital in a very positive frame of mind. He said he wanted to use this as an opportunity to redesign his office, make it more streamlined. Been thinking about it for ages, apparently. He's asked me to handle it, so it's actually going to put a bit more work my way, which is nice. He's thinking of going paperless. I warned him it'll be a tough one to achieve, but he seems determined.'

'I see. And er, did he say anything about me? Or our meeting?'

Dad considered for a moment. 'He *did* say something, actually.'

'Oh, yes?'

'He said how remarkable it was that somebody of your age was showing so much initiative. He said he thought you were a very confident young man – and that if he could be of any more help with your project, you shouldn't hesitate to ask him.'

Alfie stared at him. 'He said that? Really?'

'Yes, really. Why, what were you expecting? That he'd blame you for wrecking his office?' Dad chuckled. Alfie just sat there, looking at him.

'And . . . what about his face?'

'Oh, it's nothing serious. A flesh wound. Didn't even need a stitch.'

'Well, that's great. So, he . . . he's not angry with me?'

'No, of course he's not. Why should he be? It was just bad luck that you were there when it happened, right?'

Alfie nodded. 'Yeah. Sure it was.'

Selina came back with the drinks. 'That was quick,' said Dad.

'It's like we've been turbocharged,' said Selina. 'That kitchen is running like clockwork.' She set a large latte down in front of Dad, with evident pride. Malcolm had even managed to do that thing where it looked as though an intricate leaf had been drawn into the foam. 'Wow,' said Dad. 'Looks impressive. Has he been on a course or something?'

'He watched one of those tutorials on YouTube,' confided Selina. 'I don't know what's come over him. I've never seen him so full of confidence. He's like Gordon Ramsey and Jamie Oliver all rolled into one.' Dad lifted the mug to his lips and Selina and Alfie watched in silent apprehension as he took a cautious sip.

His eyes widened in surprise. He took the mug away from his mouth and smiled, a thick white foam on his top lip. 'Absolutely perfect,' he said.

Selina let out a long sigh of relief, before turning on her heel and trotting happily back into the kitchen.

OK, thought Alfie. *Things have settled down a bit. Good.* But how long would that last? He glanced at his watch. While he'd been sitting here, another fifteen minutes had slipped away like grains of sand in an hourglass.

'So, what have you got planned for today?' Dad asked him.

'Hmm? Oh, I'm going into Preston with —'

'. . . Mia,' finished Dad. 'Don't worry, it's not a criticism,' he added, noting Alfie's downcast expression. 'It's clear she's made a big impression on you. All right, I give up. How soon before I get to meet her?'

Alfie shrugged. 'Are you sure you want to?'

'Yeah, why not?' Dad thought for a moment. 'Is there

something wrong with her?' he asked. 'Is she as tall as a giraffe with tartan hair?'

Alfie sniggered. 'Naturally,' he said.

'Oh well, she should do nicely then.' Dad smiled. 'You know, I was thinking. Once I've finished up on this job, maybe we could afford that fancy holiday you've been pining for. Go to Spain somewhere, hire a villa with a pool, drive around in a little hire car . . . what do you think?'

'Maybe,' said Alfie, without enthusiasm. Somehow, a holiday seemed unimportant now. 'Whatever.'

Dad looked astonished. 'All right,' he said, 'Two questions. Where is my son, Alfie? And what have you done with him?'

'What do you mean?'

'Well, before we came here, it was pretty much all you were talking about. How all your friends had gone somewhere nice for the summer and you were stuck in this boring country with . . .' A look of realisation dawned. 'Oh, I get it. Maybe you've found something here that's more enticing than a holiday, right?'

Alfie looked at him. 'What are you on about?' he muttered.

'Mia, of course! Clearly, she's far more interesting than a trip to the Costa Blanca.'

'Dad . . .'

'What is with you, anyway? How did you turn out to be such a romantic?'

'It's nothing to do with Mia! She's nice and everything but . . .

I've got other stuff on my mind, right now. Important stuff.'

'Oh yes, such as . . .'

Something in Alfie's head clicked. *Right*, he thought. *You asked for it.* He took a deep breath. 'OK, so there's this witch called Meg. She's been dead for hundreds of years, but I somehow managed to say the words that brought her up from the grave and she's been following me everywhere, ever since. Now she says she's going to destroy everything I care about if I don't work out where her son is buried.'

There was a long silence while they sat there looking at each other.

'I thought you promised me, you were going to spend less time playing those video games,' said Dad. Alfie stared at him, speechless. Dad lifted his coffee cup andtook another sip of his latte. 'You know, this is really good,' he said. 'Seriously, it could be the nicest I've ever had.'

'Did you hear what I said?' Alfie told him. 'There's this witch called . . .'

He paused as Selina swept back into the room, holding two plates out in front of her like trophies. She placed a perfectly respectable-looking portion of beans on toast before Alfie and then, with a flourish, put a huge fried breakfast down for Dad. 'Ta daaah!' she announced. Dad and Alfie stared down at the plate in mute amazement. It looked perfect. There were rashers of crispy bacon, succulent sausages, grilled mushrooms and golden hash browns. And, best of all, there were two perfectly poached eggs. Dad lifted his knife and poked one with the tip of it. Thick, yellow yoke gushed from it and spilt enticingly across the plate. 'Wow,' he murmured. He looked up at Selina. 'Give my compliments to the chef,' he said.

'I certainly shall,' said Selina, and away she went, looking for all the world as if, at any moment, she might break into a song and dance routine. Dad looked at Alfie, mystified. 'What the hell's going on?' he murmured.

Alfie knew, but apparently there was no point in trying to explain. Nobody took you seriously when you tried. He offered up a silent wish that Hannah would have some information for him, later that day.

**

She was standing on the imposing steps of the Harris Library as Alfie and Mia approached, a big leather bag slung over one shoulder. She saw them coming and lifted a hand to wave, then came down the steps to greet them. 'Right on time,' she said.

'Did you find anything?' asked Alfie, aware as he did so that another six hours had slipped by since breakfast.

Hannah gave him a look. 'Let's go somewhere where we can talk over a coffee,' she suggested. 'It's been a busy morning. I need my caffeine fix.'

'Yes, but can't you just tell me —'

'All in good time. This way!!'

They followed her across the busy square and along Harris Street to a small cafe. It wasn't too crowded in there and once they had located a vacant table, a waiter came straight over and took their order. Alfie waited impatiently while Hannah perused the menu and finally ordered a cup of tea and a fruit scone. As soon as the waiter had moved away, Alfie leant urgently forward over the table.

'Well?' he asked Hannah. 'What have you got for me?'

Hannah frowned and glanced at Mia. 'He's an impatient sort, your friend,isn't he?' she observed, as though Alfie wasn't there.

'I think he's pretty anxious about this,' agreed Mia. 'He hasn't stopped looking at his watch all the way here.'

Hannah chuckled. She unfastened the strap of her bag and took out some notebooks. She opened the largest of them and perused the neatly written pages. 'I thought it best to go straight to the most reliable source,' she said. 'Wimbley.'

Alfie stared at her. 'What's that?' he muttered.

'Not "what" but "who"?' she corrected him. 'Frederick Wimbley, the historian. He's barely remembered these days, but he wrote what is, essentially, the first local history of Preston and its surrounding area. It was published in 1715 . . .'

Alfie lifted a hand to interrupt. 'But . . . hang on a minute. Meg was buried in 1705, so how is that going to help us?'

Hannah smiled. 'As I was saying, it was *published* in 1715, but he'd been writing it for many years before that. Also,

I decided to concentrate on the annotated version by Tobias Wilson.'

'Annotated?' echoed Mia.

'Yes. That just means . . . scribbled on. Wilson was an antiquarian, and he often added bits of information to the original, when he had some fresh insight regarding it. The remarks are sometimes humorous, but it's clear he had immense respect for Wimbley . . .'

'Right,' said Alfie, nodding, trying to hurry her along.

'The volume I looked at is very rare and worth thousands of pounds, you can only handle it with the greatest of care. Luckily, I know Doris, who works in the archive, and she always turns a blind eye when I —'

'Yes, yes, that's all great,' said Alfie. 'But Hannah, I really need to know, did you find anything on Lord Vincent Blackwood? Because I spent all last night looking on the internet and didn't even scare up a mention of him.'

Hannah sneered. 'The internet,' she said, as if it was a dirty word. 'Wimbley, on the other hand, *did* know about him.' She picked up her notebook and peered at the rows of text through her tortoiseshell-rimmed glasses. 'Now, to save time, I have taken the trouble to render the rather archaic spelling into a more modern approximation. But you'll see here . . .' She tapped a page with a plump forefinger, '. . . Wimbley has a mention of a Lord Vincent Blackwood and his wife, Lady

Evelyn, in 1710, living in a place called Hunter's Lodge, along with their son . . . William.'

Alfie almost groaned at this news. 'William?' he murmured. 'What about Edgar?'

'Well, let's not be too hasty,' Hannah advised him. 'I couldn't find any record of another child, male or female. But think about it. If your theory is correct . . .'

'It's not a theory, it's what Meg told me!'

'Erm . . . yes.' A troubled look flickered across Hannah's face, but she managed to push it away. 'Just think for a moment. If you had stolen somebody's newborn child in order to pass it off as your own, it's unlikely isn't it, that you would keep his original name? That would be a dead giveaway. Now, as I said, this particular entry was made in October 1710, where the age of William is recorded as five years old . . .'

Alfie and Mia exchanged looks. 'That fits perfectly,' said Mia. 'Meg was killed in 1705. Edgar would have been exactly that age.'

'OK, but how would the Blackwoods account for a new baby suddenly appearing out of nowhere?' reasoned Alfie. 'People would have noticed that this Evelyn had never been pregnant.'

'A good point,' said Hannah. 'I had the same thought. So, I backtracked a few years and found a mention of the Blackwoods being away from the Lodge for a long period in 1705. It says that both Lord Vincent and his wife spent a year away from home, travelling around Europe. Now, there's no mention of dear

Meg in Wimbley's book – he wouldn't involve himself in anything so fanciful – and we have no way of knowing what time of year it was when she died, but I *did* find a brief mention in another text to say that William was born in Italy and that the Blackwoods returned to Hunter's Lodge with their son when he was around a year old.' She looked at their puzzled faces. 'Well, think about it, for goodness' sake! It would be easy for them to smuggle baby Edgar away with them to Europe and then fabricate his supposed "birth" in a foreign country, wouldn't it? It would also be easy to have a certificate of birth forged by some shady character they employed over there. When they returned, a full year after the events at Cuckoo Hall, anybody who wanted to challenge the fact that the baby was not Lady Evelyn's would be obliged to travel to Italy in order to prove the deception, something that would be quite beyond the means of most people in Preston, at that time.'

Alfie nodded. 'It seems to make sense,' he agreed.

'Well, it gets better than that. My hunch about Tobias Wilson's annotations may have paid off.' She pointed to another entry in her notebook. 'Look here, I found this scribbled in the margin alongside the original entry about the Blackwoods and their son. It was quite hard to make out, but I think it contains a useful clue.' She lifted the notebook. 'Next to the name, "William", Wilson has written the words, "he has his father's eyes and I pray, not his mother's skills." She set the book down and gave them a triumphant look. 'What do you make of that?' she asked them.

There was a silence and then Mia said, 'Oh, right!'

Alfie looked at her. 'I don't get it,' he said.

'Sure, you do! It's like this Wilson guy knows the truth, yeah? "His father's eyes", because he knows Lord Vincent is the boy's father; and "I pray *not* his mother's skills", because he also knows that his real mother was a witch!'

Alfie let out a gasp. 'That's perfect,' he said. 'It has to be right. Hannah, you're a star!'

'I have my uses,' admitted Hannah, smiling at the compliment. The waiter arrived with their order and Alfie was obliged to sit simmering impatiently while the food and drinks were carefully set out in front of them. As soon as the waiter had moved away, Alfie leant across the table again.

'But we still don't know where the grave is,' he reminded Hannah.

'No.' Hannah was buttering a fruit scone. 'And I'm afraid in that area, I've been rather less successful. I've learned that the Blackwoods emigrated to the New World in 1724, when William would have been in his early teens. They sold the lodge – lock, stock and barrel – to a local businessman. Lord Vincent, it seems, had ideas about farming tobacco in Virginia. But after that, I'm afraid I found no mention of them.'

Alfie slumped back in his seat. 'Oh no,' he said. 'You're saying that Edgar is buried somewhere in America?'

Hannah shook her head. 'No, I'm not saying anything of the kind. I found Vincent and Evelyn on the passenger lists of a boat bound for America in that year, together with several of their servants. But of Edgar – or rather, of William – there was no record.'

'No record?' Alfie stared at her. 'What does that mean?'

'I rather think it means that he didn't go with them.' She raised the scone to her mouth and took a generous bite, then chewed in silence for a while, letting the information sink in.

'Well, if he didn't go to America,' ventured Mia, 'then we have to assume he stayed in Lancashire, right? So, all we need to do is look for any more mentions of William Blackwood.'

Hannah swallowed the mouthful of scone. 'Believe me, my dear, I have looked,' she said. 'Everywhere I could think of. And besides, how likely is it that the Littlewoods would leave a boy of twelve or thirteen years to fend for himself?'

'They could have left him with a relative,' suggested Alfie. 'An aunt or something.'

Hannah took a sip of tea to clear her throat. 'After going to such lengths to obtain him in the first place? I seriously doubt it. No, my first thought was to check parish records to see if the boy had died and been buried somewhere, locally.'

'But he'd have only been a teenager,' reasoned Alfie.

'True. But deaths in childhood were, sadly, very commonplace then, it wouldn't be an unusual occurrence for a teenager to fall foul of some dreaded disease or other . . . cholera, smallpox . . . take your pick. There's a whole clutch of possibilities. But I came up empty on that score. I found no record of a burial. And I started thinking about it . . .' Hannah paused.

'Go on,' said Alfie.

'Let's say we have a couple with a stolen baby, a couple who have already taken considerable trouble to conceal their original crime. Then the boy falls unexpectedly ill and dies. What are they to do? Can they risk burying him in a church? Lord Vincent has already gone through the tricky process of having the child's mother interred in consecrated ground – and he surely knows that there are many who are suspicious of him because of that. He also knows that there are local people who doubt that Evelyn is William's mother, maybe a few who actually know the truth about the situation. Tobias Wilson's comment proves that much! Is Lord Vincent going to expose himself to yet more suspicion by having his dead son officially buried in a local churchyard? Or will he just arrange a secret burial, in some out of the way place, so he and his wife can quietly flee the country to begin their new life in America?' She set down her teacup with a loud clink. 'It's only a wild guess,' she added, 'but the more I think about it, the more it seems to make perfect sense. I think the Blackwoods did what used to be called a moonlight flit.'

'Oh my God,' murmured Alfie. 'You're saying . . . you're saying that maybe *nobody* knows where Edgar is buried! That it happened in secret.'

'It seems like a distinct possibility,' admitted Hannah. 'I'm sorry. I know it's not the answer you were hoping for.'

'But . . . what am I going to tell Meg?' whispered Alfie.

Again, that troubled look crossed Hannah's face. 'Alfie,' she murmured. 'I know you believe this whole thing is real —'

'It *is* real!'

'But you can surely appreciate how it sounds to others. Now, I undertook this work, because Mia told me how desperate you were to have some answers . . . and, I suppose, because I really *love* doing this kind of research. But when you say things like that, it makes me concerned about you.'

Alfie glared at her. 'How d'you think I knew about Lord Vincent Blackwood?' he cried. 'Answer me that! Do you think I just plucked him out of thin air? I only know because Meg told me about him.'

'Yes, but you could have heard that name anywhere. It's quite common around this area, there's even a local estate agents with —'

'I know about Blackwood and Phibes. My Dad works there. I nearly burned the place down the other day!'

Hannah stared at him. 'You did what?' she cried.

'Er, no, that came out wrong . . . I don't mean deliberately.'

Alfie thought for a moment. 'The milk! What about that?'

'The milk?'

'Yes. It's been turning sour everywhere I go.' He looked at Mia. 'You've witnessed that, right? Tell her I'm not making it up.'

She nodded. 'It *has* been happening,' she told Hannah. 'I've seen it.'

'Mia, it's a hot summer, of course milk can go bad . . .'

Alfie pointed to the cup in Hannah's hand. 'But it tastes OK now, doesn't it? And do you know why? Because Meg's given me this amnesty.'

'But listen to yourself, Alfie!' Hannah gazed at him in concern. 'You have to admit, what you're saying does sound a bit . . .'

'I know how it sounds! It sounds like I've lost my mind. And, what makes it even more ridiculous, I'm the only one who can see her. But listen to me, please, whatever you think about it, Hannah, I promise you this is the truth. She's given me a deadline. I now have . . .' He did a frantic mental calculation, '. . . a bit less than twenty-four hours to sort this out. Otherwise, she is going to start hurting people. Mia, my dad . . . maybe even you, now you've helped me. I can't just sit around and wait for that to happen, can I? There has to something I can do . . .' He thought for a moment. 'What have we missed?'

'I don't think we've missed anything,' said Hannah. 'I've given you pretty much everything I found.'

Yes, but there *has* to be something else . . . Wait a minute, you said something about a lodge, didn't you? The place where the Blackwoods lived?'

'Er . . . yes, Hunter's Lodge. Now, I believe I *did* have something about that. Just a minute . . .' Hannah set down the first notebook and picked up another one. She started leafing through the pages. 'Yes, here it is. The lodge *is* still standing, apparently, but it's derelict now. There was some talk of it being turned into an Outward Bound centre a few years back, but apparently the funding for the project fell through. It's out on the moors beyond Beacon Fell, in the Forest of Bowland.'

Alfie looked at Mia. 'We have to go there,' he said.

She looked doubtful. 'The Forest of Bowland? That's quite a yomp. We can't just up and leave now . . .'

'Why not? Time's running out.'

'Yes, but . . . well, I'd at least need to head home and explain to my mum that I'm going off on a trip. I can't just leave her, there's things I need to organise for her. And you'd have to let your dad know, surely?'

'I could just send him a text on the way there.'

'Yes, but it would be dark before we even got there and he'd worry and send someone after us, the police or whatever. No. You need to make it sound casual. Tell him we're going hiking with some friends for the weekend.' She thought for a moment. 'And there's stuff we'll need to take with us – food, walking boots, money for fares – things like that. I know you want to get on with it, but I really think the best idea would be to leave tomorrow morning at first light.'

'But that's going to waste even more time!'

'Hunter's Lodge isn't even open to the public,' Hannah warned them. 'I believe it's all boarded up and fenced off. I doubt you'll be able to get in.'

'Even so, we have to try,' insisted Alfie. 'It's the only lead we've got.' He looked at Mia. 'Listen,' he said. 'I'm going to go there anyway, whatever you say, so . . . maybe, well, maybe it's best if I do this trip on my own.'

'What?' She looked shocked at the very idea. 'Why do you say that?'

'Because Meg can only reach people through me and if we should run out of time before we find anything . . . well, you'll be a lot safer away from me.'

A determined look came into Mia's eyes. 'You're not getting rid of me that easy,' she said.

'I'm not trying to get rid of you,' he assured her. 'I just want to protect you.'

'Don't bother,' she assured him. 'I can look after myself.'

'But you don't under —'

'Think about it for a moment,' Mia interjected. 'You know I'm right about this. If we head off tonight, without giving proper reasons for going, people will be spooked, and they'll come after us. How is that going to help?'

'Nobody even knows where we're headed!' protested Alfie.

'*I* know,' Hannah reminded him. 'And Mia is right. If you even think about going there tonight, I'll phone the police and send them after you. And that's a promise.'

'Oh, thanks, that's really helpful!' growled Alfie. 'I thought you were on my side.'

'There are no sides in this,' Hannah told him. 'But you need to use your head.'

'We can spend tonight finding out as much as we can about this Hunter's Lodge place,' Mia urged him. 'And we can be on our way at first light, before anyone else is even awake. By the time anyone misses us, we can be there and back.'

Hannah was shaking her head. 'I don't like the sound of it one little bit,' she said. 'Even if you do leave it till tomorrow morning, it sounds like it could go horribly wrong. What if one of you is injured? I'd never be able to forgive myself.'

Alfie looked at her. 'We'll be really careful,' he assured her. 'We're just going for a hike on the moors. That's not so bad, is it? People do it all the time.'

'Properly equipped people,' Hannah corrected him.

'I've got some decent gear at home,' Mia told her. 'I'll make sure we've got everything we need. We won't take any unnecessary risks.'

Hannah shook her head. 'You'll have to promise me you'll keep in regular phone contact,' she told them. 'I mean it.

If I don't get a call or a text every hour or so, I *will* send the police after you. That's a promise.'

'I'll text you,' said Mia. 'As soon as we're on our way.'

'And every hour after?'

'Yes, sure, no problem!'

Alfie studied Hannah for a moment, seeing the doubt in her eyes. 'I know what you're really worried about,' he said. 'Me being out there with Mia. You think I'm dangerous, don't you? Some crazy person.'

She gazed back at him. 'I don't know what to think,' she admitted. 'But it's clear the two of you are going through with this, whatever I say. And I suppose you're both old enough to make your own decisions.' She reached across the table and squeezed Alfie's hand. 'I'm just saying, be careful,' she told him. 'Both of you. I don't want anything awful to happen. I don't want to be thinking that I could have done something to prevent it.' She thought for a moment. 'When is this deadline, exactly?'

'Four-thirty tomorrow,' said Alfie. 'At least, that was the time when she set the curse. Which means we've got exactly twenty-four hours left.'

Mia glanced at her watch. 'Twenty-three hours and forty-six minutes,' she corrected him.

'And you really think Mia and I are in danger?' asked Hannah.

Alfie nodded. 'Yeah, I'm afraid so. But only when you're with *me*. All the bad things that have happened have been when I'm there.'

'And that doesn't worry you?' murmured Hannah.

He nodded. 'I see what you're saying,' he murmured. 'And yes, of course it worries me! But I swear to you, Hannah, this isn't something in my head. It's not something I made up after watching too many video games. This is one hundred per cent real.' He turned back to Mia. 'Listen, it's not too late to back out. Perhaps I really should do this on my own.'

'Are you kidding?' Mia shook her head. 'You wouldn't even know how to find the place without my help.' She lifted her hand from under the table to show him her phone, the screen displaying a map. On the screen, there was a red marker, in the midst of a wide stretch of green.

'Where's that?' asked Alfie.

'That's Hunter's Lodge,' said Mia. 'I've been working it out. If we leave at 6 a.m., we'll be there by midday.'

CHAPTER EIGHTEEN

COMPLICATIONS

Back in his bedroom at The Excelsior, Alfie threw all of the contents of his battered school rucksack into the back of the wardrobe and filled it with things he thought might prove useful for his trip tomorrow – a metal bottle of drinking water, a couple of bars of chocolate and a waterproof jacket. He found the closest thing he had to hiking boots – a knackered pair of red leather Kickers, which he'd had for years. They were virtually coming apart at the seams but at least they were comfortable.

Then, too agitated to relax, he opened his laptop and did a search on Hunter's Lodge. It turned out there were several places by that name, hotels mostly, in a variety of widespread locations, from Scotland to Wincanton. It was also, weirdly, the name of a secret organisation formed in America in the 1800s – something to do with an armed rebellion in Canada. So, he attempted to narrow things down a little by searching for Hunter's Lodge near Preston. He found a motel in Chorley by that name and even a housing development for retired people in Walton-Le-Dale. He flicked distractedly through page after page of dead ends and was just about to give up when a familiar name caught his eye in the short paragraph under a link. *Blackwood.*

He clicked on the link and found he was looking at a blog written by a local historian under the title A Lancashire Lad. The lengthy section he had chanced on was about the ruins of an old house that the writer used to play near when he was a youngster. More recently, he'd been dismayed to discover that there was very little information about the place, so he'd decided to do some research on it and confessed that he had become 'a bit obsessed' with the place. Alfie scrolled through the pages impatiently, dismissing much of the content as too ponderous to waste any time on, but then he finally found the bit he had glimpsed on the search page.

The Lodge was of course, for a few years at least, the home of the ill-fated Blackwood family until their doomed departure for America in 1724 . . .

COMPLICATIONS

Alfie sat back in his seat. Ill-fated? In what way? And why had their departure for America been 'doomed'? He went back to reading.

But it was the subsequent purchase of the house by the renowned cotton merchant, Montague Welby, that initiated its development into one of the grandest homes in the North West of England. It was Welby, too, who decided to establish the Lodge's extraordinary and extensive gardens. He brought in the renowned landscape architect Humphrey Paxton who took the Lodge's wild acres, which had formally boasted nothing more than a little greenhouse and a dogs' graveyard, and installed an extraordinarily complicated maze, a vast arboretum and a beautiful formal garden extending over several acres. Welby, of course, is the man who went on to become one of the key figures in the fight for workers' rights, establishing a series of ...

Scanning through the remainder of the article, Alfie was unable to find another mention of the Blackwoods, but there was loads of stuff about Montague flipping Welby and his fancy gardener, which he figured was of no use to him whatsoever. Again, he came back to those troubling bits about the Blackwoods. Ill-fated. Doomed. What did that refer to? He wondered if there was any way of contacting the author to ask him the question, but frustratingly, he could find no email or Twitter handle.

'How stupid is that?' he asked the screen. 'Don't you want people to get in touch with you?'

He was just about to go on with his search when there was a polite tapping at his bedroom door. 'Come in,' he said.

The door creaked open and Dad popped his head inside. 'Hi there,' he said. 'Hard at work I see. Can I come in for a moment?'

'Sure.' For some reason, Alfie automatically lowered the lid of his laptop, as though he had been looking at something he wanted to hide. He swivelled in his chair as Dad came into the room, looking uncharacteristically sheepish. 'Working on your project?' he asked.

'Yeah. You're home a bit earlier than usual.'

'Yes, something came up.' Dad noticed the rucksack on the bed and waved a hand at it. 'Going somewhere?' he asked.

'Oh . . . yeah, I am actually. Early tomorrow morning. I'm going hiking with Mia. And some of her friends.'

Dad raised his eyebrows. 'Hiking?' he asked. 'Blimey, she *is* having an effect on you, isn't she? Where are you going?'

'Umm . . . out near a place called Beacon Fell. It's supposed to be dead nice out there. The Forest of Bowland. You know, hills and dales and all that stuff.'

'I'll take your word for it. You'll have time for breakfast before you go, I suppose?'

'No. We're leaving at first light. Long trip. But I'll be back tomorrow evening, obviously.'

'Maybe I could ask Selina to make you up some sandwiches to take?'

'Ah no, don't bother. I've got money, I'll get something on the way.'

'I see. There'll be cafes, I suppose?'

'Sure. I guess.'

Dad's manner was odd, Alfie thought, quite unlike his usual relaxed self. He went over to the bed and sat down on it, his expression grave. He looked tired, Alfie thought, as though badly in need of sleep. And there was clearly something on his mind.

'Problems at work?' ventured Alfie.

'No, no, nothing like that. That's all good. But ... I did have a phone call, while I was *at* work. Your mother rang me.'

'Mum?' Alfie was puzzled. His parents didn't tend to have much contact with each other these days. 'She's not ill, is she?'

'Ah, no, nothing like that. No, she phoned to say that she'd heard about something back in Bristol and she ... wondered if I knew anything about it.'

'Oh yeah? What's that, then?'

Dad sighed. 'There's no easy way to say this, Alfie, so I'll just come straight out with it.'

'OK ...'

'It's Sophie. She's ... well, she's pregnant.'

Alfie felt as though he'd been punched in the gut. He let out a long gasp of air, then sat there, staring back at Dad, his mouth open.

'What do you mean, "she's pregnant"?' he gasped.

'As far as I'm aware, Alfie, those words can only have one meaning. I'm telling you that Sophie is going to have a baby.'

'I see.'

'And my next question . . . as I'm sure you'll understand, has to be this. Is there . . . Alfie, is there any way the baby could be yours?'

Alfie had the brief and rather disconcerting sensation that the floor had just dropped away beneath him and that he was hurtling into an abyss. As he fell, he considered the question. Could the baby be his? He sat there, numbed, trying to piece it all together. How long ago had they split up? About three months. And how long had she been going out with Brendan? Well, that one was tricky to say the very least. Sophie had told him that it had happened suddenly, out of the blue, that she'd split with Alfie the moment she realised she felt something for his friend, Brendan. But Alfie also knew that these things were rarely so cut and dried. She could have been seeing Brendan behind his back for weeks, maybe even months. And of course, when Alfie and Sophie had been going strong, naturally there'd been stuff going on. But he'd never been stupid enough not to take precautions. Brendan, on the other hand, was the reckless sort . . .

Alfie looked across at Dad who was still patiently awaiting an answer.

'I honestly don't know,' he said. 'I don't think it's mine. I certainly *hope* it isn't, but I . . . I can't be one hundred per cent sure.'

Dad nodded. 'Well, let's not go jumping to conclusions,' he said. 'Apparently, it's still early days, and it's not too late for Sophie to have a termination . . . if that's what she decides to do. I appreciate that decision would be completely up to her and that's absolutely as it should be, but it's not an easy one to make . . .'

'I can't believe it,' murmured Alfie. 'What a disaster!'

'Well, not necessarily. I'm sure there are many girls of her age who decide to make a go of it and succeed. But, she's a clever girl, I seem to remember and I know she always had her heart pinned on going to university, to study . . . what was it?'

'Politics,' muttered Alfie.

'Yes. It would be a shame, wouldn't it, if being a mother got in the way of that?' Dad shook his head. 'It's pointless speculating, we'll have to wait and see what develops. But, well, don't you think it might be a good idea to talk to her?'

'Talk to her?' Alfie's alarm must have shown on his face.

'Yes, I know it won't be easy, but you still have her phone number, I suppose?'

Alfie nodded.

'Well, no pressure, but you should think very seriously about it. She'll have a much better idea than anyone else about what's happening. And of course, I've got your back. Whatever you decide to do, I'll be there for you. You do know that, don't you?'

'Yeah, sure. Thanks, Dad.' Alfie thought for a moment. 'Dad?'

'Yes, Son?'

'How did Mum know about it?'

'Oh, she spoke to Sophie's Mum, Jane? The two of them go to the same gym. They got talking, I suppose. Obviously, Jane is aware of what happened between the two of you, so she thought your mum ought to know about it. And of course, she wasn't going to keep it to herself, even if she promised Jane that she would. So, she gave me a call.' He shrugged his shoulders. 'Anyway, give it some thought, yeah?'

'I will. Thanks, Dad.'

'And try not to worry. Things often have a way of turning out for the best in the end.' He got up from the bed. 'Anyway, I'll see you in a bit for dinner, yeah? Give me a knock when you're ready to go down. We'll see what Malcolm's latest gastronomic adventure tastes like . . . that is, if you feel up to eating?'

'I can always eat,' Alfie assured him. 'I just need a bit of time to think things over.'

'Of course. OK, Son. See you in a bit. And like I said, try not to worry.'

Dad went quietly out of the room, closing the door behind him. Alfie sat there for a moment staring at his hands, trying to remember every detail of his relationship with Sophie. He couldn't help feeling scared. He really wasn't ready to be a father. The very idea terrified him.

'Well, well, well. Very interesting. I didn't think you had it in you.'

The voice nearly made him fall off his chair. He looked up in alarm to see that Meg was sitting on the bed exactly where Dad had been a few moments earlier. She had her chin in her hands, her elbows resting on her knees and she was smiling maliciously across the room at him.

'What are you doing here?' he snapped. 'It's not time, yet!'

She made a face. 'That's not very welcoming,' she observed. 'Don't worry, I'm very aware of how long you've got. It's just that this is an interesting little development and . . . well, I couldn't help but overhear, so . . .'

'Do you listen in to everything I say?' Alfie asked her. 'Because, you know, some things are supposed to be private.'

She chuckled. 'How else am I expected to pass the time?' she asked him. 'I can only live my life through you, so of course I listen in. And this is something I have personal experience of.'

'What do you mean? Oh right. You mean Edgar. He was . . . an unplanned pregnancy, right?'

Her eyes seemed to momentarily blaze with anger.

'Most pregnancies back then were unplanned,' she hissed. 'We women were always at the mercy of some man in a position of power. So yes, I fell, like so many others before me. And I was obliged to go to Sir Vincent to tell him what had happened and beg him for help.' She grimaced. 'And strangely, at first it proved to be a blessing in disguise – a way out of the endless grind of poverty I'd been forced to endure for so many years.'

Alfie frowned. 'You're saying that it was a good thing?'

'At first it was. Oh, I didn't fall. I soared! I was given Cuckoo Hall to live in, far better than the pitiful hovel I grew up in. If there was anything I wanted, I only had to snap my fingers and Lord Vincent would come running to supply it. He would take care of everything, he told me, and when the baby was born, he would find ways to advance my position. He would make me a lady-in-waiting to his wife and I would never go hungry again. I allowed myself to be seduced by his honeyed words.' Her expression softened. She got up from the bed and walked a few steps across the room. 'But then I saw him, my little Edgar, and something unexpected happened. I fell instantly in love with him. And then, suddenly, none of it mattered any more. None of it. I told Sir Vincent that I wanted nothing more from him – that I wanted Edgar for my very own and I didn't care what inducements he offered me. And I told him, in no uncertain terms, that I would never give my child up to the care of that barren wife of his. Edgar was a part of me, I said. Lady Evelyn, for all her wealth, would never be his mother so long as I had breath in my body.' She laughed bitterly. 'Saying those words, I little realised that I was signing my own death warrant. I thought, you see, that motherhood had granted me incredible power. That it made me somehow invincible. But I was soon to learn that in these situations, women are generally powerless. Men will always have the advantage over them. Sir Vincent coldly drew up his plans to rid himself of me and to take Edgar for his own.'

Alfie waved a hand at his laptop. 'I've been trying to find out more about the Blackwoods,' he said. 'But there's so little written about them.'

'Time is running out,' Meg reminded him.

'I know that. But I do have one lead. Tomorrow I'm —'

'I know what you're doing tomorrow,' she interrupted him. 'Did you forget? I see and hear everything you plan. And if I were you, I wouldn't be wasting time sitting here on my backside, I'd be on my way to Hunter's Lodge already.'

'I wanted to go but Hannah fixed it so I couldn't risk it. She said she'd send the police after me, if I did!'

'You still have time. Use it wisely. You will know the consequences if you don't have an answer for me by tomorrow.' She got up from the bed and then thought for a moment. 'Your father was right, by the way.'

'About what?'

'You really should talk to the girl. Sophie, is that her name? You should contact her and find out what you can.'

'It's not as easy as that.'

'Of course, it's easy! D' you think I don't see how it is done nowadays? Hmm? Those little magic boxes you carry that allow you to talk across distances. Oh, if we'd had those things in my day! Thoughts had to be written on parchment and sent away . . . assuming you knew how to write in the first place! And then you'd wait weeks, perhaps even months, for a reply. Now it is a matter of moments. You could settle this in an instant. And yet you sit here brooding over it like some lovesick whelp.'

'I only just found out about it,' protested Alfie. 'I need time to —'

'That's all you can say, isn't it? Give me time! Give me more time! But let me assure you, boy, time waits for no one and the sooner you take matters into your own hands, the better. And what about your new *inamorata*?'

'My new *what*?'

'The other girl. Mia. Does she know you are a father?'

'No, she doesn't. And anyway, I might *not* be. Me and Sophie broke up ages ago.'

'But not long enough for you to be sure, eh, boy? Clearly some things haven't changed.' She laughed, as though amused by his predicament and pointed a finger at him. 'Take my advice. Talk to the girl. And make sure she doesn't divert your thoughts from the matter at hand. Otherwise I will give you something real to worry about.'

Alfie got up from his seat. 'All you do is threaten me!' he said. 'What have I ever done to deserve it? I need to know now that you won't harm —'

But she was gone, as suddenly as she had appeared. He stood for a moment, gazing at the spot where she had been standing a moment earlier. Then he began to pace around the room, thinking about what she'd said. *You could settle this in an instant.* And he knew she was right. It felt awkward but he needed to overcome that. He reached into his pocket and took out his phone. He looked at it for a long time. Then he opened the contacts and thumbed through them until Sophie's face appeared, smiling out at him. Sophie in happier times, wearing a wide-brimmed red hat and making comical crossed eyes for the camera. He hadn't looked at her face for quite a while and he was surprised to find that he didn't feel the usual jolt of sadness he'd become accustomed to. Perhaps he had already started to heal. But still, the thought of talking to her again filled him with apprehension. He shook his head. 'I can't do this,' he muttered. 'I can't.' But he didn't swipe the screen away. He walked over to the bed and sat down, staring at her picture, realising that both Dad and Meg had been right. He had to make this call.

He tapped the phone and waited anxiously, listening to it ringing a long way off. It was one of the loneliest sounds he could imagine. Sophie didn't answer and he began to lose confidence. She might hate him calling her, he told himself, she might accuse him of all kinds of things . . .

The phone clicked over to voicemail and he heard her

familiar tones. 'Hi, it's me. I'm not here right now. Leave a message and I'll get back to you.'

A bleep. He took a deep breath. 'Umm . . . Hi Sophie, it's . . . Alfie. Look, I'm sorry to call you out of the blue like this, but —'

The phone was suddenly answered. 'Hello, Alfie.' The voice calm, measured, sounding close enough to be in the same room as him.

'Oh! Sophie, hi! I didn't think there was anybody there . . .'

'No. I'm screening my calls at the moment, that's all. So, this is a surprise. Why would you be phoning me after all this time? As if I didn't know.'

'Umm . . . yeah. Look, I'm sorry. I get it if you don't want to talk right now, but, well, my Dad just told me about what's happened and I . . . I thought I'd better ring.'

A bitter laugh. 'And how did your dad come to know about it?'

'Erm . . . I think your mum spoke to my mum and . . .'

Sophie made a small sound of irritation. 'I asked her not to tell anyone!'

'Yes, but I guess she thought, you know, that it could be —'

'Yes, you don't have to spell it out for me. Obviously, you're worried.'

'Of course, I'm worried! About you and . . . I mean, is there any way . . .?'

'Spit it out, Alfie.'

'Is there any way the baby could be mine?' He realised he'd said that a lot louder than he meant to. He waited in an agony of apprehension.

A long sigh. 'You know what?' she said. 'I honestly don't know.'

'You don't? But you must have some idea!'

'Well, obviously, I'm thinking most likely it's Brendan's, but . . . I can't be sure.'

'Does he know that you're pregnant?'

'Yes, of course he does. And he's over the moon about it.'

'Really?'

'Well, don't sound so surprised! He does care about me, you know. He's already going around acting like the proud father. It's kind of embarrassing.'

'Well, OK, but . . . Brendan? As a dad?'

A long silence and then a low chuckle. 'Yeah, I get it. He's not exactly good father material, is he? Anyway, I don't even know if I'm going to have the baby. It's not too late to, you know, to have it . . . stopped.'

Her voice was so cold and matter of fact that Alfie did a double take. 'What, just like that?' he muttered.

'No, not just like that! I'm sure it will be bloody horrible and I'm not looking forward to it one little bit. But here's the thing. I had all these big plans for my future, Alfie, and being a mum never figured in them. At least, not for several years. I want to go to university and have a career and all that stuff and it's not going to be easy if I'm sitting up every night feeding a baby, is it?'

'I guess not. What does Brendan think about it?'

'He really wants me to have it! He thinks it's the best thing ever! But it's not up to him, is it? And it's not up to you either, even if it turns out it's your baby. It's my body, and it has to be my decision. I look at my mum and I can see there's a part of her that wants me to keep it so she can be like the proud grandma, and all that crap, but it's easy for her. She won't be the one giving birth. It's supposed to be the most painful thing that ever happens to you. I'm not very brave.'

'No, I get that.'

'Mum was talking about going down the adoption route. But I read somewhere that you shouldn't wait to see the baby, because you take one look and you're in love with it.'

'That's what Meg said,' murmured Alfie.

'Meg? Is that the new girl you've been knocking around with?'

'God, no! Meg is . . . just somebody I . . .' His voice trailed off. 'How did you know I was knocking around with someone?'

'Oh, your mum told my mum. That kind of thing.'

Alfie wondered how Mum had known about it. *Maybe*, he thought, *she talks to Dad more than I realise.*

'Well, anyway,' said Alfie. 'I have met somebody and she's pretty cool.'

A pause. 'I'm glad.'

'You don't have to say that.'

'I know I don't, but I really mean it. Looking back, I treated you pretty horribly, didn't I?'

'Oh, no, not really . . .'

'Yes, I did! Of course, I did. That was always your problem, Alfie. Too nice. Always trying to please everyone, instead of pleasing yourself. I think my parents always liked you more than Brendan . . . not that they'd ever say that to me. And Brendan is . . .' She made a sound of irritation. 'Brendan is Brendan. Anyway, what do you think? There's a chance the baby is yours, after all.'

'I think you have to decide for yourself, Sophie. Like you said, it's your body. But if I'm honest . . .'

'Yes?'

'I'm not exactly thrilled at the idea of being a dad. Not at sixteen.'

'OK, well at least you won't be kicking up a fuss if I decide to have the abortion.'

'Sophie!' Alfie was surprised to find that he was shocked by her words.

'What's the matter?' she asked him. 'Don't like the word? A bit squeamish?'

'No, but —'

'You have to understand, I don't know what to do for the best. One minute, I'm thinking yes, have the baby – it'll work out OK.

The next I'm thinking no, no, no way, I can't do it! I want to . . .
I want to . . .' Her voice broke down and Alfie could hear her
dissolve into tears. 'You don't get it, do you? However you feel
about it, it's in me. Me! I'm the one who's got to deal with it. You
and Brendan, you'll never have that problem. You'll always be
on the outside, saying how terrible it all is, how sorry you feel
for me . . . but I'll be the one who does all the . . .' Her voice broke
again and Alfie couldn't be sure of the last words he'd heard. He
waited while her crying gradually subsided. 'I'm sorry,' she said
at last. 'I'm not being very rational.'

'Don't be sorry,' he told her. 'Look, here's the thing. I've been
trying to pretend you don't exist, that there was never anything
between us. But that's silly. So if you need to talk to someone,
you've got my number.'

She sniffed. 'Thanks, Alfie. I appreciate that. And good luck
to you and Meg.'

'No, she's called Mia! Like I said, Meg is . . . Meg is something
else.'

'And you'll accept whatever decision I make."

'Absolutely.'

'OK, I'll go now. It was . . . surprisingly nice to talk to you.
Bye.'

'Bye.' He hung up and sat on the bed, looking at the phone,
telling himself that it was a good thing that he'd called. It hadn't
settled anything – he'd still have the extra worry of it hanging

over him as he made his way up to Hunter's Lodge. Once again, he considered grabbing his rucksack and heading there now by whatever means he could, but after some consideration he realised that Mia was right. If he left now, Dad would smell a rat. First thing tomorrow he could leave without anybody questioning him, and then he'd have until four-thirty to come up with an answer. If it didn't work . . . well, he had already decided that there was only one option. He'd have to run away, far from everyone and everything he cared about – become a lonely vagrant with just a dead witch for company. It would be the only way to keep others safe from Meg's retribution.

An old line he'd read somewhere came to him. *The condemned man ate a hearty meal.* And weirdly, despite everything, he did feel strangely hungry.

With a sigh, he got up off the bed and went out of his room to meet Dad for dinner.

CHAPTER NINETEEN

TAKING OFF

Alfie's phone alarm jolted him out of that terrible, too familiar, dream where he was being pursued through a dark forest by something unseen – something with sharp teeth. He lay on his back for a moment, staring up at the ceiling, while he allowed his breathing to settle back to something approaching normality. He glanced at his phone and saw that it was 3 a.m. Shaking off the last shreds of slumber, he got up out of bed and went to the bathroom to shower himself awake. He steeled himself as he opened the glass door of the cubicle, just in case Meg was lurking in there, but for once he had the place to himself. He ran the water and stepped under the flow, not waiting for it to heat up properly, the cold stinging assault making his skin tingle. Once done, he towelled himself dry, dressed himself in the closest things he had to hiking gear and then swung the rucksack up on to his shoulders. He took a last look around, wanting to be sure that he hadn't forgotten anything, and then let himself quietly out of the room. He walked quickly along the landing to number six and slipped the brief note he had scribbled the night before, under the door.

Dad
Taking off now. See you tonight.
Alfie.

He sincerely hoped that he would be able to keep that appointment, but the way things were he couldn't be sure. It seemed to him that his whole future was hanging in the balance. He was about to go to a place he'd never been before, in order to try and stave off a witch's curse. Which, when you thought about it, was pretty terrifying. Oh, and one other thing. He might be a father. The thought of *that* filled him with even more dread.

In the small hours of the morning, it had occurred to him that he could call Meg's bluff – tell her that he'd tried to help but had failed, then challenge her to do her worst. After all, he only had her word for it that she could actually inflict real harm on the people he loved. What if she was lying? But then he remembered the awful crushing power he had felt when she'd lifted him from his bed to the ceiling. Reliving that experience made up his mind. He couldn't risk it. He had to give this his best shot.

Alfie moved quietly to the front door of The Excelsior, turned the lock and let himself out. He closed the door gently behind him and stood for a moment on the steps, gazing up at the sky. He had fully expected it to be getting light by now – but the seemingly endless run of clear weather had come up against the unexpected arrival of thick layers of turbulent, grey cloud, moving restlessly overhead. He was glad he'd remembered to pack his waterproof jacket, because it looked like he might be needing it before the day was through. He walked a short distance along the street to the agreed meeting place, just outside the little corner shop, which wasn't yet open for business. Alfie had thought it best to be away from The Excelsior when his taxi arrived, just in case somebody was up and about and started asking him awkward questions. He could picture Selina, looking at him with interest. 'Now where are you off to so early? Does your father know you're out?'

Alfie glanced at his watch. He had ten minutes to wait and right now that seemed like a very long time indeed. He and Mia had discussed the quickest way of getting to their starting point and, after investigating the nearly non-existent bus and train options, had decided that a taxi was the only sensible way.

It would use up more of Alfie's rapidly depleting stash of money, but the alternatives would waste far too much time and Mia had assured him she knew the number of a reliable firm. And money wouldn't matter if Meg went through with her threat.

While he waited, Alfie thought about the dinner he and Dad had eaten the night before. They'd sat in the dining room of The Excelsior and he'd told Dad all about his phone call to Sophie – about her indecision. Dad had cautioned him to keep an open mind about it. 'She's in a tough position at the moment,' he said. 'She needs to make her mind up and, of course, we have to give her space to do that. It won't be easy for her.'

'And if she does decide to have the baby, how will they know who the father is?'

Dad had explained about paternity tests – how a simple blood sample would establish that much. 'But it might never come to that,' Dad reminded him. 'Try to put it out of your mind for now.'

Strangely, Alfie had been absolutely ravenous and had eaten every bit of Malcolm's ragout of beef with sautéed potato, while Dad had opted for seafood linguine. The dining room had been nearly full, and Selina had presided over the evening with evident delight – clearly convinced that The Excelsior's future was assured.

And so it would be, Alfie thought, provided he never went back there. That was a terrible thought. He'd have to get as far away from Dad and Mia as possible, and he'd never be able to risk showing up again, because who knew how long a witch's curse might stay active?

The taxi appeared right on time and there was Mia sitting in the back, all togged out in what looked like decent hiking gear. Alfie jumped in beside her and she gave him a quick peck on the cheek as the vehicle moved off.

'How are you feeling?' she asked him. 'Did you get much sleep?'

He shook his head.

'Me neither,' she said. 'Let's hope we come up with something today.'

'Yes, fingers crossed,' he said, trying not to let his inner dread show through. He looked at her. 'There's something I need to tell you,' he murmured.

'Oh yeah, what's that?'

He cast a brief look towards the back of the taxi driver's head. 'Not yet,' he said quietly. 'When we're out of the car.'

She nodded. 'OK. Did you pack any food?' she asked him.

'Er . . . chocolate bars and water,' he said.

She rolled her eyes. 'Is that it?'

'I had stuff on my mind,' he protested.

'Well luckily, when I was putting out food for Mum this morning, I remembered to make us some sandwiches. Cheese and pickle, OK? And I put a couple of bags of crisps in as well.'

'That's fine,' he said. 'You're good at this stuff, aren't you?'

'I do my best. Oh, and Hannah sent me a text last night. Said she's going back to the library later today, for one more session, just in case she missed something the first time around. She said she'd let us know if she found anything new.'

'That's good of her.'

'I think she just wants to help. I must remember to text her every hour or so or she'll . . .' She too glanced at the driver, 'do what she said. Remind me to, will you?'

'Right.' Alfie sat there, staring out of the window as the quiet streets of Woodplumpton village gave way to leafy country lanes. He looked up at the sky again and frowned. If anything, the clouds looked worse than they had before. Just his luck . . .

Mia placed her hand on his and gave it an encouraging squeeze. 'We'll find something,' she said. 'I'm sure we will.'

The taxi driver, a big heavyset man, was watching them in his rear-view mirror. 'Going hiking?' he asked, in a flat Lancastrian drawl.

'Yes,' said Mia.

'You haven't picked the best day for it,' said the man bluntly. 'The forecast is for heavy rain and thunderstorms.'

'Perfect,' whispered Alfie.

'Well, it couldn't last forever, could it?' continued the taxi driver, sounding almost pleased at the prospect. 'I mean, this is Lancashire not Torremolinos.'

'I suppose so,' agreed Mia, trying not to sound bored.

'Now there's a place! Torremolinos. I don't suppose you've ever been?'

They shook their heads.

'That's where I go every year. I don't get it meself,' added the driver. 'Hiking.'

'What don't you get?' asked Mia.

'Well, it's just walking, in't it? For miles. It's quicker in a car. Less effort.'

'A car can't get to where we're going,' Mia assured him.

'Oh yeah, where's that then?'

'The back of beyond.'

'Why, what's out there?'

A good question, thought Alfie. Answers, he hoped. But he didn't say that. In fact, he didn't speak again until they had got to their drop-off point on the edge of the moors and the driver asked them for money. Alfie handed over the notes without comment and didn't wait for change. He shouldered his rucksack and he and Mia got out of the car. The taxi moved away and accelerated back in the direction from which it had come. They turned to survey the way ahead. There was a vast stretch of moorland in front of them across which a dirt track led onward for as far as the eye could see, underneath a turbulent bruise-coloured sky.

'What did you want to tell me?' asked Mia.

'Let's talk on the way,' Alfie suggested. They started walking.

***

They trudged along for a good half hour without saying anything, Alfie setting the pace, head down, his hands in his pockets.

'Do we have to go quite so fast?' Mia asked him eventually.

'I think we do,' he replied without looking up. 'We don't even know what we're looking for and we need to give ourselves as much time as possible to have a proper look around. How long is it going to take us to get there?'

Mia took out her phone and glanced at the screen. 'Just under two hours,' she told him.

'Really? Why would anyone live so far from civilisation?'

'It was probably even further from towns or villages back then. But when you're rich, I don't suppose that matters. People bring stuff to your door whenever you snap your fingers.' She slid the phone back into her pocket and glanced at him. 'What did you want to say to me, by the way?'

He sighed, considered telling her to forget about it, but then realised that he couldn't do that. He owed it to her to fill her in on the situation. 'I found something out last night,' he said.

'About Meg?'

He shook his head. 'About me,' he said gloomily.

'Oh yeah, what's that?'

'I . . . well, I . . . might be a father soon,' he said. He appreciated it sounded shocking, but he couldn't think of a better way of putting it.

Mia stopped in her tracks for a moment, but Alfie didn't slow his pace and so after a few moments she was obliged to run after him until she'd caught up. 'I really hope you're joking,' she said.

'I wish I was. But it's true.'

'How could you be a father?' she asked him, and he gave her a look.

'Take a wild guess,' he said.

They walked on in silence for a moment. Somewhere off in the distance, thunder rumbled ominously, and the air seemed to blow several degrees colder.

'Is that it?' she asked him. 'Is that all you've got to say?'

'No, of course not.' He shrugged his shoulders. 'Back in Bristol there was a girl called Sophie. We were going out together for quite a while. We were serious. But we split up a couple of months ago, when she went off with one of my best mates.'

'Oh, nice,' murmured Mia. 'Go, Sophie.'

'Yes, well, I thought that was the end of it, obviously. And I didn't see the point in mentioning her to you.'

'No, why would you?'

'But I found out last night that she's pregnant and she's not really sure who the father is.'

'Oh, boy. So, it could be this other guy's?'

'His name's Brendan. Yes – more than likely, it's his. But she can't be sure. And she can't decide whether to have a termination or not.'

'Whoa! Tough one.' Mia studied her moving feet for a moment. 'So, you're basically waiting for her to make her mind up, right?'

He nodded. 'Pretty much. It's all I needed. First, I have Meg to worry about and now this. Not great timing.'

'So, what will you do? If she has the baby and it turns out to be yours?'

He gave her a hopeless look. 'I don't have a clue,' he admitted. 'I'm just praying that it doesn't happen that way.'

A flurry of raindrops spattered him and looking to the far horizon, Alfie saw a dull flicker of electricity light up a roiling patch of cloud. 'That's all we need,' he snarled. 'A thunderstorm.' He swung the rucksack off one shoulder and around to his front, then pulled out his waterproof jacket and struggled into it without breaking his pace. He got it zipped up and then studied Mia for a moment. 'Any thoughts?' he muttered.

Mia mimicked the cab driver. 'Should 'ave gone to Torremolinos,' she said.

'I'm being serious,' he persisted.

'Thoughts about what?'

'About my situation. I mean, do you even *care*?'

'Of course, I care!' She frowned. 'Any way you look at it, it's a bummer. Me, I think she'd be crazy to have a child so young but people do crazy things all the time, don't they? One of my cousin's had three kids by the age of eighteen and she seems happy enough.'

'But Sophie wants to go to university.'

'Who says she can't? There are lots of women with kids who do exactly that.'

'It can't be easy for them.'

'No, I guess not. But they manage somehow. Have you told this Sophie you don't *want* to be a dad?'

'Sure. In a roundabout way . . .'

'I think you need to be direct with her.'

'My dad said to give her space.'

Mia nodded. 'Yeah, she'll need that all right. I bet she's feeling pretty scared. But just the same, she needs to know exactly how you feel about it.' She seemed to consider for a moment. 'I've got a feeling it's Brendan's baby,' she said.

'Yeah? Based on what, exactly?'

'Based on what I know about you. You strike me as the careful type.'

He stared at her. 'That would be more convincing if I wasn't the guy who walked three times around Meg Shelton's grave and said, 'I don't believe in witches!'

'True. But then everyone knows that's just a silly old story, right?' She waited for a reaction but when she didn't get one, she continued. 'What's she like, by the way?'

'What, Sophie?'

'No, not *her*. Meg. You've never really told me much about her, except that she's not what you expected.'

'Yeah . . . I thought she'd be this weird old woman, you know, with warts and a crooked nose and all that. But she's . . . not like that at all. She's kind of attractive in a weird way. She's clever and knowing and . . . well, I don't really think she's evil.'

Mia raised her eyebrows. 'She's threatened me and your dad,' she reminded him.

'Yes, I know that . . . but you can tell she's only doing it because she's desperate to find out something about the son that was stolen from her. I mean, that's why she made those threats – because she's waited for so long to find Edgar and she's gone kind of mad with waiting. I'm her only hope of finding him, so . . .' His voice trailed off. 'I don't even know why I'm telling you this,' he said. 'You don't really believe me, do you? You think the same as Hannah. That I'm off my head.'

'I did believe that at first,' confessed Mia. 'I had this idea that you were just trying to impress me, in some weird way. But now . . .'

'Now, what?'

'Well, most lads would have kept it a secret about being a dad . . .'

'*Maybe* a dad,' he corrected her.

'Sure. That's what I'm saying, though. Most lads would have kept it to themselves until they were absolutely sure – until they had no other choice than to own up. But you came right out with it. Which makes me think you're basically the honest sort.'

'Hmm.' Alfie was unconvinced. 'I couldn't tell Dad about it, though. Well, I sort of did in a jokey way, and he just thought I was talking about a video game.'

'Well, he's your dad. Of course you didn't tell *him*. He'd only worry. Where does he think you are, by the way?'

'On a hiking trip with friends.'

She reached out and took one of his hands in hers. 'Well, that much is true,' she assured him. 'With one friend, anyway.'

He looked at her. 'If it turns out that I am a dad,' he murmured. 'Will that be it for me and you? I mean, will you run away screaming or something?'

She smiled at him but didn't answer.

The sky suddenly turned a shade darker and the rain descended with a vengeance. They both reached back and lifted their hoods up over their heads.

'Well, this is fun,' observed Alfie tonelessly. 'How long now?'

Mia didn't even bother to consult her phone. 'About seven minutes less than the last time you asked me,' she said.

They didn't speak for a long time after that.

CHAPTER TWENTY

HUNTER'S LODGE

They walked for what seemed like hours and the weather continued to deteriorate, until it felt like they were travelling at night. The sky was a mass of restless black cloud, illuminated only occasionally by a vivid flash of forked lightning – which they could see was actually arcing jagged streaks of white light down into the ground. It occurred to Alfie that one misplaced bolt could end his worries in an instant, and it troubled him that it didn't seem such an ordeal when put like that.

The rain worsened, lashed directly into their faces by the wind, as though some unseen power was trying to prevent them from reaching their destination. They made much worse time than predicted, but eventually the map on Mia's phone informed them that they were getting close to their destination. The last ten minutes or so seemed to ooze past like cold honey dripping from a frosted spoon. Finally, they crested a rise and found themselves looking down into a valley where a huge derelict house stood beneath the driving rain. It was completely enclosed by a circle of high wire fencing. Even at this distance, they could see the 'DANGER! KEEP OUT!' signs.

'How are we supposed to get over those fences?' asked Mia. But, for the moment at least, Alfie didn't have an answer. He led the way down the slope and Mia trudged wearily after him. Despite their waterproof jackets, they were soaked to the skin and Alfie's body felt almost numb with the cold. He tried to ignore the squelching of his feet inside his inadequate boots. They came to the nearest stretch of fence and stood looking up at it, noting that itappeared to be edged with razor wire. 'At least it isn't electrified,' murmured Alfie.

Mia looked warily at the flickering pulses in the restless clouds above them. 'It could very easily be,' she said. 'Maybe we should walk around it, just in case there's an easier way in.'

'We can't afford to waste any more time,' Alfie told her. 'I'm going over.'

Mia said nothing, and so he stepped up to the fence and tested it gingerly with his fingers – just to make sure it really wasn't electrified. Once reassured, he reached up as high as he could, dug his fingers into the wire and lifted a foot until he could get his toe into a position where it might hold his weight. He pushed down hard on the foot and his body lifted a short distance. He flung up his other hand and pulled himself higher, then repeated the process. In this way, Alfie managed to claw his way higher and higher, until finally he got to the razor wire at the top. He paused, swaying in the wind, momentarily unsure of what to do now he was here. But after some thought, he unslung his rucksack and, using that to cushion himself against the rusting metal blades, he performed an ungainly roll over the tangle of wire and fell in a heavy sprawl down the far side of the fence. He landed awkwardly, lost his footing and fell, face down, in the grass. He lay for a moment, gathering his breath, then twisted around into a sitting position. He looked up and saw that his rucksack was still stuck on the razor wire and he muttered a series of vivid curses, before lowering his gaze expecting to see Mia standing on the far side of the fence, watching him.

She wasn't there. He experienced a momentary sense of panic, then, aware of movement to his right, he turned his head and saw her coming towards him with a smile on her face. She was on his side of the fence! He struggled upright. 'How the bloody hell did you . . .?' he spluttered and she jerked a thumb over her shoulder.

'I found a place where somebody had gone in with wire cutters,' said Mia. 'Just a few metres further on. You should have hung on a moment.' She looked up at his stranded rucksack. 'What do we do about that?' she asked. 'Isn't there chocolate in it?'

'Never mind the rucksack!' he exclaimed and he started towards the house, intent on getting inside the place. When he eventually thought to look back at her, Mia was following him, holding his rucksack. He stopped in his tracks. 'How did you —?'

'I found a long branch,' she said, returning his incredulous look. 'Well, I wasn't going to risk losing the chocolate,' she added, by way of explanation. She held the sodden rucksack out to him, which he took and slung across his shoulders.

'Thanks,' he muttered, grudgingly, and they went onwards again, crossing a stretch of weed-encrusted gravel leading to what looked like the front entrance of the lodge. A short flight of stone steps led up to a grandiose edifice of arched stone, decorated with carved animals – a wild boar being pursued by a pack of dogs and a couple of men on horseback. The original door was set into the arch but had been boarded up with sheets of plywood. At some point, however, somebody had seen fit to tear back a large section of the wood with a crowbar, leaving a jagged opening. Beyond that, the rotting oak door hung half open on broken hinges.

'Looks like somebody was here before us,' muttered Alfie.

Mia nodded. She took out her phone and clicked on the torch. 'Shall we?' she asked him.

He nodded, took out his own phone and led the way through

the opening into the gloom beyond. It was a relief to be out of the rain, but the feeling was short-lived as there was something horribly eerie about the great cavernous interior of the room in which they now stood. Devoid of any furniture, it was just a huge, oblong of roughly flagged floor, above which a cobweb-festooned ceiling arched. The longest wall was dominated by a gigantic stone fireplace big enough to stand in. As they walked, their footsteps echoed eerily on the flagstones. Alfie noticed a couple of empty lager cans and some cigarette butts in one corner. They traversed the room and went through a doorway at the far end of it, which led to a mouldering wooden staircase beside which somebody had affixed a sign that read 'KEEP AWAY! UNSAFE!'

Alfie and Mia exchanged uncertain looks, but it was Mia who led the way – testing each step carefully with her foot before putting her full weight on to it. In this halting manner, they went slowly up, eventually emerging on to a long gallery which ran above all four sides of the main room. Open doorways led off in all directions and they began to investigate, but they all led to nothing more than a series of empty rooms, each with its own stone fireplace. Whatever clues might have been left by the original occupants, had clearly long been removed. They spent several fruitless hours looking aimlessly around, their frustration mounting.

'This is hopeless!' cried Alfie, and his voice seemed to echo through the building. 'We don't even know what we're looking for – it's a complete waste of time.'

'We have to keep looking,' Mia urged him. 'We can't just give up. There's still a couple of doors we haven't tried yet. We need to check them all.'

They continued their thankless task of going from room to room, scanning the walls with their torches, to find nothing more than the occasional bit of modern day graffiti. '*I will kill again*,' read one message. '*This house is haunted*,' said another. But if there were any ghosts here, they preferred to keep themselves to themselves.

They had nearly searched the entire place when Mia's phone trilled unexpectedly, almost making them jump out of their respective skins. She glanced at the screen, 'It's Hannah.' She answered and started talking frantically. 'Hannah, I'm sorry, I was just about to call you, honestly I was! Alfie was supposed to remind me, but I . . . what? Oh, OK, wait. I'll put you on speaker.' Mia tapped the screen and Hannah's distinctive voice seemed to fill the entire house.

'Where are you?' she asked.

'We're in Hunter's Lodge,' said Mia. 'Been here a couple of hours. But it's hopeless, the place is completely empty.'

'That doesn't surprise me. I should think the contents have been either auctioned or donated to museums a long time ago. I did warn you about the place.'

'Well, yes,' began Mia, 'but we had to give it a try. I'm not sure —'

'Never mind that! Listen! I've had a stroke of luck at the library.'

'Are you there now?' asked Mia.

'Yes, but I've just stepped out for a moment to call you. Can you both hear me?'

'Yes,' said Alfie impatiently. 'Have you found something? We're running out of time.'

'I appreciate that. But listen – I have chanced upon a couple of things that could be very useful indeed. First of all, I've found out why there's no record of Sir Vincent and his wife after they sailed for America. I chanced upon the passenger lists for a ship called The Mary Louise, bound for America. Both Sir Hugo and his wife were listed, but no child was with them. Anyway . . . whether it was bad luck or fate, the ship sank off the coast of America and was lost with all hands.'

Mia gasped. 'You mean . . . they drowned?'

'I'm afraid so.'

Alfie frowned. Now he understood what that blogger had meant when he described Sir Hugo's 'ill-fated' voyage.'

'I don't see how that's useful,' he growled. 'It's not. But there's something else. You remember Sir Humphrey Paxton, don't you?'

Mia looked puzzled. 'Who?' she murmured.

The name rang a bell in Alfie's head. 'He was the gardener guy,' he muttered. 'The one who worked for the man who

273

bought the hall after Sir Vincent left it.'

'Yes, well remembered! He was employed by Sir Montague Welby to adapt the Blackwood's extensive grounds.'

'Yes, but what's that got to do with anything?' protested Alfie. 'They wouldn't know about Edgar and all that side of things – it must have happened long before they even got here.'

'Yes, I appreciate that, but hear me out. In my search today, I found an account written by Paxton about how he'd undertaken the adaptation of the Blackwood's land. You remember, he turned their fairly simple grounds into a complex garden? It got me thinking . . .'

'Go on,' Mia urged her.

'Well, it makes perfect sense to me. If you want to hide a body you aren't going to keep it indoors, are you? Wherever you hide it, it's going to rot and stink the place out. No, you're going to bury it outdoors. Somewhere quiet enough so you can visit it, leave flowers and so forth, but remote enough so that no stranger is ever going to chance upon it and wonder what it's doing there . . .'

Alfie was rapidly losing his patience. He glanced at his watch and saw that the day was sliding past all too quickly. There were now only a couple of hours left to the deadline. 'Hannah, I don't understand what you're saying!' he protested.

'Well, I remembered something from the first time I read about Paxton's work for Welby. It said that the Blackwoods had possessed a vast stretch of land but that there were only a few things of interest there. And then I remembered that one of them was —'

'A dogs' graveyard,' said Mia, suddenly remembering.

'Exactly! Not an uncommon thing in those days – there were plenty of stately homes that had one, usually in a remote setting where members of the family could go and visit their faithful hounds from the past . . .'

Alfie let out a slow breath. 'You're saying that Edgar might be buried in this one?'

'Yes, think about it. You couldn't ask for better cover! You could even put a gravestone there, amongst the other ones, and nobody would think anything of it. It's what's called hiding in plain sight.'

There was a short silence while Alfie considered her words.

'That's it,' he said. 'It has to be.'

'Well, let's not be hasty. Right now, it's only a theory . . .'

'But it's the best one we have,' said Alfie.

'It's the *only* one we have,' Mia reminded him. She looked down at the phone. 'Where is this graveyard, Hannah?'

'It's about a mile from the house,' said Hannah. 'I have a copy of Paxton's original plans right here in front of me . . .' But there was something in her tone that suggested she had bad news to impart. 'I'm afraid it's not going to be easy,' she added.

'What do you mean?' asked Alfie. 'Why not?'

'In Paxton's account, he mentions that he planted a maze on the grounds. It was all the rage back then. A really big, complicated maze.'

'And . . .?'

'I'm afraid he chose the dogs' graveyard to be at the very centre of it.'

'And this maze is still there?'

'As far as I'm aware, it is.'

Alfie let out a moan. 'Could they make it any more difficult for us?' he cried. 'A bloody maze? How are we supposed to find our way through that?'

'Well, in theory, it's not impossible. I have the design in front of me. I ought to be able to guide you through it over the phone . . .'

'But?'

'Well, it's a traditional yew hedge maze. It will have been untended for a very long time. Badly overgrown, I expect. It might not even be possible to make your way through it.'

'We have to try.' Alfie was already heading for the open doorway. Mia scrambled after him, holding out the phone. 'Where is this graveyard?' he yelled over his shoulder.

'Well, it will be outside of the fenced area, obviously. But there is a path, if you can locate it. You need to start from the back door of the house and head due south-west.'

'How are we supposed to know which way that is?' asked Alfie.

'There's a compass app on my phone,' Mia assured him.

'We'll use that.' She glanced at the screen. 'But listen, Hannah, I'm getting a bit low on battery. I'm going to ring off and call you back as soon as we're ready to start,' she said.

'OK,' said Hannah.

Mia hung up and followed Alfie along the gallery to the staircase.

'We need to get back to that gap in the fence you found,' he told her. 'Then we'll make our way around to the back of the house.' He stepped through the opening that led to the staircase and placed a foot on the top step. 'We can ring Hannah and —'

The step seemed to sway alarmingly beneath his foot, throwing him off balance. He opened his mouth to yell a warning to Mia when, quite suddenly, the step tumbled away from under him and he was falling, headlong, amid a clutter of twisting, turning debris. The ground came rushing up to meet him and he felt an impact that seemed to river through his entire body. Lightning flashed before his eyes and blackness rushed like an inky flood into his skull.

For quite a while, he knew nothing.

***

'Wake up, boy. Wake up!'

He groaned and tried to lift his head. He was lying on his side on cold stone, amidst a jumble of wooden detritus. He glanced blearily around, and his head seemed to spin. There was no sign of Mia anywhere. He tried to speak but his voice was little more than a feeble croak.

'What . . . how . . . where . . .?"

'Boy! Concentrate. I'm talking to you.' He turned his head the other way and saw Meg's face. She was kneeling beside him in the gloom, looking impatiently down at him – her eyes seeming almost to burn into his. 'What are you doing?' she chided him. 'Was there ever another who was as skilled as you at falling asleep on the job?'

'I . . . I'm not sleeping,' he whispered. 'The stairs . . . I fell . . .'

'Well, never mind about that! You've been given a clue, haven't you? An important one! Now go and seek it out.'

He managed to get himself into a sitting position and looked frantically around. 'Where's Mia?' he asked. 'She was right behind me.'

'Never mind about *her*. I need you to focus on the job in hand.'

He looked at the dusty stone flags beneath him and noticed a black rectangle lying on it. His phone. It must have fallen from his pocket. He picked it up and saw that the screen was crazed. He tried pressing the on switch, but nothing happened. 'Oh, that's great,' he muttered. 'Now I don't even have a phone.' A sense of utter futility flooded through him. He lifted his head and glared at Meg. 'You'll have to go and look for Edgar yourself,' he told her. 'You heard what Hannah said. 'There's a dogs' graveyard, somewhere in a maze. I don't know exactly where, but —.'

'What part of this do you not understand?' she snarled. 'You should know by now – I can't go anywhere without you. You are my eyes! Come on. Get on your feet!'

She reached out and grabbed the collar of his jacket, yanking him unceremoniously upright. He stood there, swaying slightly like a marionette, shaking his head in an attempt to clear it. 'Why me?' he asked her. 'Why can't you get someone else to do your dirty work for you?'

'What?' Her voice seemed puzzled now. 'What do you mean?'

'You're always pushing me! Do this! Do that! But I can't go on – don't you get it? I've had enough. I've gone as far as I can.

I quit. You'll have to do the rest on your own.'

'Alfie, what are you talking about? Are you all right?'

Meg's face seemed to dissolve in front of him, and now it was Mia's worried features that peered at him through the dusty gloom.

'Mia? What . . . what happened?'

'A section of the stairs fell away while you were on them. I thought you were dead! I had to find another way down and it took ages. Are you hurt?'

He considered for a moment. His left elbow and his right hip ached like hell, and he'd definitely bumped his head at some point – but otherwise he seemed to have survived the fall without major injury. He lifted his phone to show her. 'This is completely wrecked,' he said. He thought for a moment. 'How long ago did I fall?'

'About half an hour to forty minutes, I guess. Like I said, it took me ages to find a safe way down from there. If I don't phone Hannah soon, she'll be sending the cops after us.' She looked at him. 'Who were you talking to when I was climbing down?'

Alfie shook his head. 'Meg,' he said. 'Meg was here. She was mad at me. I think she thought I wasn't going to get up again.' He turned and gazed up the stairwell, at the ragged gap near the top, the timbers from which now formed a jumbled heap beneath his feet. 'It's a wonder I didn't break my neck,' he murmured. 'Right, which way is out?' He took a tentative step and staggered, so Mia stepped closer and put her shoulder under his. 'This way,' she said, and she guided him through a doorway and across the big room. When they finally stepped out into the grey light of afternoon, Alfie stood for a moment on the steps and allowed the chill rain to hit his face and bring him fully back to his senses. Mia, meanwhile, was back on the phone and he could hear her placating Hannah. 'No, sorry, it just took a bit longer than we thought. But we're outside now. Yes, we're perfectly OK! Really. Listen, I'm going to ring off and I'll call again when we're at the back of the house. Yes, I know, we need to be opposite the back door.'

Then she was beside him again. 'Are you OK to walk?' she asked him.

'I'm good.' He studied his watch in disbelief. 'How can it be so late?' he murmured.

She gave him a fierce grin. 'Time flies when you're having fun,' she said and, despite himself, he giggled.

'Listen,' he said, placing a hand on her shoulder. 'If we run out of time and I give you the word, you must promise me you'll run as far away from me as possible. You hear me? If I say the word – don't stop to think, just go . . .'

'Yes, yes,' she soothed him. 'But it isn't going to come to that. We're going to find this dogs' graveyard, I know we are! I've got a good feeling about it.'

'And if Hannah is wrong?' he ventured.

Mia didn't have an answer for that. 'Come on,' she said. And they headed back down the steps, into the pouring rain.

CHAPTER TWENTY-ONE

LABYRINTH

They were finally in position at the back of the house, in line with the main door, and Mia's compass app had shown them the direction in which they ought to be facing. She rang Hannah, who answered immediately. Looking over Mia's shoulder, Alfie was uncomfortably aware that the battery life on Mia's phone was now only a little over ten per cent and that the phone itself was absolutely soaking wet. His own phone was already out of action. What were they supposed to do if Mia's gave out?

'Right,' said Hannah's voice. 'As I said, point yourselves southwest and start walking. Eventually, you should see some kind of wooden signpost on your right-hand side.'

They needed no second bidding. They took off as fast as the slippery rain-slicked grass would allow, while Hannah kept talking on speaker. 'Once you find the signpost there should be some kind of a path to follow, though it will quite probably be overgrown after all this time. A stone path, it says here.'

They hurried onwards, eyes peeled for anything sticking up from the ground – but they seemed to walk for ages without seeing anything at all.

'This is beginning to feel like a wild goose chase!' exclaimed Alfie. 'Are you sure we're going in the right direction?'

'It's a long way from the house,' Hannah reminded him. 'It's going to take time to reach it.'

They walked on, eyes straining for a sight of something that might fit Hannah's description. Finally, Mia pointed off to their right. 'Could that be it?' she asked. She was indicating a rotten wooden stump, no more than a foot in height, jutting up from the sodden grass. They moved closer and, crouching beside it, Alfie could see that the ancient wood was at least regularly shaped and might once have been a proper post. 'I think this could be it,' he announced. 'But there's not enough of it left to see which way it's meant to be pointing.'

'All right, let me check . . .' A long pause. 'From here, you need to go due south,' said Hannah. 'Keep an eye out for that path.'

Mia turned the phone around in her hand and then pointed in a new direction. 'This way,' she said. They walked along for a short distance, eyes fixed to the ground, and then Alfie paused to kick at the moss-covered earth with the heel of one boot. A thick wad of sodden growth scudded aside to reveal that there was indeed an old flagged track beneath it.

'We're definitely on the path!' announced Mia and they moved on again, the rain still hammering relentlessly on their hoods. Every so often, Alfie paused to kick at the ground just to ensure they hadn't diverged from the trail. It led them steeply downhill, through a copse of trees, while Hannah provided a soundtrack. 'Somewhere up ahead of you, you should eventually see the entrance to the maze,' she told them. 'It's set in a stone wall and is meant to represent . . .' Her voice trailed away.

'Represent what?' Mia prompted her.

'The . . . mouth of hell.'

'Oh, that's nice,' said Alfie.

'Apparently, Paxton was a fan of Dante . . .'

'Who?'

'The writer, Dante Alighieri. He wrote *The Divine Comedy*, which is about a journey to hell.'

'I'm beginning to know how that feels,' muttered Alfie. He peered ahead through the pouring rain, but the visibility wasn't great. He had to talk himself out of glancing repeatedly at his watch because whenever he did, whole swathes of time seemed to have slipped by. 'I think we may have gone wrong.' he said.

'No wait,' said Mia, pointing. 'There *is* something ahead . . .'

They kept on walking and eventually the thing came into focus – a long stretch of high-stone wall, crossing in front of them. Set into it there was indeed an entrance – a huge grey gateway, shaped like an open set of jaws complete with jagged teeth. 'That looks welcoming,' muttered Alfie. They came up to it and looked inside. Alfie let out a long breath. The interior was filled almost to bursting point with what looked like an impenetrable tangle of bushes, stretching seemingly unbroken in every direction.

'Hannah, we're going to need your help,' he told Mia's phone. 'This looks more like a jungle than a maze.'

'That's what I was worried about,' she told him. 'It's had a very long time to grow wild. But hopefully I can guide you through it.'

'How are you planning to do that?' asked Mia, exasperated.

'I'm going to read you the directions. I have them right in front of me. Paxton left instructions for his gardeners, so they could navigate their way through it. OK, first bit. "*As you pass through the gates, take six paces forward . . .*" Tell me when you've done that.'

Alfie nodded. He pushed his arm against what appeared to be a wall of dense green foliage, but it gave beneath his hand. He glanced quickly back at Mia. 'Stay with me,' he advised her, and then pushed his whole body into the vegetation. In an instant he was completely enclosed by the chill embrace of wet, spiky yew.

It clawed at his face threatening to scratch out his eyes, but he closed them and told himself not to panic. He took six strides forward, having to use all his strength to make any progress. It felt, uncannily, as though the yew hedge was pushing back against him – reluctant to admit him. Mia's fingers hooked themselves into the belt of his jeans, reminding him that she was following him step for step. He took the sixth stride and then stopped, mired in what seemed like total darkness. 'Done!' he gasped.

'OK, next instruction. *"Turn hard left and take four paces forward".'*

For a moment he was so disoriented he wasn't even sure which direction *was* left, but he talked himself out of panicking and made himself turn. He snatched a breath and pushed onwards. The foliage dragged the hood from his head and something scratched his cheek, making it sting. For a moment, Mia's hand fell away from his belt and he hesitated, but then it was back again, clinging on with an urgency that reassured him. He managed to take four staggering steps. 'Done!' he said, and was obliged to cough out a strand of yew that had intruded into his open mouth.

'Good.' Hannah's voice sounded from just behind him. 'What condition is the maze in?'

'Terrible. It's just a mass of greenery.'

'Look, perhaps this isn't a good idea. Maybe you should come back another time with proper equipment ...'

'There *is* no time. Next instruction!'

'But what if you're injured in there? It would take ages to get help to you and —'

'Hannah! Next instruction, please!'

Hannah coughed, and there was the sound of rustling of paper. '"*Turn hard right and take twelve paces forward*".'

'Twelve?'

'That's what it says.'

'Then twelve it is.' Alfie gritted his teeth and forged onwards, blind to everything but his need to get to the centre of the maze. Hannah continued to read the instructions to him. He settled into a monotonous series of moves, turning left, right, heading straight on, until he hardly knew what was happening. He had almost given up hope of ever emerging from those hellish green depths when, quite without warning, he stepped into daylight. He stood for a moment, blinking in surprise – but if he thought he had reached his goal, he was in for a disappointment. In the small open courtyard in which he and Mia now stood, there was nothing but a statue – the image of an elderly man wearing a toga, one hand pointing off to the right.

'Hannah, we've found a statue,' he announced. 'Some old guy wearing a dress.'

'Excellent! That's Virgil. He was Dante's guide through the Nine Circles of Hell.'

'That's very interesting,' said Mia, and Alfie could tell from her brittle tone that she too was running out of patience. 'But I've got eight per cent of battery left, so please keep the information for when we get back and just tell us what to do next.'

'Yes, of course. Sorry. The statue should be pointing.'

'He is,' said Alfie.

'Good.' Hannah paused to read. ' *"Follow the direction indicated by the great poet and take nine strides forward ..."*'

Once again, Alfie found himself plunging headlong into a wall of suffocating green foliage. Just before he stepped in, he glanced at his watch and noted that there was now less than forty minutes to the deadline. Where had all that time gone? It was as if the surrounding vegetation was soaking it up and dissolving it.

Mia seemed to read his thoughts. 'We'll make it,' he heard her say, just before the chill green blanket enveloped them once more. 'We just have to keep going.' Hannah continued reading and Alfie kept reacting instinctively to her instructions, horribly aware that the minutes were slipping rapidly away. When they next emerged into daylight, they found themselves in another small clearing and, for a moment, he was convinced that the statue awaiting them was the same one as before and that they had somehow managed to go around in a circle. But closer examination revealed that although this was indeed another half-naked old man, he had different features to his predecessor.

'You should be with Homer now,' said Hannah. 'Is he pointing?'

'Yes.'

'OK, head in that direction. You're pretty close to the centre now.'

'I hope so.' Alfie glanced at his watch. 'There's less than fifteen minutes left.'

'Here's what the instructions say. *"Follow the path indicated by Homer and take seven steps straight ahead . . ."'*

Alfie was beginning to feel as if he was going mad. Once again, he was plunged into darkness, a clinging, overpowering sludge of chilly, wet foliage, pressing on him from every side, tearing at him, tickling him, dripping icy rain down the back of his neck. And then, as he took his sixth step, something bad happened. He suddenly felt stuck – unable to move at all.

'Why have we stopped?' he heard Mia gasp.

'Can't seem to . . . get free.' He flexed his muscles and shrugged his shoulders. Green fingers snagged in his hair and seemed to wrap themselves around his wrists and ankles. He felt a powerful tide of panic rising within him, as he imagined himself trapped there forever like a luckless insect caught in a spider's web. He imagined people in years to come, cutting down the maze and finding two ragged skeletons hanging from the branches. Cold though he was, sweat oozed from his forehead and went trickling down his face. He began to shake uncontrollably.

'Alfie!' Mia's voice – urgent and pleading. 'You've got to get us through. We're nearly out of time!'

'Mia, I can't do it. I'm finished!'

'No, you're not. Come on!' She thumped him hard on the back and the pain of it galvanised him back into action.

He gathered his strength and made a monumental effort – a wrenching, spasmodic lunge forward. He felt the green fingers that held him tearing apart. And suddenly, he burst through a final curtain of green and emerged, once more, into daylight. At first glance, Alfie thought he was looking at another statue – but it turned out to be something else entirely. It was Meg, and she didn't look happy. He stopped in his tracks, just as Mia came blundering out behind him. 'Are we there?' she gasped. 'Is this the . . .?'

She hesitated, sensing something was badly wrong. Alfie saw the way Meg's gaze fixed on Mia – the way her thin mouth twisted into an expression of disapproval. He spun around, realising that Mia was in danger. 'Get away from me!' he yelled. 'Go back – NOW!'

She hesitated, staring at him, and then briefly glanced past him. Her eyes widened in surprise and her mouth fell open. Then she seemed to come to her senses. She turned, intending, no doubt, to throw herself back into cover – but Meg pointed a finger and Mia stopped in her tracks, her arms outstretched. Her phone slipped from her shaking hand and tumbled to the earth. Now Meg let out a hissing sound and crooked one finger. Mia was yanked suddenly backwards, as if by prodigious force, shouldering Alfie to one side as she went flailing past him. She fell hard on to her back and lay on the ground, shuddering, her eyes rolling back in their sockets to reveal the whites and her mouth wide open making choking sounds. Alfie stared down at her in dismay and then turned to confront Meg.

'NO!' he yelled. 'No, don't hurt her! Please. It's not time yet.' He pointed desperately at his watch. 'There's still a few minutes . . . and we're almost there.'

Hannah's voice spilt from the phone's speaker. 'Alfie? What's happening? Alfie? ALFIE?'

Meg glared down at the phone and then made an impatient gesture with one hand. The phone clicked off. Now Meg was looking down at Mia's shuddering body. 'I warned you what would happen,' she told Alfie. 'I said what I would do if you failed me.'

'But I haven't failed you!' he protested. 'I'm almost there. Give me more time. You have to!'

'I'm tired of your excuses.' Meg raised a threatening hand. 'All you do is ask for more time. But I gave you some, and now it's up. Say goodbye to your friend.'

'NO!' In desperation, Alfie did the only thing left to him. He flung himself straight at Meg. He wrapped his arms around her and threw her off balance, pushing her back hard against the green hedge behind her.

'Take your hands off me!' she roared, and suddenly, crazily, the two of them were flailing upwards into the empty air, lifting high above the hedges. Alfie was horribly aware of the power in her, the way her body seemed to shudder and vibrate under his hands like something made of pure electricity. She made a gesture, flinging her arms out to either side, and something hit Alfie in the chest with a power that snatched the breath out of him. He was falling back to earth – stunned, gasping – his whole body tingling with shock. His left side connected with the top of a wall of hedgerow and he rolled over and fell, landing with a thud on something hard and unyielding. For a moment, he lost consciousness, the world see-sawing crazily around him, but then he came back to himself. He was lying on his side and when he put his hand down, it came to rest on flat stone. With an effort, he got himself into a sitting position and twisted round to look at what he was lying on. He dimly registered a name, etched into granite. PRINCE. He stared at it open-mouthed, realising he had found what he was looking for.

Then the hedgerow to the side of him seemed to explode apart and Meg strode through the midst of it as if it had no more substance than smoke. She was dragging Mia's lifeless body behind her, pulling her along by the hood of her jacket. She lifted a hand and flung Mia directly at Alfie. She came tumbling across the ground, to crash to a halt beside him. Mia's eyes were closed. He stared fearfully down at her. 'Is she dead?' he whispered.

'Not yet,' Meg assured him. 'But soon, I assure you. As promised.'

'But . . . wait. Look!' Alfie scrambled up from the fallen gravestone. 'This is what we were looking for. The graveyard.' He stood for a moment and gazed around at the small circle of stones in the clearing – some fallen, some still standing. 'This is the place,' he assured Meg. 'The place where they buried Edgar. You must have heard what Hannah said about the dog's graveyard.'

'She looked unconvinced. 'If you're playing for time . . .'

'No, I promise you. He's in one of these graves, I'm sure of it.' He stumbled to the next marker, a small black oblong, and kneeled to brush dirt from the inscription with his fingers, revealing a single word etched into the stone. MAJOR. He shook his head. 'Not . . . not this one,' he said, and scrambled on his hands and knees to the next. 'But one of them. It has to be one of them.' Meg followed him, at least for the moment, prepared to listen.

'Go on,' she murmured.

'Didn't you hear what Hannah said? She believes that the Blackwoods . . . when Edgar died, they . . . they hid his body here,' stammered Alfie. 'In one of these graves . . .' He crouched beside the next marker, a grey granite headstone, and he scrabbled at the ancient inscription with already sore fingertips.

But the occupant of this grave was called LUCKY. The inscription blurred as Alfie's eyes filled with tears.

Meg began to turn away. 'I tire of this game,' she said. She looked at Mia's still form on the ground and started back towards it. 'Let's get it over with,' she said.

'No, no, wait. Please, wait! I know it's here somewhere, if you'll just give me more time. It has to be here!' Sobbing, Alfie reeled to the next grave and dropped to his knees in front of it. He dashed the tears from his eyes and glanced at Meg. She was lifting a hand over Mia's sprawled body, preparing to strike the final blow.

Alfie turned desperately back to the gravestone and saw the inscription.

Billy.

He was about to scramble away but something stopped him. Billy . . . that was . . .

'Yes!' he screamed. '*This* one! This is Edgar's grave!'

Meg hesitated and looked towards him, her expression one of distrust. 'You're bluffing,' she said. 'Playing for time.'

'No, I swear to you! This is where they put your son. Look. See that? Billy!'

'My son's name is Edgar,' she assured him.

'But that's not what the Blackwoods called him! Please, listen to me. They named him William. See . . . Billy. Billy is short for William.'

She lowered her hand. She turned and came slowly towards

Alfie. She stood for what felt to him like an age, looking at the gravestone, her expression softening. 'You are . . . certain?' she whispered.

'Positive,' he told her. 'Hannah saw it in an old journal. Didn't you hear what she said? They called him William Blackwood.'

Meg dropped to her knees and placed her hands flat on the earth. She closed her eyes and began to mutter something under her breath, her voice a low, sensual murmur. Alfie became gradually aware of a vibration in the ground – a low seismic rumbling. He took a few uncertain steps back, stumbled and then dropped to the ground, next to Mia's sprawled figure. He watched in silence. The ground beneath Meg's hands appeared to be vaporising – rising as clouds of steam in the rainy air. As Alfie stared, mesmerised, the earth seemed to turn to mist and then a pair of transparent skeletal arms rose up from beneath the haze. Two bony hands clasped Meg's. Then the hands appeared to gather flesh and become more solid. Meg was laughing now, as though hardly believing that her long wait was finally over. She pulled hard and, quite suddenly, she was holding the body of a young boy against her – a boy wearing a tattered white nightgown. As she held him, he seemed to gradually solidify and take proper form. Still she laughed, but now tears trickled down her cheeks. She got herself upright and set the boy down on his own feet. He stood there, gazing up at her, an angelic looking child with straight shoulder length hair. Alfie could see that he had his mother's features, the same long, thin face and the same proud nose. She was smiling adoringly down at him, her eyes brimming with fresh tears. 'Edgar,' she whispered. 'My Edgar. It really is you.'

The boy said nothing, just continued to gaze up at her as if transfixed.

Finally, she turned to look at Alfie. 'It is done,' she said. 'Now I can finally rest.'

He sat there, staring back at her. 'And Mia?' he whispered.

She made a dismissive gesture with her free hand. 'She'll wake up soon enough,' she assured him. She noted his doubtful expression and laughed. 'Did you really think I meant to hurt her?' she asked him. 'I was only applying pressure, I can assure you.' When Alfie didn't answer, she turned away and lead the boy towards the great gully she had already burned through the hedgerow. 'Time to go,' she announced. She glanced at Edgar. 'We have much to catch up on.'

'Wait,' said Alfie. Meg paused and looked back over her shoulder. 'Are we done now?' he asked.

She seemed to consider the question for quite a while. Then she nodded. 'Your debt is paid,' she said. 'I relieve you of your obligation.'

'And . . . I won't see you again?'

She looked at him. 'Not unless you summon me,' she said. 'You remember how to do that, don't you?' She returned her attention to her son. 'Come, Edgar,' she said. 'I have so much to tell you.' As she led the boy away, the dense greenery seemed to dissolve away from them like smoke, leaving an easy path to follow. Finally, when they had gone quite some distance, they too began to fade. In moments they were gone.

The rain began to ease off. Alfie slumped back on to the ground, letting out a long, slow breath. He couldn't remember when he had last felt this exhausted. As he lay there, looking up at the sky, he saw that a dark edge of cloud was passing over him revealing clear blue sky behind it. The rain stopped abruptly, and warm sunshine took its place.

Mia stirred beside him. She let out a soft groan and her eyelids fluttered. Alfie sat up again and leant over her. As he watched, relieved, she gradually came back to herself. She registered him watching her, and smiled.

'I had the weirdest dream,' she murmured. She sat up and looked around at the circle of gravestones. 'We found it,' she observed.

He nodded, and indicated Edgar's recently vacated grave. The ground looked perfectly normal now. 'That's what we were looking for,' he said.

She studied the single name inscribed on the stone and then nodded. 'Billy,' she said. 'William.'

He smiled. 'Well remembered,' he said.

'And Meg?'

'She's happy now. She's taken Edgar, and gone.'

'Gone where?' she asked.

He shrugged. 'To wherever you go when you're at peace,' he murmured. 'But she said I won't be seeing her again.'

A shrill noise broke the silence. 'That's my phone,' said Mia. She looked blearily around. 'But where is it?'

He pointed through the breach in the yew hedge. 'Over that way somewhere,' he murmured. 'You dropped it. It's a miracle it's still working.'

'I guess it will be Hannah.'

'Yeah. She'll be wondering what happened to us.'

'What *did* happen to us?' murmured Mia.

He smiled. 'We'd better find the phone before your battery gives out,' he said.

He got unsteadily to his feet and helped her up. He held her to him for a moment, marvelling at the touch of her and the realisation that she was finallysafe from harm. 'What do you remember?' he asked her gently.

'I remember you telling me to run. And the . . . woman . . .' Her eyes widened in surprise. 'Oh, my God,' she whispered.

'What?' he asked her.

'Just before I tried to get away. Alfie, I . . . I *saw* her. I saw Meg. She was just as you described her.'

They stood looking at each other in silence for a moment, while somewhere unseen, the phone continued to ring.

'We'd better go and find that,' said Alfie. 'We're going to need some help to get home.'

She nodded.

She took his hand in hers and the two of them went to search for the phone together.

THE END

EPILOGUE

Alfie strolled slowly along the path to the church, barely pausing to glance at Meg's grave as he went by. It was several days since his return from Hunter's Lodge and the various aches and pains he'd suffered there had started to ease. The scratches on his arms and face were well on their way to healing. Dad had been horrified at the state of him when he'd finally shown up at home and had threatened to drive him straight back to Bristol, if that was what it took to keep him out of trouble. But he'd calmed down eventually. Alfie's explanation of how he and his 'friends' had been caught in a storm out on the moors had finally been accepted and things had soon settled back into a more relaxed mood.

The weather had returned to its former glory and the feel of the sun on Alfie's face was decidedly comforting. Mia was sitting on the wooden bench, a short distance from Meg's grave. She had a sketch book open on her lap and was concentrating on that, her hand moving a charcoal pencil expertly across the page. Alfie crept quietly up behind her and stood for a moment, looking over her shoulder, admiring her work. He recognised instantly the character she was depicting and decided she was doing a great job of capturing Meg's look – the tall slim frame, the long tangle of hair on either side of her long, handsome face. And those eyes. Dark and glowering – they seemed to burn off the page.

'That's amazing,' he said at last, and Mia turned to look up at him in surprise.

'How long have you been standing there?' she asked him.

'Long enough,' he said. 'They are going to love you at that art college,' he added.

'Well, only if I get the right results this year,' she reminded him.

'You're good,' said Alfie. 'Of course you'll get them.' He came round and sat beside her. She started to put the book aside, but he placed a hand on hers to stop her. 'No, that's OK,' he told her. 'Carry on, we're in no big hurry.'

Mia nodded. 'I just wanted to get her down on paper,' she said, by way of explanation. 'Before she starts to fade. Do you think I've got her look right?'

Alfie studied the sketch again, and nodded. 'You've nailed it,' he said. He looked at Mia for a moment. 'I'm really glad you saw her in the end,' he said. 'Makes me feel better about the whole thing. Like before, I could never really be sure she wasn't just in my head, you know?'

'I get it. Now she's in both our heads. And I'm not going to thank you for it.' She went back to her drawing, adding a little shading to the side of Meg's face to emphasise the curve of a cheekbone. 'You got any news?' she asked Alfie, without looking up.

'Might have.'

'Oh yeah, what's that then?'

'Dad's been asked if he wants to stay on at Blackwood and Phibes and be their regional online co-ordinator, or something. Full-time post. He asked me what I thought of the idea.'

Mia hesitated and glanced up. 'What did you say?' she asked.

Alfie shrugged. 'I told him I was starting to like it here. That I'd made a really good friend. And that there was this excellent college she was planning to go to, that might just be right for me, too . . . if they'll have me.'

Mia smiled. 'Sounds like a plan,' she said, and bowed her head to her sketchbook again. 'So, do you think he's going to say yes to the idea?'

'I think he may already be doing that right now.'

'Cool.' A troubled pause. 'Any news on the *other* thing?'

He affected a puzzled look. '*Other* thing?' he echoed.

'You know what I'm talking about. Sophie.'

'Oh, her.' He shrugged his shoulders. 'No, still nothing on that score. Dad spoke to Mum and she reckons Sophie might have decided to keep the baby. But that's only a guess. Nothing's decided.'

Mia looked up again and frowned. 'What will you do, if that happens?'

'I'll try and do the right thing, whatever that is. But . . . she's with Brendan now, so that isn't going to mean me running off to be with her or anything. I'll just have to accept whatever happens and get on with my own life.

'It's Brendan's kid, anyway,' said Mia, confidently. Her pencil moved across Meg's eyebrows, emphasising the arch of them.

'You don't know that,' he reminded her.

'No, but I feel it in my blood.' She waved her free hand at the page. 'Perhaps a bit of Meg rubbed off on me.' She looked up again. 'You never pinned that down, did you? I mean, your family being from Singleton and everything, back in the day. About whether you might be related to Meg.'

He nodded. 'No, I didn't get around to it,' he admitted. He glanced slyly over towards the stone. 'I suppose I could always summon her back and ask her.'

Mia glared at him. 'Don't,' she said, managing to fill the single word with enough dread to make it final. 'Don't even think about it,' she added, just to ensure he got the message.

He grinned. 'No worries. I'm not that desperate to know. And there are easier ways to find out that stuff.' He smiled. 'I bet Hannah could help me out on that. How is she, by the way?'

'She's just about forgiven us. Told me if I ever get her mixed up in something like that again, she'll give us hell.'

'I think we've already had that,' said Alfie.

'She's asked us to go up there some time and tell her the whole story. She wants all the juicy details. I told her, though, no way was any of it for publication. Not unless she turns it into fiction –

but she told me she doesn't write that kind of thing.' She looked at Alfie uncertainly. 'Unless, you feel differently about it?'

He shook his head. 'No way. I'd rather forget all about it, if I can.'

Reassured, Mia carried on with her work. 'Where do you want to go after this?' she murmured.

'Hmm? Oh, I don't know.' Alfie leant back on the bench and stretched luxuriously. After the recent turmoil he'd endured, it felt wonderful just to relax and take things easy. 'Maybe I'll sit here for a while and watch you work,' he concluded. 'I like doing that.'

She didn't argue, so for the next half hour, that's exactly what he did.

AUTHOR BIOGRAPHY

Philip Caveney was born in North Wales in 1951 and now lives in Edinburgh.

His first novel, *The Sins of Rachel Ellis* was published in 1977 and he produced a series of adult thrillers over the following decades. His first novel for younger readers, Sebastian Darke: Prince of Fools was released in 2007 and was published all around the world. Since then, he has concentrated on writing exclusively for younger readers.

He also writes under the pseudonym Danny Weston. Danny's debut novel *The Piper* won the Scottish Children's Book Award in 2016 and in 2018, *The Haunting of Jessop Rise* was shortlisted for the Scottish Teenage Book prize and nominated for a Carnegie Medal.

ACKNOWLEDGEMENTS

As ever, there are a few people to thank.

When I started to write this book, the world was a fairly rational place. Now, thanks to Covid 19, it has changed out of all recognition. So I would like to thank all the people who have helped me carry on with the daily task of creating worlds in my head. First up of course, there's the team at UCLan - Hazel, and more recently, Brian and Charlotte, who have been guiding me through the complicated process of recording an audiobook, and Toni, who did the fabulous cover design.

And, of course there's Susan, my wife, who is always the first person I show my work to – an excellent critic and an unabashed grammar nerd. Oh yes, plus the members of Writers Inc, recently reunited via the internet.

I should also like to thank Creative Scotland for their generosity.

But mostly, this one is for Meg Shelton. So little is known about her life that I had to make up quite a bit of it. I hope she approves of the story I gave her. And just in case she doesn't like what I've done, let me add this.

'I do believe in witches. I do believe in witches.

I DO BELIEVE IN WITCHES!'

HERE LIES THE GRAVE OF MEG SHELTON, "THE
WITCH OF WOODPLUMPTON" OR OTHERWISE
KNOWN AS "THE FYLDE HAG". LOCAL LEGEND
SPEAKS OF MEG AS A MISCHIEVIOUS WITCH
WHO HAD POWERS TO TRANSFORM HERSELF
INTO ANIMALS.

IT IS BELIEVED THAT MEG'S BODY WAS CRUSHED
BETWEEN A BARREL AND A WALL IN THE 18TH
CENTURY. IT IS SAID WHEN MEG WAS BURIED SHE
WAS PLACED UPSIDE DOWN TO STOP HER FROM
DIGGING HER WAY OUT. A BOULDER WAS PUT
ON TOP TO KEEP HER IN BUT SOME SUSPECT
THIS DIDNT WORK!

"This is an excellent book with compelling characters,
a creepy atmosphere and a clever plot. It was hard
to put down and I finished it in one day."

Joseph Delaney

A. J. HARTLEY

COLD BATH STREET

From the *New York Times* bestselling author

Written Stone Lane is the direct sequel to *Cold Bath Street* and is a fast-paced ghost thriller that will set your heart racing until the very end.

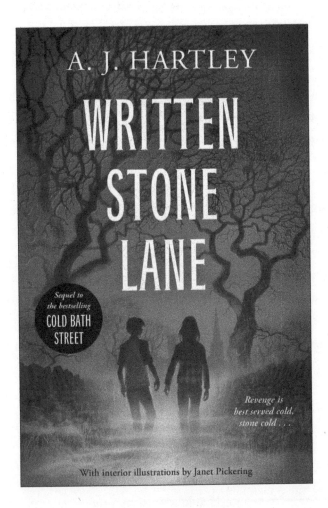

A. J. HARTLEY

WRITTEN STONE LANE

Sequel to the bestselling
COLD BATH STREET

Revenge is best served cold, stone cold . . .

With interior illustrations by Janet Pickering

HAVE YOU EVER WONDERED
HOW BOOKS ARE MADE?

UCLan Publishing are based in the North of England and involve
BA Publishing and MA Publishing students from the University
of Central Lancashire at every stage of the publishing process.

BA Publishing and MA Publishing students are based within
our company and work on producing books as part of their
course – some of which are selected to be published and printed
by UCLan Publishing. Students also gain first-hand experience
of negotiating with buyers, conceiving and running innovative
high-level events to leverage sales, as well as running content
creation business enterprises.

Our approach to business and teaching has been recognised
academically and within the publishing industry. We have
been awarded Best Newcomer at the Independent Publishing
Guild Awards (2019) and a *Times* Higher Education Award
for Excellence and Innovation in the Arts(2018).

As our business continues to grow, so too does the experience
our students have upon entering UCLan Publishing.

To find out more, please visit
www.uclanpublishing.com/courses/